PRAISE FOR PATRICIA HIGHSMITH

"Highsmith writes the verbal equivalent of a drug—easy to consume, darkly euphoric, totally addictive. . . . Highsmith belongs in the moody company of Dostoevsky or Angela Carter."

—*Time Out*

"No one has created psychological suspense more densely and deliciously satisfying."

—*Vogue*

"Patricia Highsmith's novels are peerlessly disturbing . . . bad dreams that keep us thrashing for the rest of the night."

—*The New Yorker*

"Though Highsmith would no doubt disclaim any kinship with Jonathan Swift or Evelyn Waugh, the best of [her work] is in the same tradition. . . . It is Highsmith's dark and sometimes savage humor, and the intelligence that informs her precise and hard-edged prose, which puts one in mind of those authors."

—*Newsday*

"For eliciting the menace that lurks in familiar surroundings, there's no one like Patricia Highsmith."

—*Time*

"Mesmerizing . . . not to be recommended for the weak-minded and impressionable."

—*Washington Post Book World*

"A writer who has created a world of her own—a world claustrophobic and irrational which we enter each time with a sense of personal danger. . . . Miss Highsmith is the poet of apprehension."

—*Graham Greene*

"An atmosphere of nameless dread, of unspeakable foreboding, permeates every page of Patricia Highsmith, and there's nothing quite like it." —*Boston Globe*

"Highsmith's novels skew your sense of literary justice, tilt your internal scales of right and wrong. The ethical order of things in the real world seems less stable [as she] deftly warps the moral sense of her readers." —*Cleveland Plain Dealer*

"Highsmith . . . conveys a firm, unshakable belief in the existence of evil—personal, psychological, and political. . . . The genius of Highsmith's writing is that it is at once deeply disturbing and exhilirating." —*Boston Phoenix*

"Murder, in Patricia Highsmith's hands, is made to occur almost as casually as the bumping of a fender or a bout of food poisoning. This downplaying of the dramatic . . . has been much praised, as has the ordinariness of the details with which she depicts the daily lives and mental processes of her psychopaths. Both undoubtedly contribute to the domestication of crime in her fiction, thereby implicating the reader further in the sordid fantasy that is being worked out." —Robert Towers, *New York Review of Books*

Also by Patricia Highsmith

The Black House

Patricia Highsmith

W. W. NORTON & COMPANY

NEW YORK LONDON

Manufacturing by The Courier Companies, Inc.
Production manager: Amanda Morrison

Library of Congress Cataloging-in-Publication Data

Highsmith, Patricia, 1921–
The black house / Patricia Highsmith.
p. cm.
ISBN 0-393-32631-4 (pbk.)
1. Suburban life—Fiction. 2. Horror tales, American. I. Title.
PS3558.I366B53 2004
813'.54—dc22
2004024360

W. W. Norton & Company, Inc.
500 Fifth Avenue, New York, N.Y. 10110
www.wwnorton.com

W. W. Norton & Company Ltd.
Castle House, 75/76 Wells Street, London W1T 3QT

1 2 3 4 5 6 7 8 9 0

To Charles Latimer

CONTENTS

Something the Cat Dragged In

A few seconds of pondering silence in the Scrabble game was interrupted by a rustle of plastic at the cat door: Portland Bill was coming in again. Nobody paid any attention. Michael and Gladys Herbert were ahead, Gladys doing a bit better than her husband. The Herberts played Scrabble often and were quite sharp at it. Colonel Edward Phelps—a neighbor and a good friend—was limping along, and his American niece Phyllis, aged nineteen, had been doing well but had lost interest in the last ten minutes. It would soon be teatime. The Colonel was sleepy and looked it.

"Quack," said the Colonel thoughtfully, pushing a forefinger against his Kipling-style mustache. "Pity—I was thinking of earthquake."

"If you've got *quack*, Uncle Eddie," said Phyllis, "how could you get quake out of it?"

The cat made another more sustained noise at his door, and now with black tail and brindle hindquarters in the house, he moved backwards and pulled something through the plastic oval. What he had dragged in looked whitish and about six inches long.

"Caught another bird," said Michael, impatient for Eddie to make his move so he could make a brilliant move before somebody grabbed it.

"Looks like another goose foot," said Gladys, glancing. "Ugh."

The Colonel at last moved, adding a P to SUM. Michael moved, raising a gasp of admiration from Phyllis for his INI stuck onto GEM, the N of which gave him DAWN.

Portland Bill flipped his trophy into the air, and it fell on the carpet with a thud.

"Really *dead* pigeon that," remarked the Colonel who was nearest the cat, but whose eyesight was not the best. "Turnip," he said for Phyllis's benefit. "Swede. Or an oddly shaped carrot," he added, peering, then chuckled. "I've seen carrots take the most fantastic shapes. Saw one once . . ."

"This is white," said Phyllis, and got up to investigate, since Gladys had to play before her. Phyllis, in slacks and sweater, bent

over with hands on her knees. "Good *Chr*—Oh! Uncle Eddie!"
She stood up and clapped her hand over her mouth as if she had
said something dreadful.

Michael Herbert had half risen from his chair. "What's the
matter?"

"They're human *fingers!*" Phyllis said. "Look!"

They all looked, coming slowly, unbelievingly, from the card
table. The cat looked, proudly, up at the faces of the four humans
gazing down. Gladys drew in her breath.

The two fingers were dead white and puffy, there was not a
sign of blood even at the base of the fingers, which included a
couple of inches of what had been the hand. What made the
object undeniably the third and fourth fingers of a human hand
were the two nails, yellowish and short and looking small because
of the swollen flesh.

"What should we do, Michael?" Gladys was practical, but liked
to let her husband make decisions.

"That's been dead for two weeks at least," murmured the
Colonel, who had had some war experiences.

"Could it have come from a hospital near here?" asked Phyllis.

"Hospital amputating like that?" replied her uncle with a
chuckle.

"The nearest hospital is twenty miles from here," said Gladys.

"Mustn't let Edna see it." Michael glanced at his watch. "Of
course I think we—"

"Maybe call the police?" asked Gladys.

"I was thinking of that. I—" Michael's hesitation was interrupted by Edna—their housekeeper-cook—bumping just then
against a door in a remote corner of the big living room. The tea
tray had arrived. The others discreetly moved toward the low table
in front of the fireplace, while Michael Herbert stood with an air
of casualness. The fingers were just behind his shoes. Michael
pulled an unlit pipe from his jacket pocket, and fiddled with it,

blowing into its stem. His hands shook a little. He shooed Portland Bill away with one foot.

Edna finally dispensed napkins and plates, and said, "Have a nice tea!" She was a local woman in her mid-fifties, a reliable soul, but with most of her mind on her own children and grandchildren—thank goodness under these circumstances, Michael thought. Edna arrived at half past seven in the morning on her bicycle and departed when she pleased, as long as there was something in the house for supper. The Herberts were not fussy.

Gladys was looking anxiously toward Michael. "Get a-*way*, Bill!"

"Got to do something with this meanwhile," Michael murmured. With determination he went to the basket of newspapers beside the fireplace, shook out a page of the *Times*, and returned to the fingers which Portland Bill was about to pick up. Michael beat the cat by grabbing the fingers through the newspaper. The others had not sat down. Michael made a gesture for them to do so, and closed the newspaper around the fingers, rolling and folding. "The thing to do, I should think," said Michael, "*is* to notify the police, because there might have been—foul play somewhere."

"Or might it have fallen," the Colonel began, shaking out his napkin, "out of an ambulance or some disposal unit—you know? Might've been an accident somewhere."

"Or should we just let well enough alone—and get rid of it," said Gladys. "I need some tea." She had poured, and proceeded to sip her cup.

No one had an answer to her suggestion. It was as if the three others were stunned, or hypnotized by one another's presence, vaguely expecting a response from another which did not come.

"Rid of it where? In the garbage?" asked Phyllis. "*Bury* it," she added, as if answering her own question.

"I don't think that would be right," said Michael.

"Michael, do have some tea," said his wife.

"Got to put this somewhere—overnight." Michael still held the little bundle. "Unless we ring the police now. It's already five and it's Sunday."

"In England do the police care whether it's Sunday or not?" asked Phyllis.

Michael started for the armoire near the front door, with an idea of putting the thing on top beside a couple of hat boxes, but he was followed by the cat, and Michael knew that the cat with enough inspiration could leap to the top.

"I've got just the thing, I think," said the Colonel, pleased by his own idea, but with an air of calm in case Edna made a second appearance. "Bought some house slippers just yesterday in the High Street and I've still got the box. I'll go and fetch it, if I may." He went off toward the stairs, then turned and said softly, "We'll tie a string around it. Keep it away from the cat." The Colonel climbed the stairs.

"Keep it in whose room?" asked Phyllis with a nervous giggle.

The Herberts did not answer. Michael, still on his feet, held the object in his right hand. Portland Bill sat with white forepaws neatly together, regarding Michael, waiting to see what Michael would do with it.

Colonel Phelps came down with his white cardboard shoe box. The little bundle went in easily, and Michael let the Colonel hold the box while he went to rinse his hands in the lavatory near the front door. When Michael returned, Portland Bill still hovered, and gave out a hopeful "Meow?"

"Let's put it in the sideboard cupboard for the moment," said Michael, and took the box from Eddie's hands. He felt that the box at least was comparatively clean, and he put it beside a stack of large and seldom-used dinner plates, then closed the cabinet door which had a key in it.

Phyllis bit into a Bath Oliver and said, "I noticed a crease in one finger. If there's a ring there, it might give us a clue."

Michael exchanged a glance with Eddie, who nodded slightly. They had all noticed the crease. Tacitly the men agreed to take care of this later.

"More tea, dear," said Gladys. She refilled Phyllis's cup.

"M'wow," said the cat in a disappointed tone. He was now seated facing the sideboard, looking over one shoulder.

Michael changed the subject: the progress of the Colonel's redecorating. The painting of the first-floor bedrooms was the main reason the Colonel and his niece were visiting the Herberts just now. But this was of no interest compared to Phyllis's question to Michael:

"Shouldn't you ask if anyone's missing in the neighborhood? Those fingers might be part of a *murder*."

Gladys shook her head slightly and said nothing. Why did Americans always think in such violent terms? However, what could have severed a hand in such a manner? An explosion? An ax?

A lively scratching sound got Michael to his feet.

"Bill, do *stop* that!" Michael advanced on the cat and shooed him away. Bill had been trying to open the cabinet door.

Tea was over more quickly than usual. Michael stood by the sideboard while Edna cleared away.

"When're you going to look at the ring, Uncle Eddie?" Phyllis asked. She wore round-rimmed glasses and was rather myopic.

"I don't think Michael and I have quite decided what we should do, my dear," said her uncle.

"Let's go into the library, Phyllis," said Gladys. "You said you wanted to look at some photographs."

Phyllis had said that. There were photographs of Phyllis's mother and of the house where her mother had been born, in which Uncle Eddie now lived. Eddie was older than her mother by fifteen years. Now Phyllis wished she hadn't asked to see the photographs, because the men were going to do something with the *fingers*, and Phyllis would have liked to watch. After all, she was dissecting frogs and dogfish in zoology lab. But her mother had

warned her before she left New York to mind her manners and not
be "crude and insensitive," her mother's usual adjectives about
Americans. Phyllis dutifully sat looking at photographs fifteen and
twenty years old, at least.

"Let's take it out to the garage," Michael said to Eddie. "I've
got a workbench there, you know."

The two men walked along a graveled path to the two-car
garage at the back of which Michael had a workshop with saws
and hammers, chisels and electric drills, plus a supply of wood and
planks in case the house needed any repairs or he felt in the mood
to make something. Michael was a freelance journalist and book
critic, but he enjoyed manual labor. Here Michael felt better with
the awful box, somehow. He could set it on his sturdy workbench
as if he were a surgeon laying out a body, or a corpse.

"What the hell do you make of this?" asked Michael as he
flipped the fingers out by holding one side of the newspaper. The
fingers flopped onto the well-used wooden surface, this time palm
side upward. The white flesh was jagged where it had been cut,
and in the strong beam of the spotlight which shone from over the
bench, they could see two bits of metacarpals, also jagged, project-
ing from the flesh. Michael turned the fingers over with the tip of
a screwdriver. He twisted the screwdriver tip, and parted the flesh
enough to see the glint of gold.

"Gold ring," said Eddie. "But he was a workman of some kind,
don't you think? Look at those nails. Short and thick. Still some
soil under them—dirty, anyway."

"I was thinking—if we report it to the police, shouldn't we
leave it the way it is? Not try to look at the ring?"

"Are you going to report it to the police?" asked Eddie with
a smile as he lit a cigar. "What'll you be in for then?"

"In for? I'll say the cat dragged it in. Why should I be in for
anything? I'm curious about the ring. Might give us a clue."

Colonel Phelps glanced at the garage door, which Michael
had closed but not locked. He too was curious about the ring.

Eddie was thinking, if it had been a gentleman's hand, they might have turned it in to the police by now. "Many farmworkers around here still?" mused the Colonel. "I suppose so."

Michael shrugged, nervous. "What do you say about the ring?"

"Let's have a look." The Colonel puffed serenely, and looked at Michael's racks of tools.

"I know what we need." Michael reached for a Stanley knife which he ordinarily used for cutting cardboard, pushed the blade out with his thumb, and placed his fingers on the pudgy remainder of the palm. He made a cut above where the ring was, then below.

Eddie Phelps bent to watch. "No blood at all. Drained out. Just like the war days."

Nothing but a goose foot, Michael was telling himself in order not to faint. Michael repeated his cuts on the top surface of the finger. He felt like asking Eddie if he wanted to finish the job, but Michael thought that might be cowardly.

"Dear me," Eddie murmured unhelpfully.

Michael had to cut off some strips of flesh, then take a firm grip with both hands to get the wedding ring off. It most certainly was a wedding ring of plain gold, not very thick or broad, but suitable for a man to wear. Michael rinsed it at the cold water tap of the sink on his left. When he held it near the spotlight, initials were legible: *W.R.—M.T.*

Eddie peered. "Now *that's* a clue!"

Michael heard the cat scratching at the garage door, then a meow. Next Michael put the three pieces of flesh he had cut off into an old rag, wadded it up, and told Eddie he would be back in a minute. He opened the garage door, discouraged Bill with a "*Whisht!*" and stuck the rag into a dustbin which had a fastening that a cat could not open. Michael had thought he had a plan to propose to Eddie, but when he returned—-Eddie was again examining the ring—Michael was too shaken to speak. He had meant to say something about making "discreet inquiries." Instead he said in a voice gone hollow:

"Let's call it a day—unless we think of something brilliant tonight. Let's leave the box here. The cat can't get in."

Michael didn't want the box even on his workbench. He put the ring in with the fingers, and set the box on top of some plastic jerricans which stood against a wall. His workshop was even ratproof, so far. Nothing was going to come in to chew at the box.

As Michael got into bed that night, Gladys said, "If we don't tell the police, we've simply got to bury it somewhere."

"Yes," said Michael vaguely. It seemed somehow a criminal act, burying a pair of human fingers. He had told Gladys about the ring. The initials hadn't rung any bell with her.

Colonel Edward Phelps went to sleep quite peacefully, having reminded himself that he had seen a lot worse in 1941.

Phyllis had quizzed her uncle and Michael about the ring at dinner. Maybe it would all be solved tomorrow and turn out to be—somehow—something quite simple and innocent. Anyway, it would make quite a story to tell her chums in college. And her mother! So this was the quiet English countryside!

The next day being Monday, with the post office open, Michael decided to pose a question to Mary Jeffrey, who doubled there as postal clerk and grocery salesgirl. Michael bought some stamps, then asked casually:

"By the way, Mary, is anybody missing lately—in this neighborhood?"

Mary, a bright-faced girl with dark curly hair, looked puzzled. "Missing how?"

"Disappeared," Michael said with a smile.

Mary shook her head. "Not that I know. Why do you ask?"

Michael had tried to prepare for this. "I read somewhere in a newspaper that people do sometimes—just disappear, even in small villages like this. Drift away, change their names or some such. Baffles everyone, where they go." Michael was drifting away himself. Not a good job, but the question was put.

He walked the quarter of a mile back home, wishing he had had the guts to ask Mary if anyone in the area had a bandaged left hand, or if she'd heard of any such accident. Mary had boyfriends who frequented the local pub. Mary this minute might know of a man with a bandaged hand, but Michael could not possibly tell Mary that the missing fingers were in his garage.

The matter of what to do with the fingers was put aside for that morning, as the Herberts had laid on a drive to Cambridge, followed by lunch at the house of a don who was a friend of the Herberts. Unthinkable to cancel that because of getting involved with the police, so the fingers did not come up that morning in conversation. They talked of anything else during the drive. Michael and Gladys and Eddie had decided, before taking off for Cambridge, that they should not discuss the fingers again in front of Phyllis, but let it blow over, if possible. Eddie and Phyllis were to leave on the afternoon of Wednesday, day after tomorrow, and by then the matter might be cleared up or in the hands of the police.

Gladys also had gently warned Phyllis not to bring up "the cat incident" at the don's house, so Phyllis did not. All went well and happily, and the Herberts and Eddie and Phyllis were back at the Herberts' house around four. Edna told Gladys she had just realized they were short of butter, and since she was watching a cake . . . Michael, in the living room with Eddie, heard this and volunteered to go to the grocery.

Michael bought the butter, a couple of packets of cigarettes, a box of toffee that looked nice, and was served by Mary in her usual modest and polite manner. He had been hoping for news from her. Michael had taken his change and was walking to the door, when Mary cried: "Oh, Mr. Herbert!"

Michael turned round.

"I heard of someone disappearing just this noon," Mary said, leaning toward Michael across the counter, smiling now. "Bill Reeves—lives on Mr. Dickenson's property, you know. He has a cottage there, works on the land—or did."

Michael didn't know Bill Reeves, but he certainly knew of the Dickenson property, which was vast, to the northwest of the village. Bill Reeves's initials fitted the W.R. on the ring. "Yes? He disappeared?"

"About two weeks ago, Mr. Vickers told me. Mr. Vickers has the petrol station near the Dickenson property, you know. He came in today, so I thought I'd ask him." She smiled again, as if she had done satisfactorily with Michael's little riddle.

Michael knew the petrol station and knew how Vickers looked, vaguely. "Interesting. Does Mr. Vickers know why he disappeared?"

"No. Mr. Vickers said it's a mystery. Bill Reeves's wife left the cottage too, a few days ago, but everyone knows she went to Manchester to stay with her sister there."

Michael nodded. "Well, well. Shows it can happen even here, eh? People disappearing." He smiled and went out of the shop.

The thing to do was ring up Tom Dickenson, Michael thought, and ask him what he knew. Michael didn't call him Tom, had met him only a couple of times at local political rallies and such. Dickenson was about thirty, married, had inherited, and now led the life of gentleman farmer, Michael thought. The family was in the wool industry, had factories up north, and had owned their land here for generations.

When he got home, Michael asked Eddie to come up to his study, and despite Phyllis's curiosity, did not invite her to join them. Michael told Eddie what Mary had said about the disappearance of a farmworker called Bill Reeves a couple of weeks ago. Eddie agreed that they might ring up Dickenson.

"The initials on the ring could be an accident," Eddie said. "The Dickenson place is fifteen miles from here, you say."

"Yes, but I still think I'll ring him." Michael looked up the number in the directory on his desk. There were two numbers. Michael tried the first.

A servant answered, or someone who sounded like a servant, inquired Michael's name, then said he would summon Mr. Dickenson. Michael waited a good minute. Eddie was waiting too. "Hello, Mr. Dickenson. I'm one of your neighbors, Michael Herbert . . . Yes, yes, I know we have—couple of times. Look, I have a question to ask which you might think odd, but—I understand you had a workman or tenant on your land called Bill Reeves?"

"Ye-es?" replied Tom Dickenson.

"And where is he now? I'm asking because I was told he disappeared a couple of weeks ago."

"Yes, that's true. Why do you ask?"

"Do you know where he went?"

"No idea," replied Dickenson. "Did you have any dealings with him?"

"No. Could you tell me what his wife's name is?"

"Marjorie."

That fitted the first initial. "Do you happen to know her maiden name?"

Tom Dickenson chuckled. "I'm afraid I don't."

Michael glanced at Eddie, who was watching him. "Do you know if Bill Reeves wore a wedding ring?"

"No. Never paid that much attention to him. Why?"

Why, indeed? Michael shifted. If he ended the conversation here, he would not have learned much. "Because—I've found something that just might be a clue in regard to Bill Reeves. I presume someone's looking for him, if no one knows his whereabouts."

"I'm not looking for him," Tom Dickenson replied in his easy manner. "I doubt if his wife is, either. She moved out a week ago. May I ask what you found?"

"I'd rather not say over the phone . . . I wonder if I could come to see you. Or perhaps you could come to my house."

After an instant of silence, Dickenson said, "Quite honestly, I'm not interested in Reeves. I don't think he left any debts, as far as I know, I'll say that for him. But I don't care what's happened to him, if I may speak frankly."

"I see. Sorry to've bothered you, Mr. Dickenson."

They hung up.

Michael turned to Eddie Phelps and said, "I think you got most of that. Dickenson's not interested."

"Can't expect Dickenson to be concerned about a disappeared farmworker. Did I hear him say the wife's gone too?"

"Thought I told you. She went to Manchester to her sister's, Mary told me." Michael took a pipe from the rack on his desk and began to fill it. "Wife's name is Marjorie. Fits the initial on the ring."

"True," said the Colonel, "but there're lots of Marys and Margarets in the world."

"Dickenson didn't know her maiden name. Now look, Eddie, with no help from Dickenson, I'm thinking we ought to buzz the police and get this over with. I'm sure I can't bring myself to bury that—object. The thing would haunt me. I'd be thinking a dog would dig it up, even if it's just bones or in a worse state, and the police would have to start with somebody else besides me, and with a trail not so fresh to follow."

"You're still thinking of foul play?—I have a simpler idea," Eddie said with an air of calm and logic. "Gladys said there was a hospital twenty miles away, I presume in Colchester. We might ask if in the last two weeks or so there's been an accident involving the loss of third and fourth fingers of a man's left hand. They'd have his name. It looks like an accident and of the kind that doesn't happen every day."

Michael was on the brink of agreeing to this, at least before ringing the police, when the telephone rang. Michael took it, and found Gladys on the line downstairs with a man whose voice sounded like Dickenson's. "I'll take it, Gladys."

Tom Dickenson said hello to Michael. "I've—I thought if you really would like to see me—"

"I'd be very glad to."

"I'd prefer to speak with you alone, if that's possible."

Michael assured him it was, and Dickenson said he could come along in about twenty minutes. Michael put the telephone down with a feeling of relief, and said to Eddie, "He's coming over now and wants to talk with me alone. That is the best."

"Yes." Eddie got up from Michael's sofa, disappointed. "He'll be more open, if he has anything to say. Are you going to tell him about the fingers?" He peered at Michael sideways, bushy eyebrows raised.

"May not come to that. I'll see what he has to say first."

"He's going to ask you what you found."

Michael knew that. They went downstairs. Michael saw Phyllis in the back garden, banging a croquet ball all by herself, and heard Gladys's voice in the kitchen. Michael informed Gladys, out of Edna's hearing, of the imminent arrival of Tom Dickenson, and explained why: Mary's information that a certain Bill Reeves was missing, a worker on Dickenson's property. Gladys realized at once that the initials matched.

And here came Dickenson's car, a black Triumph convertible, rather in need of a wash. Michael went out to greet him. "Hellos," and "you remember mes." They vaguely remembered each other. Michael invited Dickenson into the house before Phyllis could drift over and compel an introduction.

Tom Dickenson was blond and tallish, now in leather jacket and corduroys and green rubber boots which he assured Michael were not muddy. He had just been working on his land, and hadn't taken the time to change.

"Let's go up," said Michael, leading the way to the stairs.

Michael offered Dickenson a comfortable armchair, and sat down on his old sofa. "You told me—Bill Reeves's wife went off too?"

Dickenson smiled a little, and his bluish-gray eyes gazed calmly at Michael. "His wife left, yes. But that was after Reeves vanished. Marjorie went to Manchester, I heard. She has a sister there. The Reeves weren't getting on so well. They're both about twenty-five—Reeves fond of his drink. I'll be glad to replace Reeves, frankly. Easily done."

Michael waited for more. It didn't come. Michael was wondering why Dickenson had been willing to come to see him about a farmworker he didn't much like?

"Why're you interested?" Dickenson asked. Then he broke out in a laugh which made him look younger and happier. "Is Reeves perhaps asking for a job with you—under another name?"

"Not at all." Michael smiled too. "I haven't anywhere to lodge a worker. No."

"But you said you found something?" Tom Dickenson's brows drew in a polite frown of inquiry.

Michael looked at the floor, then lifted his eyes and said, "I found two fingers of a man's left hand—with a wedding ring on one finger. The initials on the ring could stand for William Reeves. The other initials are M.T., which could be Marjorie somebody. That's why I thought I should ring you up."

Had Dickenson's face gone paler, or was Michael imagining? Dickenson's lips were slightly parted, his eyes uncertain. "Good lord, found it where?"

"Our cat dragged it in—believe it or not. Had to tell my wife, because the cat brought it into the living room in front of all of us." Somehow it was a tremendous relief for Michael to get the words out. "My old friend Eddie Phelps and his American niece are here now. They saw it." Michael stood up. Now he wanted a cigarette, got the box from his desk and offered it to Dickenson.

Dickenson said he had just stopped smoking, but he would like one.

"It was a bit shocking," Michael went on, "so I thought I'd make some inquiries in the neighborhood before I spoke to the police. I think informing the police is the right thing to do. Don't you?"

Dickenson did not answer at once.

"I had to cut away some of the finger to get the ring off—with Eddie's assistance last night." Dickenson still said nothing, only drew on his cigarette, frowning. "I thought the ring might give a clue, which it does, though it might have nothing at all to do with this Bill Reeves. You don't seem to know if he wore a wedding ring, and you don't know Marjorie's maiden name."

"Oh, that one can find out." Dickenson's voice sounded different and more husky.

"Do you think we should do that? Or maybe you know where Reeves's parents live. Or Marjorie's parents? Maybe Reeves is at one or the other's place now."

"Not at his wife's parents', I'll bet," said Dickenson with a nervous smile. "She's fed up with him."

"Well—what do you think? I'll tell the police? . . . Would you like to see the ring?"

"No. I'll take your word."

"Then I'll get in touch with the police tomorrow—or this evening. I suppose the sooner the better." Michael noticed Dickenson glancing around the room as if he might see the fingers lying on a bookshelf.

The study door moved and Portland Bill walked in. Michael never quite closed his door, and Bill had an assured way with doors, rearing a little and giving them a push.

Dickenson blinked at the cat, then said to Michael in a firm voice, "I could stand a whiskey. May I?"

Michael went downstairs and brought back the bottle and two glasses in his hands. There had been no one in the living room. Michael poured. Then he shut the door of his study.

Dickenson took a good inch of his drink at the first gulp. "I may as well tell you now that I killed Reeves."

A tremor went over Michael's shoulders, yet he told himself

that he had known this all along—or since Dickenson's telephone call to him, anyway. "Yes?" said Michael.

"Reeves had been . . . trying it on with my wife. I won't give it the dignity of calling it an affair. I blame my wife—flirting in a silly way with Reeves. He was just a lout, as far as I'm concerned. Handsome and stupid. His wife knew, and she hated him for it." Dickenson drew on the last of his cigarette, and Michael fetched the box again. Dickenson took one. "Reeves got ever more sure of himself. I wanted to sack him and send him away, but I couldn't because of his lease on the cottage, and I didn't want to bring the situation with my wife to light—with the law, I mean, as a reason."

"How long did this go on?"

Dickenson had to think. "Maybe about a month."

"And your wife—now?"

Tom Dickenson sighed, and rubbed his eyes. He sat hunched forward in his chair. "We'll patch it up. We've hardly been married a year."

"She knows you killed Reeves?"

Now Dickenson sat back, propped a green boot on one knee, and drummed the fingers of one hand on the arm of his chair. "I don't know. She may think I just sent him packing. She didn't ask any questions."

Michael could imagine, and he could also see that Dickenson would prefer that his wife never knew. Michael realized that he would have to make a decision: to turn Dickenson over to the police or not. Or would Dickenson even prefer to be turned in? Michael was listening to the confession of a man who had had a crime on his conscience for more than two weeks, bottled up inside himself, or so Michael assumed. And how had Dickenson killed him? "Does anyone else know?" Michael asked cautiously.

"Well—I can tell you about that. I suppose I must. Yes." Dickenson's voice was again hoarse, and his whiskey gone.

Michael got up and replenished Dickenson's glass.

Dickenson sipped now, and stared at the wall beside Michael.

Portland Bill sat at a little distance from Michael, concentrating on Dickenson as if he understood every word and was waiting for the next installment.

"I told Reeves to stop playing about with my wife or leave my property with his own wife, but he brought up the lease—and why didn't I speak to *my* wife. Arrogant, you know, so pleased with himself that the master's wife had deigned to look at him and—" Dickenson began again. "Tuesdays and Fridays I go to London to take care of the company. A couple of times, Diane said she didn't feel like going to London or she had some other engagement. Reeves could always manage to find a little work close to the house on those days, I'm sure. And then—there was a second victim—like me."

"Victim? What do you mean?"

"Peter." Now Dickenson rolled his glass between his hands, the cigarette projected from his lips, and he stared at the wall beside Michael, and spoke as if he were narrating what he saw on a screen there. "We were trimming some hedgerows deep in the fields, cutting stakes too for new markings. Reeves and I. Axes and sledgehammers. Peter was driving in stakes quite a way from us. Peter's another hand like Reeves, been with me longer. I had the feeling Reeves might attack me—then say it was an accident or some such. It was afternoon, and he'd had a few pints at lunch. He had a hatchet. I didn't turn my back on Reeves, and my anger was somehow rising. He had a smirk on his face, and he swung his hatchet as if to catch me in the thigh, though he wasn't near enough to me. Then he turned his back on me—arrogantly—and I hit him in the head with the big hammer. I hit him a second time as he was falling, but that landed on his back. I didn't know Peter was so close to me, or I didn't think about that. Peter came running, with his ax. Peter said, 'Good! Damn the bastard!' or something like that, and—" Dickenson seemed stuck for words, and looked at the floor, then the cat.

"And then? . . . Reeves was dead."

"Yes. All this happened in seconds. Peter really finished it with a bash on Reeves's head with the ax. We were quite near some woods—my woods. Peter said, 'Let's bury the swine! Get *rid* of him!' Peter was in a cursing rage and I was out of my mind for a different reason, maybe shock, but Peter was saying that Reeves had been having it off with his wife too, or trying to, and that he knew about Reeves and Diane. Peter and I dug a grave in the woods, both of us working like madmen—hacking at tree roots and throwing up earth with our hands. At the last, just before we threw him in, Peter took the hatchet and said—something about Reeves's wedding ring, and he brought the hatchet down a couple of times on Reeves's hand."

Michael did not feel so well. He leaned over, mainly to lower his head, and stroked the cat's strong back. The cat still concentrated on Dickenson.

"Then—we buried it, both of us drenched in sweat by then. Peter said, 'You won't get a word out of me, sir. This bastard deserved what he got.' We trampled the grave and Peter spat on it. Peter's a man, I'll say that for him."

"A man . . . And you?"

"I dunno." Dickenson's eyes were serious when he next spoke. "That was one of the days Diane had a tea date at some women's club in our village. The same afternoon, I thought, my God, the fingers! Maybe they're just lying there on the ground, because I couldn't remember Peter or myself throwing them into the grave. So I went back. I found them. I could've dug another hole, except that I hadn't brought anything to dig with and I also didn't want . . . anything more of Reeves on my land. So I got into my car and drove, not caring where, not paying any attention to where I was, and when I saw some woods, I got out and flung the thing as far as I could."

Michael said, "Must've been within half a mile of this house. Portland Bill doesn't venture farther, I think. He's been doctored, poor old Bill." The cat looked up at his name. "You trust this Peter?"

"I do. I knew his father and so did my father. And if I were asked—I'm not sure I could say who struck the fatal blow, I or Peter. But to be correct, *I'd* take the responsibility, because I did strike two blows with the hammer. I can't claim self-defense, because Reeves hadn't attacked me."

Correct. An odd word, Michael thought. But Dickenson was the type who would want to be correct. "What do you propose to do now?"

"Propose? I?" Dickenson's sigh was almost a gasp. "I dunno. I've admitted it. In a way it's in your hands or—" He made a gesture to indicate the downstairs. "I'd like to spare Peter—keep him out of it—if I can. You understand, I think. I can talk to you. You're a man like myself."

Michael was not sure of that, but he had been trying to imagine himself in Dickenson's position, trying to see himself twenty years younger in the same circumstances. Reeves had been a swine—even to his own wife—unprincipled, and should a young man like Dickenson ruin his own life, or the best part of it, over a man like Reeves? "What about Reeves's wife?"

Dickenson shook his head and frowned. "I know she detested him. If he's absent without tidings, I'll wager she'll never make the least effort to find him. She's glad to be rid of him, I'm sure."

A silence began and grew. Portland Bill yawned, arched his back and stretched. Dickenson watched the cat as if he might say something: after all the cat had discovered the fingers. But the cat said nothing. Dickenson broke the silence awkwardly but in a polite tone:

"Where are the fingers—by the way?"

"In the back of my garage—which is locked. They're in a shoe box." Michael felt quite off balance. "Look, I have two guests in the house."

Tom Dickenson got to his feet quickly. "I know. Sorry."

"Nothing to be sorry about, but I've really got to *say* something to them because the Colonel—my old friend Eddie—knows

I rang you up about the initials on the ring and that you were to call on us—me. He could've said something to the others."

"Of course. I understand."

"Could you stay here for a few minutes while I speak with the people downstairs? Feel free with the whiskey."

"Thank you." His eyes did not flinch.

Michael went downstairs. Phyllis was kneeling by the gramophone, about to put a record on. Eddie Phelps sat in a corner of the sofa reading a newspaper. "Where's Gladys?" Michael asked.

Gladys was deadheading roses. Michael called to her. She wore rubber boots like Dickenson, but hers were smaller and bright red. Michael looked to see if Edna was behind the kitchen door. Gladys said Edna had gone off to buy something at the grocery. Michael told Dickenson's story, trying to make it brief and clear. Phyllis's mouth fell open a couple of times. Eddie Phelps held his chin in a wise-looking fashion and said "Um-hm" now and then.

"I really don't feel like turning him in—or even speaking to the police," Michael ventured in a voice hardly above a whisper. No one had said anything after his narration, and Michael had waited several seconds. "I don't see why we can't just let it blow over. What's the harm?"

"What's the harm, yes," said Eddie Phelps, but it might have been a mindless echo for all the help it gave Michael.

"I've heard of stories like this—among primitive peoples," Phyllis said earnestly, as if to say she found Tom Dickenson's action quite justifiable.

Michael had of course included the resident worker Peter in his account. Had Dickenson's hammer blow been fatal, or the blow of Peter's ax? "The primitive ethic is not what I'm concerned with," Michael said, and at once felt confused. In regard to Tom Dickenson he was concerned with just the opposite of the primitive.

"But what else is it?" asked Phyllis.

"Yes, yes," said the Colonel, gazing at the ceiling.

"Really, Eddie," said Michael, "you're not being much of a help."

"I'd say nothing about it. Bury those fingers somewhere—with the ring. Or maybe the ring in a different place for safety. Yes." The Colonel was almost muttering, murmuring, but he did look at Michael.

"I'm not sure," said Gladys, frowning with thought.

"I agree with Uncle Eddie," Phyllis said, aware that Dickenson was upstairs awaiting his verdict. "Mr. Dickenson was provoked—seriously—and the man who got killed seems to have been a creep!"

"That's not the way the law looks at it," Michael said with a wry smile. "Lots of people are provoked seriously. And a human life is a human life."

"We're not the law," said Phyllis, as if they were something superior to the law just then.

Michael had been thinking just that: they were not the law, but they were acting as if they were. He was inclined to go along with Phyllis—and Eddie. "All right. I don't feel like reporting this, given all the circumstances."

But Gladys held out. She wasn't sure. Michael knew his wife well enough to believe that it was not going to be a bone of contention between them, if they were at variance—just now. So Michael said, "You're one against three, Glad. Do you seriously want to ruin a young man's life for a thing like this?"

"True, we've got to take a vote, as if we were a jury," said Eddie.

Gladys saw the point. She conceded. Less than a minute later, Michael climbed the stairs to his study, where the first draft of a book review curled in the roller of his typewriter, untouched since the day before yesterday. Fortunately he could still meet the deadline without killing himself.

"We don't want to report this to the police," Michael said.

Dickenson, on his feet, nodded solemnly as if receiving a verdict. He would have nodded in the same manner if he had been
told the opposite, Michael thought.

"I'll get rid of the fingers," Michael mumbled, and bent to get
some pipe tobacco.

"Surely that's my responsibility. Let me bury them somewhere—with the ring."

It really was Dickenson's responsibility, and Michael was glad
to escape the task. "Right. Well—shall we go downstairs? Would
you like to meet my wife and my friend Colonel—"

"No, thank you. Not just now," Dickenson interrupted.
"Another time. But would you give them—my thanks?"

They went down some other stairs at the back of the hall, and
out to the garage, whose key Michael had in his key case. Michael
thought for a moment that the shoe box might have disappeared
mysteriously as in a detective story, but it was exactly where he had
left it, on top of the old jerricans. He gave it to Dickenson, and
Dickenson departed in his dusty Triumph northward. Michael
entered his house by the front door.

By now the others were having a drink. Michael felt suddenly
relieved, and he smiled. "I think old Portland ought to have something special at the cocktail hour, don't you?" Michael said, mainly
to Gladys.

Portland Bill was looking without much interest at a bowl of
ice cubes. Only Phyllis said, "*Yes!*" with enthusiasm.

Michael went to the kitchen and spoke with Edna who was
dusting flour onto a board. "Any more smoked salmon left from
lunch?"

"One slice, sir," said Edna, as if it weren't worth serving to anyone, and she virtuously hadn't eaten it, though she might.

"Can I have it for old Bill? He adores it." When Michael came
back into the living room with the pink slice on a saucer, Phyllis
said:

"I bet Mr. Dickenson wrecks his car on the way home. That's often the way it is." She whispered suddenly, remembering her manners, "Because he feels *guilty*."

Portland Bill bolted his salmon with brief but intense delight. Tom Dickenson did not wreck his car.

Not One of Us

It wasn't merely that Edmund Quasthoff had stopped smoking and almost stopped drinking that made him different, slightly goody-goody and therefore vaguely unlikable. It was something else. What?

That was the subject of conversation at Lucienne Gauss's apartment in the East 80s one evening at the drinks hour, seven. Julian Markus, a lawyer, was there with his wife Frieda, also Peter Tomlin, a journalist aged twenty-eight and the youngest of the circle. The circle numbered seven or eight, the ones who knew Edmund well, meaning for most of them about eight years. The others present were Tom Strathmore, a sociologist, and Charles Forbes and his wife, Charles being an editor in a publishing house, and Anita Ketchum, librarian at a New York art museum. They gathered more often at Lucienne's apartment than at anyone else's, because Lucienne liked entertaining and, as a painter working on her own, her hours were flexible.

Lucienne was thirty-three, unmarried, and quite pretty with fluffy reddish hair, a smooth pale skin, and a delicate, intelligent mouth. She liked expensive clothes, she went to a good beauty parlor, and she had style. The rest of the group called her, behind her back, a lady, shy even among themselves at using the word (Tom the sociologist had), because it was an old-fashioned or snob word, perhaps.

Edmund Quasthoff, a tax accountant in a law firm, had been divorced a year ago, because his wife had run off with another man and had therefore asked for a divorce. Edmund was forty, quite tall, with brown hair, a quiet manner, and was neither handsome nor unattractive, but lacking in that spark which can make even a rather ugly person attractive. Lucienne and her group had said after the divorce, "No wonder. Edmund *is* sort of a bore."

On this evening at Lucienne's, someone said out of the blue, "Edmund didn't used to be such a bore—did he?"

"I'm afraid so. *Yes!*" Lucienne yelled from the kitchen, because at that moment she had turned on the water at the sink in order to push ice cubes out of a metal tray. She heard someone laugh. Lucienne went back to the living room with the ice bucket. They were expecting Edmund at any moment. Lucienne had suddenly realized that she wanted Edmund out of their circle, that she actively disliked him.

"Yes, what *is* it about Edmund?" asked Charles Forbes with a sly smile at Lucienne. Charles was pudgy, his shirt front strained at the buttons, a patch of leg often showed between sock and trousers cuff when he sat, but he was well loved by the group, because he was good-natured and bright, and could drink like a fish and never show it. "Maybe we're all jealous because he stopped smoking," Charles said, putting out his cigarette and reaching for another.

"I admit *I'm* jealous," said Peter Tomlin with a broad grin. "I know I should stop and I damned well can't. Tried to twice—in the last year."

Peter's details about his efforts were not interesting. Edmund was due with his new wife, and the others were talking while they could.

"Maybe it's his wife!" Anita Ketchum whispered excitedly, knowing this would get a laugh and encourage further comments. It did.

"Worse than the first by far!" Charles avowed.

"Yes, Lillian wasn't bad at all! I agree," said Lucienne, still on her feet and handing Peter the Vat 69 bottle, so he could top up his glass the way he liked it. "It's true Magda's no asset. That—" Lucienne had been about to say something quite unkind about the scared yet aloof expression which often showed on Magda's face.

"Ah, marriage on the rebound," Tom Strathmore said musingly.

"Certainly was, yes," said Frieda Markus. "Maybe we have to forgive that. You know they say men suffer more than women if their spouses walk out on them? Their egos suffer, they say—worse."

"Mine would suffer with *Magda*, matter of fact," Tom said.

Anita gave a laugh. "And what a name, Magda! Makes me think of a lightbulb or something."

The doorbell rang.

"Must be Edmund." Lucienne went to press the release button. She had asked Edmund and Magda to stay for dinner, but they were going to a play tonight. Only three were staying for dinner, the Markuses and Peter Tomlin.

"But he's changed his job, don't forget," Peter was saying as Lucienne came back into the room. "You can't say he has to be clammed up—secretive, I mean. It's not *that*." Like the others, Peter sought for a word, a phrase to describe the unlikability of Edmund Quasthoff.

"He's stuffy," said Anita Ketchum with a curl of distaste at her lips.

A few seconds of silence followed. The apartment doorbell was supposed to ring.

"Do you suppose he's happy?" Charles asked in a whisper.

This was enough to raise a clap of collective laughter. The thought of Edmund radiating happiness, even with a two-month-old marriage, was risible.

"But then he's probably never been happy," said Lucienne, just as the bell rang, and she turned to go to the door.

"Not late, I hope, Lucienne dear," said Edmund coming in, bending to kiss Lucienne's cheek, and by inches not touching it.

"No-o. I've got the time but you haven't. How are *you*, Magda?" Lucienne asked with deliberate enthusiasm, as if she really cared how Magda was.

"Very well, thank you, and you?" Magda was in brown again, a light and dark brown cotton dress with a brown satin scarf at her neck.

Both of them looked brown and dull, Lucienne thought as she led them into the living room. Greetings sounded friendly and warm.

"No, just tonic, please . . . Oh well, a smidgin of gin," Edmund said to Charles, who was doing the honors. "Lemon slice, yes, thanks." Edmund as usual gave an impression of sitting on the edge of his armchair seat.

Anita was dutifully making conversation with Magda on the sofa.

"And how're you liking your new job, Edmund?" Lucienne asked. Edmund had been with the accounting department of the United Nations for several years, but his present job was better paid and far less cloistered, Lucienne gathered, with business lunches nearly every day.

"O-oh," Edmund began, "different crowd, I'll say that." He tried to smile. Smiles from Edmund looked like efforts. "These boozy lunches . . ." Edmund shook his head. "I think they even resent the fact I don't smoke. They want you to be like them, you know?"

"Who's them?" asked Charles Forbes.

"Clients of the agency and a lot of the time *their* accountants," Edmund replied. "They all prefer to talk business at the lunch table instead of face to face in my office. 'S funny." Edmund rubbed a forefinger along the side of his arched nose. "I have to have one or two drinks with them—my usual restaurant knows now to make them weak—otherwise our clients might think I'm the Infernal Revenue Department itself putting—honesty before expediency or some such." Edmund's face again cracked in a smile that did not last long.

Pity, Lucienne thought, and she almost said it. A strange word to think of, because pity she had not for Edmund. Lucienne exchanged a glance with Charles, then with Tom Strathmore, who was smirking.

"They call me up at all hours of the night too. California doesn't seem to realize the time dif—"

"Take your phone off the hook at night," Charles' wife Ellen put in.

"Oh, can't afford to," Edmund replied. "Sacred cows, these

worried clients. Sometimes they ask me questions a pocket calcu-
lator could answer. But Babcock and Holt have to be polite, so I
go on losing sleep . . . No, thanks, Peter," he said as Peter tried to
pour more drink for him. Edmund also pushed gently aside a
nearly full ashtray whose smell perhaps annoyed him.

Lucienne would ordinarily have emptied the ashtray, but now
she didn't. And Magda? Magda was glancing at her watch as Lucienne looked at her, though she chatted now with Charles on her
left. Twenty-eight she was, enviably young to be sure, but what a
drip! A bad skin. Small wonder she hadn't been married before.
She still kept her job, Edmund had said, something to do with
computers. She knitted well, her parents were Mormons, though
Magda wasn't. Really wasn't, Lucienne wondered?

A moment later, having declined even orange or tomato juice,
Magda said gently to her husband, "Darling . . ." and tapped her
wristwatch face.

Edmund put down his glass at once, and his old-fashioned
brown shoes with wing tips rose from the floor a little before he
hauled himself up. Edmund looked tired already, though it was
hardly eight. "Ah, yes, the theater—Thank you, Lucienne. It's been
a pleasure as usual."

"But such a short one!" said Lucienne.

When Edmund and Magda had left, there was a general
"Whew!" and a few chuckles, which sounded not so much indul-
gent as bitterly amused.

"I really wouldn't like to be married to that," said Peter Tomlin, who was unmarried. "Frankly," he added. Peter had known
Edmund since he, Peter, was twenty-two, having been introduced
via Charles Forbes, at whose publishing house Peter had applied
for a job without success. The older Charles had liked Peter, and
had introduced him to a few of his friends, among them Lucienne
and Edmund. Peter remembered his first good impression of
Edmund Quasthoff—that of a serious and trustworthy man—but
whatever virtue Peter had seen in Edmund was somehow gone

now, as if that first impression had been a mistake on Peter's part. Edmund had not lived up to life, somehow. There was something cramped about him, and the crampedness seemed personified in Magda. Or was it that Edmund didn't really like *them*?

"Maybe he deserves Magda," Anita said, and the others laughed.

"Maybe he doesn't like us either," said Peter.

"Oh, but he does," Lucienne said. "Remember, Charles, how pleased he was when—we sort of accepted him—at that first dinner party I asked Edmund and Lillian to here at my place. One of my birthday dinners, I remember. Edmund and Lillian were beaming because they'd been admitted to our charmed circle." Lucienne's laugh was disparaging of their circle and also of Edmund.

"Yes, Edmund did try," said Charles.

"His clothes are so boring even," Anita said.

"True. Can't some of you men give him a hint? You, Julian." Lucienne glanced at Julian's crisp cotton suit. "You're always so dapper."

"Me?" Julian settled his jacket on his shoulders. "I frankly think men pay more attention to what women say. Why should I say anything to him?"

"Magda told me Edmund wants to buy a car," said Ellen.

"Does he drive?" Peter asked.

"May I, Lucienne?" Tom Strathmore reached for the scotch bottle which stood on a tray. "Maybe what Edmund needs is to get thoroughly soused one night. Then Magda might even leave him."

"Hey, we've just invited the Quasthoffs for dinner at our place Friday night," Charles announced. "Maybe Edmund *can* get soused. Who else wants to come?—Lucienne?"

Anticipating boredom, Lucienne hesitated. But it might not be boring. "Why not? Thank you, Charles—and Ellen."

Peter Tomlin couldn't make it because of a Friday night deadline. Anita said she would love to come. Tom Strathmore was free, but not the Markuses, because it was Julian's mother's birthday.

It was a memorable party in the Forbeses' big kitchen which served as dining room. Magda had not been to the penthouse apartment before. She politely looked at the Forbeses' rather good collection of framed drawings by contemporary artists, but seemed afraid to make a comment. Magda was on her best behavior, while the others as if by unspoken agreement were unusually informal and jolly. Part of this, Lucienne realized, was meant to shut Magda out of their happy old circle, and to mock her stiff decorum, though in fact everyone went out of his or her way to try and get Edmund and Magda to join in the fun. One form that this took, Lucienne observed, was Charles's pouring gin into Edmund's tonic glass with a rather free hand. At the table, Ellen did the same with the wine. It was especially good wine, a vintage Margaux that went superbly with the hot-oil-cooked steak morsels which they all dipped into a pot in the center of the round table. There was hot, buttery garlic bread, and paper napkins on which to wipe greasy fingers.

"Come on, you're not working tomorrow," Tom said genially, replenishing Edmund's wine glass.

"I—yam working tomorrow," Edmund replied, smiling. "Always do. Have to on Saturdays."

Magda was giving Edmund a fixed stare, which he missed, because his eyes were not straying her way.

After dinner, they adjourned to the long sun parlor which had a terrace beyond it. With the coffee those who wanted it had a choice of Drambuie, Bénédictine or brandy. Edmund had a sweet tooth, Lucienne knew, and she noticed that Charles had no difficulty in persuading Edmund to accept a snifter of Drambuie. Then they played darts.

"Darts're as far as I'll go toward exercising," said Charles, winding up. His first shot was a bull's-eye.

The others took their turns, and Ellen kept score.

Edmund wound up awkwardly, trying to look amusing, they all knew, though still making an effort to aim right. Edmund was anything but limber and coordinated. His first shot hit the wall three feet away from the board, and since it hit sideways, it pierced nothing and fell to the floor. So did Edmund, having twisted somehow on his left foot and lost his balance.

Cries of "Bravo!" and merry laughter.

Peter extended a hand and hauled Edmund up. "Hurt yourself?"

Edmund looked shocked and was not laughing when he stood up. He straightened his jacket. "I don't think—I have the definite feeling—" His eyes glanced about, but rather swimmily, while the others waited, listening. "I have the feeling I'm not exactly well liked here—so I—"

"Oh-h, Edmund!" said Lucienne.

"What're you talking about, Edmund?" asked Ellen.

A Drambuie was pressed into Edmund's hand, despite the fact that Magda tried gently to restrain the hand that offered it. Edmund was soothed, but not much. The darts game continued. Edmund was sober enough to realize that he shouldn't make an ass of himself by walking out at once in a huff, yet he was drunk enough to reveal his gut feeling, fuzzy as it might be to him just then, that the people around him were not his true friends any more, that they really didn't like him. Magda persuaded him to drink more coffee.

The Quasthoffs took their leave some fifteen minutes later.

There was an immediate sense of relief among all.

"She is the end, let's face it," said Anita, and flung a dart.

"Well, we got him soused," said Tom Strathmore. "So it's possible."

Somehow they had all tasted blood on seeing Edmund comically sprawled on the floor.

Lucienne that night, having had more to drink than usual, mainly in the form of two good brandies after dinner, telephoned Edmund at four in the morning with an idea of asking him how he was. She knew she was calling him also in order to disturb his sleep. After five rings, when Edmund answered in a sleepy voice, Lucienne found she could not say anything.

"Hello?—Hello? Qu-Quasthoff here . . ."

When she awakened in the morning, the world looked somehow different—sharper edged and more exciting. It was not the slight nervousness that might have been caused by a hangover. In fact Lucienne felt very well after her usual breakfast of orange juice, English tea and toast, and she painted well for two hours. She realized that she was busy detesting Edmund Quasthoff. Ludicrous, but there it was. And how many of her friends were feeling the same way about Edmund today?

The telephone rang just after noon, and it was Anita Ketchum. "I hope I'm not interrupting you in the middle of a masterstroke."

"No, no! What's up?"

"Well—Ellen called me this morning to tell me Edmund's birthday party is off."

"I didn't know any was on."

Anita explained. Magda last evening had invited Charles and Ellen to a birthday dinner party for Edmund at her and Edmund's apartment nine days from now, and had told Ellen she would invite "everybody" plus some friends of hers whom everybody might not have met yet, because it would be a stand-up buffet affair. Then this morning, without any explanation such as that Edmund or she were ill with a lingering ailment, Magda had said she had "decided against" a party, she was sorry.

"Maybe afraid of Edmund's getting pissed again," Lucienne said, but she knew that wasn't the whole answer.

"I'm sure she thinks we don't like her—or Edmund much—which unfortunately is true."

"What *can* we do?" asked Lucienne, feigning chagrin.

"Social outcasts, aren't we? Hah-hah. Got to sign off now, Lucienne, because someone's waiting."

The little contretemps of the canceled party seemed both hostile and silly to Lucienne, and the whole group got wind of it within a day or so, even though they all might not as yet have been invited.

"We can also invite and disinvite," chuckled Julian Markus on the telephone to Lucienne. "What a childish trick—with no excuse such as a business trip."

"No excuse, no. Well, I'll think of something funny, Julian dear."

"What do you mean?"

"A little smack back at them. Don't you think they deserve it?"

"Yes, my dear."

Lucienne's first idea was simple. She and Tom Strathmore would invite Edmund out for lunch on his birthday, and get him so drunk he would be in no condition to return to his office that afternoon. Tom was agreeable. And Edmund sounded grateful when Lucienne rang him up and extended the invitation, without mentioning Magda's name.

Lucienne booked a table at a rather expensive French restaurant in the East 60s. She and Tom and three dry martinis were waiting when Edmund arrived, smiling tentatively, but plainly glad to see his old friends again at a small table. They chatted amiably. Lucienne managed to pay some compliments in regard to Magda.

"She has a certain dignity," said Lucienne.

"I wish she weren't so *shy*," Edmund responded at once. "I try to pull her out of it."

Another round. Lucienne delayed the ordering by having to make a telephone call at a moment when Tom was able to order a third round to fill the time until Lucienne got back. Then they ordered their meal, with white wine to be followed by a red. On the first glass of white, Tom and Lucienne sang a soft chorus of "Happy Birthday to You" to Edmund as they lifted their glasses. Lucienne had rung Anita, who worked only three blocks away, and Anita joined them when the lunch ended just after three with a Drambuie for Edmund, though Lucienne and Tom abstained. Edmund kept murmuring something about a three o'clock appointment, which maybe would be all right for him to miss, because it really wasn't a top-level appointment. Anita and the others told him it would surely be excusable on his birthday.

"I've just got half an hour," Anita said as they went out of the restaurant together, Anita having partaken of nothing, "but I did want to see you on this special day, Edmund old thing. I insist on inviting you for a drink or a beer."

The others kissed Edmund's cheek and left, then Anita steered Edmund across the street into a corner bar with a fancy decor that tried to be an old Irish pub. Edmund fairly fell into his chair, having nearly slipped a moment before on sawdust. It was a wonder he was served, Anita thought, but hers was a sober presence, and they were served. From this bar, Anita rang Peter Tomlin and explained the situation, which Peter found funny, and Peter agreed to come and take over for a few minutes. Peter arrived. Edmund had a second beer, and insisted upon a coffee, which was ordered, but the combination seemed to make him sick. Anita had left minutes before. Peter waited patiently, prattling nonsense to Edmund, wondering if Edmund was going to throw up or slip under the table.

"Mag's got people coming at six," Edmund mumbled. "Gotta be home—little before—or else." He tried in vain to read his watch.

"Mag you call her? . . . Finish your beer, chum." Peter lifted his first glass of beer, which was nearly drained. "Bottoms up and many happy returns!"

They emptied their glasses.

Peter delivered Edmund to his apartment door at 6:25 and ran. A cocktail party was in swing *chez* Magda and Edmund, Peter could tell from the hum of voices behind the closed door. Edmund had been talking about his "boss" being present, and a couple of important clients. Peter smiled to himself as he rode down in the elevator. He went home, put in a good report to Lucienne, made himself some instant coffee, and got back to his typewriter.

Comical, yes! Poor old Edmund! But it was Magda who amused Peter the more. Magda was the stuffy one, their real target, Peter thought.

Peter Tomlin was to change his opinion about that in less than a fortnight. He watched with some surprise and gathering alarm as the attack, led by Lucienne and to a lesser extent Anita, focused on Edmund. Ten days after the sousing of Edmund, Peter looked in one evening at the Markuses' apartment—just to return a couple of books he had borrowed—and found both smirking over Edmund's latest mishap. Edmund had lost his job at Babcock and Holt and was now in the Payne-Whitney for drying out.

"What?" Peter said. "I hadn't heard a word!"

"We just found out today," said Frieda. "Lucienne called me up. She said she tried to call Edmund at his office this morning, and they said he was absent on leave, but she insisted on finding out where he was—said it concerned an emergency in his family, you know how good she is at things like that. So they told her he was in the Payne-Whitney, and she phoned there and talked with Edmund personally. He also had an accident with his car, he said, but luckily he didn't hurt himself or anyone else."

"Holy cow," said Peter.

"He always had a fondness for the bottle, you know," Julian said, "and a thimble-belly to go with it. He really had to go on the wagon five or six years ago, wasn't it, Frieda? Maybe you didn't know Edmund then, Peter. Well, he did, but it didn't last long. Then it got worse when Lillian walked out. But now *this* job—"

Frieda Markus giggled. "This job!—Lucienne didn't help and you know it. She invited Edmund to her place a couple of times and plied him. Made him talk about his troubles with Mag."

Troubles. Peter felt a twinge of dislike for Edmund for talking about his "troubles" after only three months or so of marriage. Didn't everyone have troubles? Did people have to bore their friends with them? "Maybe he deserved it," Peter murmured.

"In a way, *yes*," Julian said forcefully, and reached for a cigarette. Julian's aggressive attitude implied that the anti-Edmund campaign wasn't over. "He's weak," Julian added.

Peter thanked Julian for the loan of the two books, and took his leave. Again he had work to do in the evening, so he couldn't linger for a drink. At home, Peter hesitated between calling Lucienne or Anita, decided on Lucienne, but she didn't answer, so he tried Anita. Anita was home and Lucienne was there. Both spoke with Peter, and both sounded merry. Peter asked Lucienne about Edmund.

"Oh, he'll be sprung in another week or so, he said. But he won't be quite the same man, I think, when he comes out."

"How do you mean that?"

"Well, he's lost his job and this story isn't going to make it easier for him to get another one. He's probably lost Magda too, because Edmund told me she'd leave him if they didn't move out of New York."

"So . . . maybe they will move," said Peter. "He told you he'd definitely lost his job?"

"Oh yes. They call it a leave of absence at his office, but Edmund admitted they're not taking him back." Lucienne gave a short, shrill laugh. "Just as well they do move out of New York. Magda hates *us*, you know. And frankly Edmund never was one of us—so in a way it's understandable."

Was it understandable, Peter wondered as he got down to his own work. There was something vicious about the whole thing, and he'd been vicious plying Edmund with beers that day. The curious thing was that Peter felt no compassion for Edmund.

One might have thought that the group would leave Edmund alone, at least, even make some effort to cheer him up (without drinks) when he got out of the Payne-Whitney, but it was just the opposite, Peter observed. Anita Ketchum invited Edmund for a quiet dinner at her apartment, and asked Peter to come too. She did not ply him with drink, though Edmund had at least three on his own. Edmund was morose, and Anita did not make his mood any better by talking against Magda. She fairly said that Edmund could and should do better than Magda, and that he ought to try as soon as possible. Peter had to concur here.

"She doesn't seem to make you very happy, Ed," Peter remarked in a man-to-man way, "and now I hear she wants you to move out of New York."

"That's true," Edmund said, "and I dunno where else I'd get a decent job."

They talked until late, getting nowhere, really. Peter left before Edmund did. Peter found that the memory of Edmund depressed him: a tall, hunched figure in limp clothes, looking at the floor as he strolled around Anita's living room with a glass in his hand.

Lucienne was home in bed reading when the telephone rang at one in the morning. It was Edmund, and he said he was going to get a divorce from Mag.

"She just walked out—just now," Edmund said in a happy but a bit drunk-sounding voice. "Said she was going to stay in a hotel tonight. I don't even know where."

Lucienne realized that he wanted a word of praise from her, or a congratulation. "Well, dear Edmund, it may be for the best. I hope it can all be settled smoothly. After all, you haven't been married long."

"No. I think I'm doing—I mean she's doing—the right thing," said Edmund heavily.

Lucienne assured him that she thought so too.

Now Edmund was going to look for another job. He didn't think Mag would make any difficulties, financial or otherwise, about the divorce. "She's a young woman w-who likes her privacy quite a bit. She's surprisingly . . . *independent*, y'know?" Edmund hiccuped.

Lucienne smiled, thinking any woman would want independence from Edmund. "We'll all be wishing you luck, Edmund. And let us know if you think we can pull strings anywhere."

Charles Forbes and Julian Markus went to Edmund's apart-

ment one evening, to discuss business, Charles later said to Lucienne, as Charles had an idea of Edmund's becoming a freelance
accountant, and in fact Charles' publishing house needed such a
man now. They drank hardly anything, according to Charles, but
they did stay up quite late. Edmund had been down in the dumps,
and around midnight had lowered the scotch bottle by several
inches.

That was on a Thursday night, and by Tuesday morning,
Edmund was dead. The cleaning woman had come in with her key
and found him asleep in bed, she thought, at nine in the morning.
She hadn't realized until nearly noon, and then she had called the
police. The police hadn't been able to find Magda, and notifying
anybody had been much delayed, so it was Wednesday evening
before any of the group knew: Peter Tomlin saw an item in his
own newspaper, and telephoned Lucienne.

"A mixture of sleeping pills and alcohol, but they don't suspect suicide," Peter said.

Neither did Lucienne suspect suicide. "What an end," she said
with a sigh. "Now what?" She was not at all shocked, but vaguely
thinking about the others in their circle hearing the news, or reading it now.

"Well—funeral service tomorrow in a Long Island—um—
funeral home, it says."

Peter and Lucienne agreed they should go.

The group of friends, Lucienne Gauss, Peter Tomlin, the
Markuses, the Forbeses, Tom Strathmore, Anita Ketchum, were all
there and formed at least a half of the small gathering. Maybe a
few of Edmund's relatives had come, but the group wasn't sure:
Edmund's family lived in the Chicago area, and no one had ever
met any of them. Magda was there, dressed in gray with a thin
black veil. She stood apart, and barely nodded to Lucienne and the
others. It was a nondenominational service to which Lucienne
paid no attention, and she doubted if her friends did—except to
recognize the words as empty rote and close their ears to it. After-

wards, Lucienne and Charles said they didn't wish to follow the casket to the grave, and neither did the others.

Anita's mouth looked stony, though it was fixed in a pensive, very faint smile. Taxis waited, and they straggled towards them. Tom Strathmore walked with his head down. Charles Forbes looked up at the late summer sky. Charles walked between his wife, Ellen, and Lucienne, and suddenly he said to Lucienne:

"You know, I rang Edmund up a couple of times in the night—just to annoy him. I have to confess that. Ellen knows."

"Did you," said Lucienne calmly.

Tom, just behind them, had heard this. "I did worse," he said with a twitch of a smile. "I told Edmund he might lose his job if he started taking Magda out with him on his business lunches."

Ellen laughed. "Oh, that's not serious, Tom. That's—" But she didn't finish.

We killed him, Lucienne thought. Everybody was thinking that, and no one had the guts to say it. Anyone of them might have said, "We killed him, you know?" but no one did. "We'll miss him," Lucienne said finally, as if she meant it.

"Ye-es," someone replied with equal gravity.

They climbed into three taxis, promising to see each other soon.

The Terrors of
Basket-Weaving

Diane's terror began in an innocent and fortuitous way. She and her husband, Reg, lived in Manhattan, but had a cottage on the Massachusetts coast near Truro where they spent most weekends. Diane was a press relations officer in an agency called Retting. Reg was a lawyer. They were both thirty-eight, childless by choice, and both earned good salaries.

They enjoyed walks along the beach, and usually they took walks alone, not with each other. Diane liked to look for pretty stones, interesting shells, bottles of various sizes and colors, bits of wood rubbed smooth by sand and wind. These items she took back to the unpainted gray cottage they called "the shack," lived with them for a few weeks or months, then Diane threw nearly all of them out, because she didn't want the shack to become a magpie's nest. One Sunday morning she found a wicker basket bleached nearly white and with its bottom stoved in, but its frame and sides quite sturdy. This looked like an old-fashioned crib basket for a baby, because one end of it rose higher than the other, the foot part tapered, and it was just the size for a newborn or for a baby up to a few months. It was the kind called a Moses basket, Diane thought.

Was the basket even American? It was amusing to think that it might have fallen overboard or been thrown away, old and broken, from a passing Italian tanker, or some foreign boat that might have had a woman and child on board. Anyway, Diane decided to take it home, and she put it for the nonce on a bench on the side porch of the shack, where colored stones and pebbles and sea glass already lay. She might try to repair it, for fun, because in its present condition it was useless. Reg was then shifting sand with a snow shovel from one side of the wooden front steps, and was going to plant more beach grass from the dunes, like a second line of troops, between them and the sea to keep the sand in place. His industry, which Diane knew would go on another hour or so until lunchtime—and cold lobster and potato salad was already in the fridge—inspired her to try her hand at the basket now.

She had realized a few minutes before that the kind of slender twigs she needed stood already in a brass cylinder beside their small fireplace. Withes or withies—the words sounded nice in her head—might be more appropriate, but on the other hand the twigs would give more strength to the bottom of a basket which she might use to hold small potted plants, for instance. One would be able to move several pots into the sun all at once in a basket—if she could mend the basket.

Diane took the pruning shears, and cut five lengths of reddish-brown twigs—results of a neighbor's apple-tree pruning, she recalled—and then snipped nine shorter lengths for the cross-pieces. She estimated she would need nine. A ball of twine sat handy on a shelf, and Diane at once got to work. She plucked out what was left of the broken pieces in the basket, and picked up one of her long twigs. The slightly pointed ends, an angle made by the shears, slipped easily between the sturdy withes that formed the bottom rim. She took up a second and a third. Diane then, before she attempted to tie the long pieces, wove the shorter lengths under and over the longer, at right angles. The twigs were just flex-ible enough to be manageable, and stiff enough to be strong. No piece projected too far. She had cut them just the right length, measuring only with her eye or thumb before snipping. Then the twine.

Over and under, around the twig ends at the rim and through the withes already decoratively twisted there, then a good solid knot. She was able to continue with the cord to the next twig in a couple of places, so she did not have to tie a knot at each cross-piece. Suddenly to her amazement the basket was repaired, and it looked splendid.

In her first glow of pride, Diane looked at her watch. Hardly fifteen minutes had passed since she had come into the house! How had she done it? She held the top end of the basket up, and pressed the palm of her right hand against the floor of the basket. It gave out firm-sounding squeaks. It had spring in it. And strength. She stared at the neatly twisted cord, at the correct over-and-under lengths, all about the diameter of pencils, and she wondered again how she had done it.

That was when the terror began to creep up on her, at first like a faint suspicion or surmise or question. Had she some relative or ancestor not so far in the past, who had been an excellent basket-weaver? Not that she knew of, and the idea made her smile with amusement. Grandmothers and great-grandmothers who could quilt and crochet didn't count. This was more primitive.

Yes, people had been weaving baskets thousands of years before Christ, and maybe even a million years ago, hadn't they? Baskets might have come before clay pots.

The answer to her question, how had she done it, might be that the ancient craft of basket-weaving had been carried on for so long by the human race that it had surfaced in her this Sunday morning in the late twentieth century. Diane found this thought rather frightening.

As she set the table for lunch, she upset a wine glass, but the glass was empty and it didn't break. Reg was still shoveling, but slowing up, nearly finished. It was still early for lunch, but Diane had wanted the table set, the salad dressing made in the wooden bowl, before she took a swat at the work she had brought with her. Finally she sat with a yellow pad and pencil, and opened the plastic-covered folder marked RETTING, plus her own name, DIANE CLARKE, in smaller letters at the bottom. She had to write three hundred words about a kitchen gadget that extracted air from plastic bags of apples, oranges, potatoes or whatever. After the air was extracted, the bags could be stored in the bottom of the fridge as usual, but the product kept much longer and took up less space because of the absence of air in the bag. She had seen the gadget work in the office, and she had a photograph of it now. It was a sixteen-inch-long tube which one fastened to the cold water tap in the kitchen. The water from the tap drained away, but its force moved a turbine in the tube, which created a vacuum after a hollow needle was stuck into the sealed bag. Diane understood the principle quite well, but she began to feel odd and disoriented.

It was odd to be sitting in a cottage built in a simple style more than a hundred years ago, to have just repaired a basket in the manner that people would have made or repaired a basket thousands of years ago, and to be trying to compose a sentence about a gadget whose existence depended upon modern plumbing, sealed packaging, transport by machinery of fruit and vegetables grown hundreds of miles (possibly thousands) from the places where they would be consumed. If this weren't so, people could simply carry fruit and vegetables home in a sack from the fields, or in baskets such as the one she had just mended.

Diane put down the pencil, picked up a ballpoint pen, lit a cigarette, and wrote the first words. "Need more space in your fridge? Tired of having to buy more lemons at the supermarket than you can use in the next month? Here is an inexpensive gadget that might interest you." It wasn't particularly inexpensive, but no matter. Lots of people were going to pay thousands of dollars for this gadget. She would be paid a sizable amount also, meaning a certain fraction of her salary for writing about it. As she worked on, she kept seeing a vision of her crib-shaped basket and thinking that the basket—per se, as a thing to be used—was far more important than the kitchen gadget. However, it was perfectly normal to consider a basket more important or useful, she supposed, for the simple reason that a basket was.

"Nice walk this morning?" Reg asked, relaxing with a pre-lunch glass of cold white wine. He was standing in the low-ceilinged living room, in shorts, an unbuttoned shirt, sandals. His face had browned further, and the skin was pinkish over his cheekbones.

"Yes. Found a basket. Rather nice. Want to see it?"

"Sure."

She led the way to the side porch, and indicated the basket on the wooden table. "The bottom was all broken—so I fixed it."

"*You* fixed it?" Reg was leaning over it with admiration. "Yeah, I can see. Nice job, Di."

She felt a tremor, a little like shame. Or was it fear? She felt uncomfortable as Reg picked up the basket and looked at its underside. "Might be nice to hold kindling—or magazines, maybe," she said. "We can always throw it away when we get bored with it."

"Throw it away, no! It's sort of amusing—shaped like a baby's cradle or something."

"That's what I thought—that it must have been made for a baby." She drifted back into the living room, wishing now that Reg would stop examining the basket.

"Didn't know you had such talents, Di. Girl Scout lore?"

Diane gave a laugh. Reg knew she'd never joined the Girl Scouts. "Don't forget the Gartners are coming at seven-thirty."

"Um-m. Yes, thanks. I didn't forget.—What's for dinner? We've got everything we need?"

Diane said they had. The Gartners were bringing raspberries from their garden plus cream. Reg had meant he was willing to drive to town in case they had to buy anything else.

The Gartners arrived just before eight, and Reg made dacquiris. There was scotch for any who preferred it, and Olivia Gartner did. She was a serious drinker and held it well. An investment counselor, she was, and her husband Pete was a professor in the math department at Columbia.

Diane, after a swim around four o'clock, had collected some dry reeds from the dunes and among these had put a few long-stemmed blossoming weeds and wild flowers, blue and pink and orangy-yellow. She had laid all these in the crib-shaped basket which she had set on the floor near the fireplace.

"Isn't this pretty!" said Olivia during her second scotch, as if the drink had opened her eyes. She meant the floral arrangement, but Reg at once said:

"And look at the basket, Olivia! Diane found it on the beach today and *repaired* it." Reg lifted the basket as high as his head, so Olivia and Pete could admire its underside.

Olivia chuckled. "That's fantastic, Diane! Beautiful! How long did it take you?—It's a sweet basket."

"That's the funny thing," Diane began, eager to express herself. "It took me about twelve minutes!"

"Look how proud she is of it!" said Reg, smiling.

Pete was running his thumb over the apple twigs at the bottom, nodding his approval.

"Yes, it was almost terrifying," Diane went on.

"Terrifying?" Pete lifted his eyebrows.

"I'm not explaining myself very well." Diane had a polite smile on her face, though she was serious. "I felt as if I'd struck some hidden talent or knowledge—just suddenly. Everything I did, I felt sure of. I was amazed."

"Looks strong too," Pete said, and set the basket back where it had been.

Then they talked about something else. The cost of heating, if they used their cottages at all in the coming winter. Diane had hoped the basket conversation would continue a little longer. Another round of drinks, while Diane put their cold supper on the table. Bowls of jellied consommé with a slice of lemon to start with. They sat down. Diane felt unsatisfied. Or was it a sense of disturbance? Disturbance because of what? Just because they hadn't pursued the subject of the basket? Why should they have? It was merely a basket to them, mended the way anyone could have mended it. Or could just anyone have mended it that well? Diane happened to be sitting at the end of the table, so the basket was hardly four feet from her, behind her and to her right. She felt bothered somehow even by the basket's nearness. That was very odd. She must get to the bottom of it—that was funny, in view of the basket repair—but now wasn't the time, with three other people talking, and half her mind on seeing that her guests had a good meal.

While they were drinking coffee, Diane lit three candles and the oil lamp, and they listened to a record of Mozart *divertimenti*. They didn't listen, but it served as background music for their conversation. Diane listened to the music. It sounded skillful, even modern, and extremely civilized. Diane enjoyed her brandy. The brandy too seemed the epitome of human skill, care, knowledge. Not like a basket any child could put together. Perhaps a child in years couldn't, but a child as to progress in the evolution of the human race could weave a basket.

Was she possibly feeling her drinks? Diane pulled her long cotton skirt farther down over her knees. The subject was lobbies now, the impotence of any president, even Congress against them.

Monday morning early Diane and Reg flew back to New York by helicopter. Neither had to be at work before eleven. Diane had supposed that New York and work would put the disquieting thoughts re the basket out of her head, but that was not so. New York seemed to emphasize what she had felt up at the shack, even though the origin of her feelings had stayed at the shack. What were her feelings, anyway? Diane disliked vagueness, and was used to labeling her emotions jealousy, resentment, suspicion or whatever, even if the emotion was not always to her credit. But this?

What she felt was most certainly not guilt, though it was similarly troubling and unpleasant. Not envy either, not in the sense of desiring to master basketry so she could make a truly great basket, whatever that was. She'd always thought basket-weaving an occupation for the simpleminded, and it had become in fact a symbol of what psychiatrists advised disturbed people to take up. That was not it at all.

Diane felt that she had lost herself. Since repairing that basket, she wasn't any longer Diane Clarke, not completely, anyway. Neither was she anybody else, of course. It wasn't that she felt she had assumed the identity, even partially, of some remote ancestor. How remote, anyway? No. She felt rather that she was living with a great

many people from the past, that they were in her brain or mind
(Diane did not believe in a soul, and found the idea of a collective
unconscious too vague to be of importance), and that people from
human antecedents were bound up with her, influencing her,
controlling her every bit as much as, up to now, she had been controlling herself. This thought was by no means comforting, but it
was at least a partial explanation, maybe, for the disquietude that
she was experiencing. It was not even an explanation, she realized,
but rather a description of her feelings.

She wanted to say something to Reg about it and didn't,
thinking that anything she tried to say along these lines would
sound either silly or fuzzy. By now five days had passed since she
had repaired the basket up at Truro, and they were going up to the
shack again this weekend. The five working days at the office had
passed as had a lot of other weeks for Diane. She had had a set-to
with Jan Heyningen, the art director, on Wednesday, and had come
near telling him what she thought of his stubbornness and bad
taste, but she hadn't. She had merely smoldered. It had happened
before. She and Reg had gone out to dinner at the apartment of
some friends on Thursday. All as usual, outwardly.

The unusual was the schizoid atmosphere in her head. Was
that it? Two personalities? Diane toyed with this possibility all Friday afternoon at the office while she read through new
promotion-ready material. Was she simply imagining that several
hundred prehistoric ancestors were somehow dwelling within
her? No, frankly, she wasn't. That idea was even less credible than
Jung's collective unconscious. And suddenly she rejected the simple schizo idea or explanation also. Schizophrenia was a catch-all,
she had heard, for a lot of derangements that couldn't otherwise
be diagnosed. She didn't feel schizoid, anyway, didn't feel like two
people, or three, or more. She felt simply scared, mysteriously terrified. But only one thing in the least awkward happened that
week: she had let one side of the lettuce-swinger slip out of her
hand on the terrace, and lettuce flew everywhere, hung from the

potted bamboo trees, was caught on rose thorns, lay fresh and clean on the red tile paving, and on the seat of the glider. Diane had laughed, even though there was no more lettuce in the house. She was tense, perhaps, therefore clumsy. A little accident like that could happen any time.

During the flight to the Cape, Diane had a happy thought: she'd use the basket not just for floral arrangements but for collecting more *objets trouvés* from the beach, or better yet for potatoes and onions in the kitchen. She'd treat it like any old basket. That would take the mystique out of it, the terror. To have felt terror was absurd.

So Saturday morning while Reg worked on the nonelectric typewriter which they kept at the shack, Diane went for a walk on the beach with the basket. She had put a piece of newspaper in the basket, and she collected a greater number than usual of colored pebbles, a few larger smooth rocks—one orange in color, making it almost a *trompe l'oeil* for a mango—plus an interesting piece of sea-worn wood that looked like a boomerang. Wouldn't that be odd, she thought, if it really were an ancient boomerang worn shorter, thinner, until only the curve remained unchanged? As she walked back to the shack, the basket emitted faint squeaks in unison with her tread. The basket was so heavy, she had to carry it in two hands, letting its side rest against her hip, but she was not at all afraid that the twigs of the bottom would give. *Her work.*

Stop it, she told herself.

When she began to empty the basket on the porch's wooden table, she realized she had gathered too many stones, so she dropped more than half of them, quickly choosing the less interesting, over the porch rail onto the sand. Finally she shook the newspaper of its sand, and started to put it back in the basket. Sunlight fell on the glossy reddish-brown apple twigs. Over and under, not every one secured by twine, because for some twigs it hadn't been necessary. New work, and yet—Diane felt the irrational fear creeping over her again, and she pressed the newspaper quickly into the basket, pressed it at the crib-shaped edges, so that all her work was hidden. Then she tossed it carelessly on the floor, could have transferred some potatoes from a brown paper bag into it but she wanted to get away from the basket now.

An hour or so later, when she and Reg were finishing lunch, Reg laughing and about to light a cigarette, Diane felt an inner jolt as if—What? She deliberately relaxed, and gave her attention, more of it, to what Reg was saying. But it was as if the sound had been switched off a TV set. She saw him, but she wasn't listening or hearing. She blinked and forced herself to listen. Reg was talking about renting a tractor to clear some of their sand away, about terracing, and maintaining their property with growing things. They'd drawn a simple plan weeks ago, Diane remembered. But again she was feeling not like herself, as if she had lost herself in millions of people as an individual might get lost in a huge crowd. No, that was too simple, she felt. She was still trying to find solace in words. Or was she even dodging something? If so, what?

"What?" Reg asked, leaning back in his chair now, relaxed.

"Nothing. Why?"

"You were lost in thought."

Diane might have replied that she had just had a better idea for a current project at Retting, might have replied several things, but she said suddenly, "I'm thinking of asking for a leave of absence. Maybe just a month. I think Retting would do it, and it'd do me good."

Reg looked puzzled. "You're feeling tired, you mean? Just lately?"

"No. I feel somehow upset. Turned around, I don't know. I thought maybe a month of just being away from the office . . ." But work was supposed to be good in such a situation as hers. Work kept people from dwelling on their problems. But she hadn't a problem, rather a state of mind.

"Oh . . . well," Reg said. "Heyningen getting on your nerves maybe."

Diane shifted. It would have been easy to say yes, that was it. She took a cigarette, and Reg lit it. "Thanks. You're going to laugh, Reg. But that basket bothers me." She looked at him, feeling ashamed, and curiously defensive.

"The one you found last weekend? You're worried a child might've drowned in it, lost at sea?" Reg smiled as if at a mild joke he'd just made.

"No, not at all. Nothing like that. I told you last weekend. It simply bothers me that I repaired it so easily. There. That's it. And you can say I'm cracked—I don't care."

"I do not—quite—understand what you mean."

"It made me feel somehow—prehistoric. And funny. Still does."

Reg shook his head. "I can sort of understand. Honestly. But—another way of looking at it, Di, is to realize that it's a very simple activity after all, mending or even making a basket. Not that I don't admire the neat job you did, but it's not like—sitting down and playing Beethoven's Emperor Concerto, for instance, if you've never had a piano lesson in your life."

"No." She'd never had a basket-making lesson in her life, she might have said. She was silent, wondering if she should put in her leave of absence request on Monday, as a gesture, a kind of appeasement to the uneasiness she felt? Emotions demanded gestures, she had read somewhere, in order to be exorcised. Did she really believe that?

"Really, Di, the leave of absence is one thing, but that basket— It's an interesting basket, sure, because it's not machine-made and you don't see that shape any more. I've seen you get excited about stones you find. I understand. They're beautiful. But to let yourself get upset about—"

"Stones are different," she interrupted. "I can admire them. I'm not upset about them. I told you I feel I'm not exactly myself—me—any longer. I feel lost in a strange way—*Identity*, I mean," she broke in again, when Reg started to speak.

"Oh, Di!" He got up. "What do you mean you told me that? You didn't."

"Well, I have now. I feel—as if a lot of other people were inside me besides myself. And I feel lost because of that. Do you understand?"

Reg hesitated. "I understand the words. But the feeling—no."

Even that was something. Diane felt grateful, and relieved that she had said this much to him.

"Go ahead with the leave of absence idea, darling. I didn't mean to be so abrupt."

Diane put her cigarette out. "I'll think about it." She got up to make coffee.

That afternoon, after tidying the kitchen, Diane put another newspaper in the basket, and unloaded the sack of potatoes into it, plus three or four onions—familiar and contemporary objects. Perishable too. She made herself not think about the basket or even about the leave of absence for the rest of the day. Around 7:30, she and Reg drove off to Truro, where there was a street party organized by an ecology group. Wine and beer and soft drinks, hot dogs and jukebox music. They encountered the Gartners and a few other neighbors. The wine was undrinkable, the atmosphere marvelous. Diane danced with a couple of merry strangers and was for a few hours happy.

A month's leave of absence, she thought as she stood under the shower that night, was absurd and unnecessary. Temporary aberration to have considered it. If the basket—a really simple object as Reg had said—annoyed her so much, the thing to do was to get rid of it, burn it.

Sunday morning Reg took the car and went to deliver his Black & Decker or some appliance of it to the Gartners, who lived eight miles away. As soon as he had left, Diane went to the side porch, replaced the potatoes and onions in the brown paper bag which she had saved as she saved most bags that arrived at the shack, and taking the basket with its newspaper and a book of matches, she walked out onto the sand in the direction of the ocean. She struck a match and lit the newspaper, and laid the basket over it. After a moment's hesitation, as if from shock, the basket gave a crack and began to burn. The drier sides burned more quickly than the newer apple twigs, of course. With a stick, Diane poked every last pale withe into the flames, until nothing remained except black ash and some yellow-glowing embers, and finally these went out in the bright sunshine and began to darken. Diane pushed sand with her feet over the ashes, until nothing was visible. She breathed deeply as she walked back to the shack, and realized that she had been holding her breath, or almost, the entire time of the burning.

She was not going to say anything to Reg about getting rid of the basket, and he was not apt to notice its absence, Diane knew.

Diane did mention, on Tuesday in New York, that she had changed her mind about asking for a leave of absence. The implication was that she felt better, but she didn't say that.

The basket was gone, she would never see it again, unless she deliberately tried to conjure it up in memory, and that she didn't want to do. She felt better with the thing out of the shack, destroyed. She knew that the burning had been an action on her part to get rid of a feeling within her, a primitive action, if she thought about it, because though the basket had been tangible, her thoughts were not tangible. And they proved damned hard to destroy.

Three weeks after the burning of the basket, her crazy idea of being a "walking human race" or some such lingered. She would continue to listen to Mozart and Bartók, they'd go to the shack most weekends, and she would continue to pretend that her life counted for something, that she was part of the stream or evolution of the human race, though she felt now that she had spurned that position or small function by burning the basket. For a week, she realized, she had grasped something, and then she had deliberately thrown it away. In fact, she was no happier now than during

that week when the well-mended basket had been in her posses-
sion. But she was determined not to say anything more about it to
Reg. He had been on the verge of impatience that Saturday before
the Sunday when she had burned it. And in fact could she even
put any more into words? No. So she had to stop thinking about
it. Yes.

Under a Dark Angel's Eye

Now he was on the last leg of his journey, the bus stretch from the airport to Arlington Hills. There would be nobody to meet him at the bus terminal, and Lee didn't mind in the least. In fact he preferred it. He could walk with his small suitcase the four or five blocks to the Capitol Hotel (he assumed it was still functioning), check in, then telephone Winston Greeves to say he had arrived. Maybe they could even wind up the business with the lawyer today, because it would be only four in the afternoon by the time Lee would be phoning Winston. It was a matter of signing a paper in regard to the house where Lee Mandeville had been born. Lee owned it, and now he had to sell it, because he needed the money. He didn't care, he wasn't sentimental about the two-story white house with the green lawn in front. Or was he? Lee honestly didn't think so. He'd had some nasty, unpleasant hours in that house, as well as a few happy ones—a barefoot boyhood, tossing a football with chums from the neighborhood on the front lawn. He had lost Louise there, too.

Lee shifted in his seat, rested his cheek against his hand which was lightly closed in a fist, and stared out the window at the Indiana landscape that drifted past. He barely recognized a small town they were going through. How long had it been, nine, no ten years since he had been to Arlington Hills. Ten years ago he had come to visit his mother in the nursing home called the Hearthside, and she had either not recognized him or pretended not to, or had really thought he was someone else. At any rate she had managed to come out with "Don't come back!" just as he had been going out the door of her room. Winston who had accompanied Lee had chuckled and shaken his head, as if to say, "What can you do with the old folks—except put up with them?"

Yes, they lived on forever these days. Doctors didn't let old people die, not as long as there were pills, injections, kidney machines, new drugs, all costing dearly. That was why Lee had to sell the house. For twelve years, since his mother had entered the nursing home, the house had been rented to a couple whose two

children were in their teens now. Lee had never charged them
much rent, because they couldn't afford a high rent, and Lee val-
ued their reliability. But Lee's mother was now costing between
five and six hundred dollars a week, her savings had run out five
years ago, and Lee had borne the burden ever since, though
Medicare paid some of it. His mother Edna wasn't ill, but she did
need certain pills, tranquilizers alternating with pick-ups, plus
checkups and special vitamins. Lee paid little attention to his
mother's health, because it stayed the same year after year. She was
ambulant but crochety, and never wrote to Lee, because he didn't
write to her. Even before the nursing home, she had cursed Lee
out by letter for imaginary faults and deeds, so Lee had washed his
hands of his mother, except to pay her bills. An offspring owed that
to a parent, Lee believed, just as a parent owed to a child love, care,
and as much education as the parent could afford. Children were
expensive and time-consuming, but the parents certainly were
repaid when they became elderly and imposed the same burdens
on their children.

    Lee Mandeville was fifty-five, unmarried, and had a modestly
successful antique shop in Chicago. He dealt in old furniture, a few
good carpets, old pictures and frames, brass and silver items and sil-
verware also. He was by no means a big wheel in the antique business, but he was known and respected in Chicago and beyond. He
was trim of figure, not balding, and without much gray in his hair.
His face was clean shaven, with a crease in either cheek, and he
had rather heavy eyebrows above friendly, thoughtful blue-gray
eyes. He liked meeting strangers in his shop, summing them up,
finding out whether they wanted to buy something because it
would look nice somewhere in their house or because they really
fell in love with an object.

    As the bus rocked and lumbered into Arlington Hills, Lee
tensed himself, already uneasy, and unhappy. Well, he did not
intend to see his mother this trip. He didn't want to see her, and
he didn't have to. She was so far gone mentally that Lee had had

power of attorney for nearly ten years. Winston had at last obtained his mother's signature for that. She had held out for months, not for any logical reason but out of stubbornness, and because she enjoyed making difficulties for other people. Twenty minutes to four, Lee saw from a glance at his wristwatch. He stood up and hauled his suitcase down from the rack before the bus had quite stopped.

"Lee!—How *are* you, Lee?"

Lee was surprised by the voice, and it took him a second to spot Win in the little crowd waiting for debarkers. "Win! *Hello!* I didn't expect to see you here!" Lee's smile was broad. They patted each other on the shoulder. "How're things?"

"Oh—much the same," Win replied. "Nothing much changes around here. That's all the luggage you've got? . . . My car's over here, Lee—and Kate and I expect you to be *our guest*. All right?" Win already had Lee's suitcase in his hand. Win was in his early sixties with straight gray hair that looked always windblown. He wore navy blue trousers and a blue shirt with no tie. Win was head of an insurance company that he himself had founded, and the Mande-villes had insured their house and cars with Win for decades.

"It's kind of you, Win, but honestly, for one night—I can just as well stay at the old Capitol, you know." Lee didn't want to say that he preferred to go to a hotel.

"Won't hear of it. Kate's got your room all ready."

Win was walking toward his car, and Lee went with him. After all, Win had been helpful, very, with Edna, and Win seemed really pleased to have him. "You win, Win," Lee said, smiling, "and thank you. How's Kate? And Mort?" Mort was their son.

"Oh—the same." Win stuck Lee's lightweight suitcase onto the back seat of his car. "Mort's working now in Bloomington. Car salesman."

"Still married?" Lee recalled some awful trouble with Mort's wife—she'd run off with another man, abandoned their small child, and then, Lee thought, they had got back together again.

"No, they finally arranged a—a divorce," Win said, and started the car.

Lee didn't know whether to say "Good" or not, so he said nothing. Now his mother, Lee thought. That was the next question. He didn't care how his mother was. Instead, Lee said, "I was thinking we might wind this business up this afternoon, Win. It's just a matter of signing a paper, isn't it?" The house in Barrett Avenue was sold, to a young couple named Varick—Ralph and Phyllis, Lee remembered from the real estate agent's letter.

"Ye-es," said Win, and his heavy hands opened on the steering wheel for a couple of seconds, then closed tightly. "I suppose we could."

Lee gathered that Win hadn't made an appointment as yet. "It's still old Graham, isn't it? He knows us both so well—can't we just barge in?"

"Sure—okay, Lee."

Win Greeves steered the car into Main Street, and Lee glanced at storefronts, shop signs, seeing a lot of change since he had been here last, and for the worse aesthetically. Main Street looked more crowded, both with people and shops. Maybe Graham's old office hadn't changed. Douglas Graham was a lawyer and notary public. He had drawn up a power of attorney statement years ago, at Lee's request, so that Lee could sign checks for his mother's bills, and Winston Greeves's name had been added also in executor capacity, because Win was on the scene in Arlington Hills, and even visited his mother sometimes—though his mother didn't always recognize him, Win said—and in the last years as Edna's bank account had grown low, Lee sent five hundred dollars or a thousand to bolster it every month or so. Win sent Lee the bank statements for the account now in Lee's name, and an explanation of the bills.

"I don't need the Varicks, I suppose," Lee said. "To be present when I sign, I mean."

"I know Ralph Varick's already signed," said Win. "Fine couple, those two. You should meet them, Lee."

"Well—not really necessary. Give them my best wishes—if you ever see them." Lee didn't want to go near the old house, didn't want to see it. The nice family, the Youngs, who couldn't afford to buy the house, were still there for the rest of this month, but Lee didn't want to visit them even merely to say hello. He felt sorry for them. He forced himself to ask the unavoidable. "And I suppose my mother's just the same too?"

Win chuckled and shook his head. "She's—yes—that's about it."

Don't they *ever* kick the bucket, Lee thought bitterly, and nearly laughed at himself. And after he had banked the money for the house, how much longer, how many more years would his mother live, eating up five or six hundred dollars a week? Now she was eighty-six. Couldn't she go on till ninety and ninety-one? Why not? Lee remembered three grandparents out of four, plus one maternal uncle, who had all died in their nineties.

"Here we are," said Win, pulling in at the curb.

Lee fished for a coin, and dropped it in the meter before Win could insert his. Doug Graham had no secretary, and came out of the office himself in response to the bell they had rung on entering his waiting room.

"Well, Lee—and Win. How are you, Lee? You're looking well." Doug Graham gave Lee a warm handshake. Doug was heavier than he had been ten years ago, in his late sixties now, a big man in a baggy beige suit that showed no sign of a proper crease.

"Quite all right, Doug. And you?" Lee wished he could have said friendlier words, but they didn't come for some reason. Doug had done many a service for Lee and his mother over the years. Lee remembered with embarrassment that Doug had talked his mother out of making a will some twenty years ago, which would have cut Lee out as only offspring and nearest of kin, and bestowed all on a young black woman who cleaned the house and who had talked her way into Edna's affections.

Doug Graham quietly and calmly arranged the few papers on his desk, and pointed out where Lee was to sign. "After you've read the agreement, of course, Lee," said Doug with a smile.

Lee glanced through. It was a bill of sale for the Barrett Avenue house, pretty plain and simple. Lee signed. The deed was there too, with Lee's father's signature, also that of Lee's grandfather, but before that a name that was not of the family. Ralph David Varick was the last name. Lee did not have to sign this.

"Hope you're not too sentimental about it, Lee," said Doug in his slow, deep voice. "After all, you're not here much of late—in the last years. We've missed you."

Lee shook his head. "Not sentimental, no."

The pen was handed to Winston Greeves, who got up to sign the purchase paper as witness.

"Sorry it has to be, though," said Doug, "somehow. And sorry about your mother."

Again Lee felt a twinge of shame, because Doug knew, everyone knew, that his mother was not merely senile but quietly insane. "Well—these things happen. At least she's not in pain," Lee said awkwardly.

"That *is* true. . . . Thank you, Win. And that about winds it up, I think. . . . How long're you here for, Lee?"

Lee told him just till tomorrow, because he had to get back to his shop in Chicago. He asked what he owed Doug, and Doug said nothing at all, and again Lee felt shame, because Doug must know that he had sold the house because he couldn't otherwise meet expenses.

"We need a little drink on this," said Doug, pulling out a whiskey bottle from a lower drawer in his desk. "It's just about quitting time anyway, so we deserve it."

They each had small, neat drinks, standing up. But the atmosphere remained sad and a little strained, Lee felt.

Ten minutes later, they were at the Greeveses' house—bigger than the house Lee had just signed away, with a bigger lawn and more expensive trees. Kate Greeves welcomed Lee as if he were one of the family, pressing his hand in both hers, kissing his cheek.

"Lee, I'm so glad Win persuaded you to stay! Come, I'll show you your room, then we can relax." She took him upstairs.

There was a smell of baking and of warm cinnamon from the kitchen. His room was neat and clean, furnished with factory-made dressing table and chairs and bed, but Lee had seen worse. The Greeveses were doing their best to be nice to him.

"I'd love to take a little walk," Lee said when he went back downstairs. "Hardly six. Still a lot of daylight—"

"Oh, no! Stay and talk, Lee. Or I'll *drive* you around, if you'd like to see the old town." Win seemed willing.

But that idea didn't appeal to Lee. He wanted to stretch his legs on his own, but he knew Win would protest that he'd have to walk fifteen minutes to get out of Rosedale, the residential section, and so on and so on. Lee found himself sitting in the living room with a strong scotch in his hands. Kate brought in a bowl of hot buttered popcorn.

The telephone rang, and the Greeveses exchanged a look, then Win went to get it in the hall.

Lee picked up an old glass paperweight with a spread blue butterfly in it. The paperweight was the size of a cake of soap and very pretty. He was about to ask Kate where she had got it from, when Win's voice saying "*No!*" made Lee keep his silence.

"*No*, I said," Win said softly but in a tone of repressed wrath. "And don't phone again tonight. I mean what I *say*." There was a click as Win put the telephone down. When he returned to the living room, his hands were shaking slightly. He reached for his glass. "Sorry about that," he said to Lee with a nervous smile.

Something to do with Mort, Lee supposed. Maybe Mort himself. Lee thought it best not to ask questions. Kate also looked tense. Mort must be at least forty now, Lee thought. He was a weak type, and Lee remembered one adolescent scrape after another—a wrecked car, Mort picked up by the police for drunkenness somewhere, Mort marrying a girl because she was pregnant, the same wife Mort had just divorced, Win had said. Such troubles seemed silly to Lee, because they were so avoidable—compared to a deranged mother who lingered on and on.

"Not coming over, is he?" Kate whispered to Win as she bent to offer Win the popcorn bowl.

Win shook his head slowly and grimly.

Lee had barely heard Kate speak. They talked of other things during dinner, and only a little bit about Lee's mother. Her health was all right, she took walks in the garden there, came down to the dining room for every meal. Once a month there was a "birthday party" for everyone whose birthday fell during that month. There was TV, not in every room, but in the communal hall downstairs.

"She still reads the Bible, I suppose," said Lee, smiling a little.

"Oh, I suppose. There's one in every room there, I know," Win replied, and glanced at his wife, who responded by asking Lee how his shop in Chicago was doing.

As Lee replied, he thought about his mother, grim-lipped and gruesome without her false teeth which she didn't always care to wear, reading her Bible. What did she get out of it? Certainly not the milk of human kindness, but of course that phrase was Shakespeare's. Or had Jesus said it first? The Old Testament was bloodthirsty, vengeful, even barbaric in places. His mother had always, or frequently enough, said to him, "Read your Bible, Lee," when he was depressed, discouraged, or when he had been "tempted" maybe to buy a nice looking secondhand car on the installment plan, when he had been seventeen or eighteen. How innocent, buying a car on the installment plan, compared to what his mother had done when he was twenty-two! He had been engaged to Louisa Watts, madly in love with her, in love in a way, however, that could have lasted, that would have resulted in a good marriage, Lee believed. His mother had told Louisa that Lee had girls everywhere, prostitute favorites too, that in his car he drove to other towns for his fun. And so on. And Louisa had been only nineteen. She had believed that, and she had been hurt. *Goddamn my mother*, Lee thought. And what had his mother gained by her lies? Keeping him at home, for herself? She hadn't. Louisa had married another man in less than a year, moved somewhere, maybe New York, and Lee had left home and gone to San Francisco for a while, worked as a longshoreman, gone to New Orleans and done the same. If Louisa only hadn't been married, he would have tried again with her, because she was the only girl in the world for him. Yes, he had met other girls, four or five. He had wanted to marry, but had never been able to convince himself (and maybe not the other girls either) that marriage would work. Then he had gone to Chicago when he had been nearly thirty.

"You don't like the pie, Lee?" asked Kate.

Lee realized that he had barely touched the hot apple pie, that he was squeezing his napkin in his left hand as if it were someone's neck. "I do like the pie," Lee said calmly, and proceeded to finish it.

That night, Lee slept badly. Thoughts turned in his head, yet when he tried to devote a few minutes to thinking something out, he got nowhere. It was a pleasure for him to get out of bed at dawn, dress quietly, and sneak down the stairs for a walk before anyone else was up. He hadn't bothered shaving. Lee was out of the Rosedale area in less than ten minutes. The air was sweet and clear, coolish for May. The town was awakening. There were milk trucks making deliveries, mailmen of course, and a few workmen boarding early buses.

"Lee?—It's Lee Mandeville, isn't it?"

Lee looked into the face of a young man in his twenties with brown wavy hair, in a tweed suit with shirt and tie. Vaguely Lee remembered the face, but couldn't have come up with the name if his life had depended on it.

"Charles Ritchie!" said the young man, laughing. "Remember? I used to deliver groceries for your mother!"

"Oh, *sure*. Charlie." Lee smiled, remembering a skinny twelve-year-old who sometimes drank a soda pop in their kitchen. "Hey, aren't you missing your bus, Charlie?"

"Doesn't matter," said the young man, barely glancing at the bus that was pulling away. "What brings you here, Lee?"

"Selling the house. You remember the old house?"

"I sure do!—I'm sorry you're selling. I had the idea you might move back some time—for retirement or something."

Lee smiled. "I need the money, frankly. My mother's still alive, you know, and that costs a little. Not that I begrudge it, of course." He saw Charlie's face grow suddenly earnest.

Frowning, Charlie said, "I don't understand. Mrs. Mandeville died fo—yes, about five years ago. Yes, I—*I* went to her funeral, Lee." His eyes stared into Lee's.

Lee realized that it was true. He realized that this was why Win had insisted upon Lee's spending the night with him, so he wouldn't run into citizens of the town who might tell him the truth.

"What's the matter, sir? I'm sorry I brought it up. But *you* said—"

Lee gently took his elbow from the young man's grip, and smiled. "Sorry. I suppose I looked about to faint! Yes." Lee took a breath and made an effort to pull himself together. "Yes, of course she's dead. I don't know what I was talking about, Charlie."

"Oh, that's *okay*, Lee . . . You're really all right?"

"Sure I'm all right. And that's another bus coming, isn't it?"

Through a haze of pale yellow morning sunlight and pale green leaves, the bus approached. Lee moved away, waved goodbye, ignoring Charlie's parting words. Lee walked slowly for several minutes, not caring in what direction his steps took him.

Now Lee realized that the Hearthside people, the accountant there, or someone, must be in league with Win Greeves, because Lee had seen real bills from the Hearthside in the last five years.

Lee felt himself physically weak, as if he were walking in mud instead of on a cement pavement. And what the hell was he going to do about it? Five years. And in dollars? Twenty or twenty-four thousand dollars a year times five were—Lee smiled wryly, and stopped trying to calculate. He looked up at a street marker, and saw that he stood on a corner at which Elmhurst intersected South Billingham. He took Elmhurst, which he thought led, eastward, back to Rosedale. All he really wanted from the Greeveses' house was his suitcase.

When Lee got back to the house, he found the door unlocked, and noticed an aroma of coffee and bacon. Win came at once down the hall.

"Lee! We were a little worried! Thought maybe you'd sleepwalked right out of the house!" Win was grinning.

"No, no, just taking a walk—as I wanted to do last night." Win was staring at him. Was he pale, Lee wondered. Probably. Lee realized that he could still be polite. That was easy. It was also safe and natural to him. "Hope I didn't hold you up, Win?" Lee looked at his wristwatch. "Ten of eight now."

"Not—one—bit!" Win assured him. "Come and have some breakfast."

Now the food really refused to go down, but Lee kept his polite manner, sipped coffee and poked at his scrambled eggs. He saw Win and Kate exchange glances again, glances that Win tried to avoid, though his eyes kept being drawn back to his wife's as if he were hypnotized.

"Did you—uh—have a nice walk, Lee?" Win asked.

"Very nice, thanks. I ran into—Charles Ritchie," Lee said carefully and with some respect, as if Charles had been lifted from a grocer's delivery boy to the status of one of the disciples bearing a message of truth. "He used to deliver groceries for my mother." Lee noticed that Win was not doing much better than he with his breakfast.

The tension grew a few degrees tighter, then Kate said:

"Win said you wanted to leave today, Lee. Can't you change your mind?"

That remark was so false, Lee suddenly blew up, inwardly. But outwardly he kept his cool, except that he tossed his napkin down. "Sorry, but I can't. No." His voice was hollow and hoarse. Lee stood up. "If you'll excuse me." He left the table and went up to his room.

Just as he was closing his suitcase, Win came in. Now Win looked white in the face, and ten years older.

Lee felt almost sorry for him. "Yes, I heard about my mother. I think that's what's on your mind. Isn't it, Win?" Now Lee had his small suitcase in his hand, and he was ready to leave the room.

Win tiptoed to the door and closed it. His hand that he drew away from the doorknob was shaking, and he lifted it and his other hand and covered his face. "Lee, I want you to know I'm ashamed of myself."

Lee nodded once, impatiently, unseen by Win.

"Morton was in such trouble. That damned wife of his . . . She hasn't turned loose, there's no divorce, and it's a damned mess. The girl—I mean the wife's pregnant again and she's accusing Mort now, but I doubt if that's true, I really do. But she keeps asking for money and legally—"

"Who the hell cares?" Lee interrupted. He squeezed the suitcase handle, eager to leave, but Win blocked him like an ugly mountain. Win's eyes, wide and scared, met Lee's.

He reminded Lee of an animal, sure that it was going to be slaughtered in the next seconds, but in fact Lee had never seen an animal in such circumstances. "I suppose," Lee said, "the nursing home had some kind of understanding with you. I remember the bills, anyway—recent ones."

Win said miserably, "Yes, yes."

Now Lee recalled Doug Graham's words to him, when Lee had said that at least his mother wasn't in pain now, and Doug had replied that that was true. Doug knew that his mother was dead, but their conversation wouldn't have caused him to repeat that fact, and of course he had assumed Lee knew it. Lee made a start for the door.

"Lee!" Win nearly caught him by the sleeve, but he drew his hand back, as if he didn't dare touch Lee. "What're you going to do, Lee?"

"I don't know . . . I think I'm in a state of shock."

"I know I'm to blame. Just me. But if you only knew the straits I was in, *am* in. Blackmail—first from Mort's wife, blackmailing him, I mean, and now—"

Lee understood: Mort the son was now blackmailing his father about this business. How low could human beings sink? For some bizarre reason, Lee wanted to smile. "How did she die?" He asked in a courteous tone. "Stroke, I suppose?"

"Died in her sleep," Win murmured. "Hardly anybody came to the funeral. She'd made such enemies, y'know, with her sharp tongue . . . The man—"

"What man?" Lee asked, because Win had stopped.

"The man at the Hearthside. His name is Victor Malloway. He's—you could say he's every bit as guilty as I am. But he's the only one—else." Again Win looked pitiably at Lee. "What're you going to do, Lee?"

Lee took a breath. "Well—what, for instance?" Win did not reply to that question, and Lee opened the door. "Bye-bye, Win, and thanks."

Downstairs, Lee said the same thanks and good-bye to Kate. The words she said did not register on Lee. Something about taking him to the bus terminal, or calling a taxi. ". . . quite all right," Lee heard himself saying. "I'll make it by myself."

He was gone, free, alone, walking with the suitcase in the direction of town, of the bus terminal. He walked all the way at an easy and regular pace, arrived at the terminal around ten, and waited patiently for the bus to the bigger town with the airport.

He still felt dazed, but thoughts came anyway. They were bitter, unhappy thoughts that flowed through his mind like a polluted stream. He detested his thoughts.

And even on the moving bus, his thoughts went on, memories of his mother's odious vanity when she had been younger, her henpecking of his father (dead in his late fifties of cancer), of his mother's unremitting dislike and criticism of every girl he had ever brought to the house. Also his mother's backbiting at her own friends and neighbors, even at the ones who tried to be friendly and kind to her. His mother had always found something "wrong" with them. And now, the truly awful thing, the terrifying fact that her life had wound up like a classic tragedy played rather behind the scenes instead of on a stage in view of lots of people. His mother had been finished off, as it were, by a few shabby crooks like Win Greeves and son, and the fellow called Victor—Mallory, was it? Indeed, they had been feeding like vultures on her rotting corpse for the past five years.

Lee did not relax until he had opened the front door of his antique shop, and surveyed the familiar interior of shining furniture, the warm glint of copper, the soft curves of polished cherrywood. He left the CLOSED sign hanging in the door, and relocked it from the inside. He must return to normal, he told himself, must carry on as usual and forget Arlington Hills, or he would become ill himself—polluted, like his river of ugly memories on the bus and on the plane. Lee bathed and shaved and by five in the afternoon removed his CLOSED sign. He had one visitor after that, a man who drifted around looking, and didn't buy anything, but that was no matter.

Only occasionally, in moments when he was tired, or disappointed about something that had gone wrong, did Lee think of the false friend Win, and wish him ill. *An eye for an eye, a tooth for a tooth*, the Bible said, the Old Testament part, anyway. But he really *didn't* want that, Lee told himself, otherwise he would be doing something now to bring Win Greeves to justice, to hit back at

him. Lee could even sue him and win handily, recover expenses
and then some by forcing the Greeveses to sell their handsome
house in Rosedale. With that money, he could buy his own house
back, his birthplace. But Lee realized that he didn't want the two-
story white house where he had been born. His mother's spirit
had spoiled that house, made it evil.

From Win Greeves there was silence, not a letter or a line from
him of further explanation, or of an offer to repay part of what he
had wrongly taken. Now and then, Lee did imagine Win worried,
probably very anxious as he tried to guess what Lee might be
doing about the situation. Nearly a month had passed since Lee's
visit to Arlington Hills. Wouldn't Win and Kate and Mort be
assuming that Lee Mandeville had taken a lawyer and that he was
preparing his case against Winston Greeves and the man at the
Hearthside?

Then Lee received, to his surprise, a letter from Arlington Hills
addressed by typewriter and with Win's company's name, Eagle
Insurance, and the spread eagle trademark in the upper left corner
of the envelope. Lee turned the envelope over—no name on the
back—and for a few seconds wondered what might be in it. An
abject apology, maybe even a check, however small? Absurd! Or
was Eagle Insurance sending him a last bill for his mother's house
insurance? Lee laughed at this idea and opened the letter. It was a
short typewritten note.

Dear Lee,

After all our troubles, there is one more. Mort died
last Tuesday night, after running into a man and seriously
injuring him (but not killing him, thank God) and then
hitting a tree in his car himself. I can almost say it's a bless-
ing, considering the trouble Mort has caused himself and
us. I thought you might like to hear. We are all sad here.

Yours,
Win

Lee gave a sigh, a shrug. Well. What was he supposed to reply, or think, or care, about this? Was Win possibly expecting a letter of condolence from him? This piece of information, Lee thought, affected him not at all. Morton Greeves's life or death was simply nothing to Lee.

Later that day, when Lee was tugging off rubber boots and feeling a bit tired—he had been paint-stripping with a water hose in his back alley—he had a vision of Mort dead and bleeding, having hit a tree in his car, and thought, "Good!" *An eye for an eye* . . . For a few seconds he relished a vengeance achieved. Morton was Win's only son, only child. Worthless all his life, and now dead! Good! Now Lee had his money for the Arlington Hills house he had sold, and he could, if he wished, buy a property he had looked at in a suburb of Chicago, a pleasant house near the lake. He could have a little boat.

An image of his mother came to Lee as he undressed for bed that night, his mother in her big wicker rocking chair in the living room, reading her Bible, peering up at him grim-mouthed (though with her teeth), and asking him why he didn't read the Bible more often. The Bible! Had it made his mother any better, kinder to her fellow men? A lot of the Bible seemed to be anti-sex, too. His mother was, certainly. If sex was so bad, Lee thought, how had his mother ever conceived him, ever got married in the first place?

"No," Lee said aloud, and shook himself as if he were shaking something off. No, he wasn't going to entertain any thoughts of the Bible, or of vengeance, in regard to Win's family, or in regard to the man at the Hearthside whose name by now Lee had forgotten, except for the first name Victor. What kind of Victor was he, for instance? Lee smiled at the absurdity of his name, the vainglorious ring of it.

Lee had a few friends in the neighborhood, and one of them, Edward Newton, a man of Lee's age and owner of a nearby bookshop, dropped in on Lee one afternoon as he often did, to have a coffee in the back of the shop. Lee had told Edward and others of his friends that his mother had been ill when he visited Arlington Hills, and that she had died a few days after his visit. Now Edward had found a small item in the newspaper.

"Did you know him? I thought I'd show it to you, because I remember the name Hearthside, where your mother was." Edward pointed to an item three inches long in the newspaper he had brought.

SUICIDE OF NURSING HOME
SUPERINTENDENT, 61

The report said that Victor C. Malloway, superintendent of the Hearthside retirement and nursing home in Arlington Hills, Indiana, had killed himself by closing his car and piping in the exhaust from a running engine in his own garage at home. He left no note of explanation. He was survived by a wife, Mary, a son Philip and daughter Marion, and three grandchildren.

"No," Lee said. "No, I never met him, but I've heard his name, yes."

"I suppose it's a depressing atmosphere—old people, you know. And *they're* dying pretty frequently there, I'd suppose."

Lee agreed, and changed the subject.

Win was next, Lee supposed. What would happen to him, or what would he do to himself? Maybe nothing, after all. His own son was dead, and how much of that death might be called suicide, Lee wondered. Surely Mort had known from Win that the game was up, that no more money would be coming from Lee Mandeville. Surely too Win and Victor Malloway would have had a couple of desperate conversations. Lee still remembered Win's defeated and terrified face in that upstairs bedroom in Arlington Hills. Enough was enough, Lee thought. Win was a half-destroyed man now.

With some of his money, Lee invested in ten Turkish carpets

whose quality and colors especially pleased him. He was sure he
could sell five or six at a profit, and he put a sign in his window to
the effect that an exceptional opportunity to buy quality Turkish
carpets was now offered, inquire within. The ones he did not sell
would go well in the house in the suburbs on which Lee had put
a down payment. Lee felt increasingly happy. He gave a birthday
party on his own birthday, invited ten friends out to a restaurant,
then took them back to his apartment and turned on the lights in
his shop. One of his friends played on a piano that Lee had in his
shop section, and there was a lot of laughter, because the piano was
slightly out of tune. Everyone sang and drank champagne and
toasted Lee's health.

Lee began to furnish his new house, which was smaller than
the Arlington Hills house of his family, but still had two stories and
a lovely fruit garden around it. It was almost thirty miles from Lee's
shop, so he did not drive there every day, but used the place mainly
for weekends, though the distance was not so great that he
couldn't drive in the evening to stay the night there, if he chose.
Now and again he thought, with a shock, of his mother, and the
fact that she had been dead nearly *six* years, not the eight or ten
months that he had told all his friends. And he thought without a
tweak of resentment of the hundred thousand dollars or so down
the drain, money which Win had pocketed and shared with Mort
and the suicide Victor. The score had been evened. A score, yes, like
the score in a game that Lee was not interested in—a domino
score, an anagram-game score. Best to forget it. All deaths were sad.
Lee had not lifted a finger, yet Mort and Victor were dead. It had
not been necessary to gouge out an eye.

Autumn came, and Lee was busy with weatherstripping in his
house, when he heard a news item that caught his attention. He
had heard the name Arlington Hills, but he had missed the first
part. It was something about the death of a man in his own house
due to a bullet wound possibly self-inflicted. Lee worked on, feeling vaguely troubled. Could Winston Greeves have been the name

the announcer had said? The news would be repeated in an hour, unless something more important crowded out the Arlington Hills bit. Lee continued measuring his insulating tape, cutting, sticking down. He worked on his knees in blue jeans.

If this were Win Greeves, it was really too much, Lee thought. Enough vengeance. More than enough. Well, there were lots of people in Arlington Hills, and maybe it hadn't been Win. But Lee felt troubled, angry in a strange way, and nervous. The minutes crept as Lee worked, and when 5 p.m. came, Lee listened carefully to the news report. It was the last item before the weather: Winston Greeves, aged sixty-four, of Arlington Hills, Indiana, had died from a bullet wound that might or might not have been self-inflicted. His wife said that he had recently acquired a pistol for target practice.

Lee had listened to the news standing, and suddenly his shoulders bent and he lowered his head. He felt weak for a few seconds, then gradually his strength returned, and with it the strange anger that he had known an hour ago. It was too much. *My cup runneth over* . . . No, that wasn't it. Christ had said that. Christ wouldn't have approved of *this*. Lee was about to cover his face with his hands, when he remembered Win making the same gesture. Lee took his hands down and straightened. He went down the stairs to his living room.

To the left and right of his fireplace there were bookshelves set into the wall. He reached firmly for a black leatherbound book. This was the Bible, the same one his mother had used to read, with the top and bottom of its spine all worn and showing brown where the black had worn off the leather. Lee quickly found where the Old Testament left off and the New Testament began, and he seized the thicker Old in his left hand and tore it from the binding. He thrust it like something unclean away from him and into the fireplace where there was no fire now, and he wiped his left hand on the side of his blue jeans. The pages had all spilled apart, thin and dry. Lee struck a match.

He watched the pages burn, and become even more gossamery and quite black, and he knew he had accomplished nothing. This was not the only Old Testament in the world. He had made an angry gesture to satisfy only himself. And he felt not at all satisfied, or cleansed, or rid of anything.

A letter of condolence to Kate Greeves, Lee thought, was due. Yes, he would write it this evening. Why not now? Words came to his mind as he moved toward the table where he kept his paper and pens. A longhand letter, of course. Kate had lost her son and her husband in a span of only a few months.

Dear Kate,

By accident this afternoon I heard on my radio the sad news about Win. I can realize that it is an awful blow to receive so shortly after the death of Morton. I would like you to know that I send you my sincerest sympathies now and that I can appreciate your grief . . .

Lee wrote on smoothly and slowly. The curious thing was that he did feel sympathy for Kate. He bore her no grievance at all, though she was a partner to her husband in his deception. She was, somehow, a separate entity. This fact transcended guilt or the necessity to forgive. Lee signed his name. He meant every word of the letter.

I Despise Your Life

A hole is a hole is a hole, Ralph was thinking as he stared at the keyhole. The key was in his hand, ready to stick in, but still he hesitated. He could just as well ring the doorbell! He was expected.

Ralph turned and clumped in a circle in his cowboy boots, and faced the door again. It was his father's apartment after all, and he had the key. Ralph set his teeth, his lower lip curled forward, and he stuck the key in the lock and turned it.

There was a light in the living room, ahead and to the right.

"Hello, Dad?" Ralph called, and walked toward the living room. A battered leather handbag swung from a strap over his shoulder.

"Hi there, Ralph!" His father was on his feet, in gray flannels and sweater, house shoes, and with a pipe in his hand. He looked his son up and down.

Ralph, taller than his father, walked past him. Everything neat and orderly as usual, Ralph saw, two sofas, armchairs, one with a book on its arm where his father must just have been reading.

"And how's life?" asked his father. "You're looking . . . pretty well."

Was he? Ralph realized that his jeans were dirty, and recalled that he hadn't bothered shaving even yesterday. The left side of his short-cut, blondish hair was a dark pink, because someone had smeared a handful of dye into it suddenly, sometime last night or rather early this morning. Ralph knew his father wasn't going to mention the dye, but his father's face bore a faintly amused smile. Not nice, Ralph thought. Such people were the enemy. Mustn't forget that.

"Sit down, boy. What brings you here? . . . Like a beer?"

"Yeah, sure. Thanks." Ralph was at that moment feeling a little fuzzy in the head. He had been a lot sharper less than an hour ago, higher and sharper, when he had been smoking with Cassie, Ben and Georgie back at the dump. The *dump.* That was what had brought him here, and he'd better get down to it. Meanwhile a beer was what they called socially acceptable. Ralph took the cold can that his father extended.

"You probably don't want a glass."

Ralph didn't, and so what? He threw his head back a little, smiling, and sipped from the triangle in the can. Another hole, this triangle. "Life's full of holes, isn't it?"

Now his father grinned. "What do you mean by that? . . . Sit down somewhere, Ralph. You look tired. Had a late night?" His father took the armchair, put a bookmark in the book and laid the book on a side table.

"Well, yeah—practicing as usual. Always gets later than we think." Ralph lowered his lean figure to the sofa. "We're going—" Now where was he? He had meant to tell his father about the record they were going to cut next Sunday at a place in the Bronx. The Plastics, Ralph's group called itself. Cassie was great on the bass fiddle, unusual for a girl. Cassie was great all round. She was their mascot, their pet, and she even cooked. "There's a kitchen where we're living," Ralph said finally.

"Oh, I assumed that. It's a big apartment, isn't it?"

"Well, yeah, but it's a loft. One very big room, then a smaller room, kitchen and bath. And that's—I need a hundred dollars now to hold up my end of it. The rent. That is, till we cut this record Sunday in the Bronx. That's what we're rehearsing now."

His father nodded calmly. "Then the record will be marketed?"

"Naturally," said Ralph, aware that he lied, or that the "marketing" was at best dubious. "Ten songs. That's a big deal. We're calling it 'Night on the Tiles' by the Plastics."

His father fiddled with his pipe, poked at the tobacco with a nail-like gadget.

Well, Ralph thought with impatience as the silence went on. "It's not that I like to ask you—" But that wasn't true, he didn't mind a damn asking for a hundred. What was a hundred to his father? The price of a business lunch!

"This time it's no, Ralph. Sorry."

"What do you mean?" Ralph felt a small, polite smile grow on his face, a smile of feigned incredulity. "What's a hundred to you? We owe the rent there, we have to chip in, and we want this record cut. That's business and it's pretty important!"

"And the record before that and before that? Do these records exist?" Stephen Duncan went on over his son's protest, "You're twenty, Ralph, you're behaving like somebody *ten*, and you're asking me to keep on subsidizing it."

His father smiled, but he was hotting up. That seldom happened. Ralph said, "You're giving my mother a thousand a month and you don't even feel it."

"Would you like to ask your mother for a hundred?" Steve gave a laugh.

No, that was a stone wall. Ralph's mother had gone back to California, to her parents' hometown. His mother and dad had been divorced about a year now. His mother had wanted the divorce, and there'd been a pretty nasty story about "the other man," his mother's lover Bert, but their affair had broken up after the divorce, and that wasn't the point, as far as Ralph and his mother were concerned. His mother didn't like his lifestyle, had been surprisingly unsympathetic when Cornell had kicked him out for bad grades in the middle of his sophomore year, and when Ralph had taken up with some musicians in New York his mother had fairly stopped talking to him. Even his father had been more understanding then. And here was his father making tons of money with his tools plant in New Jersey, with his house and a boat in Long Island, and balking at a hundred dollars! Ralph felt like yelling to his father that he was a tightwad, forty-six years old and living in the past, but caution warned him to take it easy, that all might not be lost today. "It's an emergency, dad. Just these next two weeks—are really important and if we—"

"Oh, for God's sake, Ralph, how many times have you said that? Pull yourself together and get a job! Any kind of job. Work behind a counter! Better men than you have started that way."

This was the enemy coming out. Ralph's lower lip curled from his teeth, as it had when he had stuck the key in the keyhole, but he kept his tone low and polite. "That's pretty negative, what you're saying. That's really death and the destruction of life."

His father laughed and shook his head. "What've you had today? Acid? . . . You've had something. You talk about death and you can't even keep yourself in a healthy state. Who're you fooling, Ralph?"

"I haven't had anything today, but we were working late last night. Rehearsing. We do work. And we write our own music. *Ben* writes our music."

Again the superior-looking nod from his father. "You never showed any particular interest in music till a few months ago. Clarinet now. A fine instrument, Mozart wrote for it, and you use it for rubbish. Face it, Ralph. The Plastics! You're well named!" His father stood up, his lips a straight line of tension. "Sorry, Ralph, but I've got to leave the house in about ten minutes. Got to go to the Algonquin to meet a man who's just arrived from Chicago. Work, you know? . . . This music thing, Ralph—I see it all over, mediocre pop bands—"

"Rock," said Ralph.

"Rock, all right. The music phase might as well be part of a school curriculum. A year of guitar, clarinet or whatever. Third-rate music and then it's all dropped."

His father was trying, a little bit, to be friendly, Ralph could see. "All right, maybe it's a phase. But give me a hand with it for a while. Would that kill you?"

"It might kill you. You've lost weight even. I can imagine the junk food you kids eat."

Ralph got to his feet, staggering very slightly, but that was because of his boot heels. He was ready to leave, more than ready. "I frankly think your whole life is junk."

"I don't think you mean that . . . Take it easy, Ralph."

Ralph was on his way to the door. When he had opened it, he turned as if automatically, because he hadn't thought to, and said, "Bye, Dad."

Twenty minutes later, he was home at the dump on the edge of SoHo. Ralph had walked a little, walking off his disappointment, trying to, then had caught a bus downtown. And here he was, breathing again. Home! The tall white walls and the white ceiling way up there were like the wide open spaces! Cassie had the stereo up high and was dancing to it by herself, snapping her fingers gently. She gave Ralph barely a nod when she saw him, but Ralph didn't mind. He was smiling. Ben, raking his guitar along with the electronic music, yelled a "Hi!" In the bathroom, a fellow strange to Ralph stood in shorts washing his hair at the basin, and Georgie was sloshing around in the tub. Ralph wanted to use the toilet, and did. When Ralph went back into the living room, a fellow and a girl whom Ralph didn't know came out of the small bedroom in the corner. Now these two sat down on one of the two pushed-together double beds that served as a big sofa in the daytime. The two lit cigarettes, Cassie was smiling and yelling something at them—Ralph couldn't hear through the music—and Ralph saw that the two newcomers had dropped their coats in the corner by the trestle table, where all their guests dropped their coats. Was a party on for tonight? Hardly eight o'clock now. Early for arrivals.

Suddenly Ralph had an idea: they'd give a rent-raising party. Ralph wasn't the only one of the four who was short of rent money just now. They could charge five dollars for admission—or better make it three—and people could bring their own booze or wine or whatever.

Ralph approached Cassie and shouted his idea.

Cassie's blue-gray eyes lit up, she nodded, and went over to scream it at Ben.

All they had to do was notify the right people, maybe twenty or thirty, Ralph thought. These might bring along a few other people, but the fewer right people would furnish the money. It was Wednesday. They'd make the party for Saturday.

"Come at *nine*!" Cassie was shrieking into the telephone. "Tell Teddie and Marcia, will you? That'll save me a call."

The electronic tape had now come to the human voice bit, which always made Ralph think they were chanting:

> *You've had it now . . .*
> *You've had it now . . .*

Now how was that meant? That you were finished, or that you'd just had something good? Like Cassie. Cassie belonged to all three of them just now, Georgie the pianist, Ben the guitar man, and himself. That was good. No arguments, no silly jealousy anywhere. None of the crap that bothered dead people like his father.

"Dead *people*!" Ralph shouted, raising a booted foot, lifting a hand. His fingers struck the brim of his secondhand Stetson, and reminded him that he still had it on. "Saw my *dad* today!" Ralph yelled, taking his Stetson off with a flourish.

But nobody heard him. The fellow who had been washing his hair came out of the bathroom with a towel over his head, bumped into Cassie and went on, bumped into the double beds and plunged down. The pair of strangers had left.

Around midnight they ate frankfurters, boiled up by Cassie, in the kitchen. Mustard lay in a big plate on the kitchen table. The music continued. Cassie brought a stick of coke from the hiding place (which kept changing) in the little bedroom, and Georgie did the honors, scraping away with a razor blade at the white stick on a piece of flat but jagged-edged marble that he held on his leather-covered thighs. He lined up carefully and equitably fourteen rows of white powder, which they all sniffed in polite and leisurely turn. Five takers, twice taking, left four rows to spare. Ralph gallantly offered his second helping to Cassie, who rewarded him with a smile and a kiss on the lips. He was sitting next to her then, on an edge of the double bed. All five sat on the edges, lounging inward toward the marble slab in the center.

Gotta wrangle oh-and-oh-and-oh . . .

Did anyone hear those words but Ralph?

The fellow who had washed his hair later got unceremoniously thrown down the stairs by Ben, who could sometimes lose his temper.

"*That's* not very nice!" Cassie yelled, as she danced around the living room, snapping her fingers in her easy way.

Ralph didn't ask what had happened. He thought Cassie had said earlier that the boy had brought the coke, and if so, he'd surely been paid for it. Hadn't he? And did it matter? No. The rent mattered. And they'd get that. Ralph kept his eyes on Cassie, though she was dancing with Georgie. Ben was on his guitar again. Ralph didn't want to dance, he wanted to sleep.

And later it was Ralph who was in the same bed with Cassie, in the little bedroom. He couldn't make it with her, and didn't really try. It was great just to hold a girl in your arms, as they said in the old songs.

The party idea had made progress by the next noon, when the four of them were having coffee and Danish in the kitchen.

"It'll be one giant disco," said Ben, "and we'll put the eats on the beds, so people can lounge on the floor there, pickin'."

"Surrealist *fruit* deco. I know what *I'll* do." Georgie, wide-eyed, his blond hair waxed into points, munched his pastry.

"Paper cups. Safer if stuff gets broken. Have we got money for paper cups?" This from Cassie.

"We got at least fifty jam jars," Ralph put in. "Now listen, we want this to pay off. You think we should make a very *selective* guest list? Like twenty we're sure can pay, so there won't be a mob that can't?"

"Na-ah," Ben said. "We stick up an invite in the Meetcha with price of admission loud and clear, see? No three buck-see, no entree . . . They'll come!"

Saturday was only two days off. They'd get hardly any sleep Saturday, Ralph realized, but the date in the Bronx wasn't till noon, nothing ever got started there till 3 P.M. and on pills they'd make it, and maybe do the record even better. They'd be doing only five songs Sunday, half the record.

That afternoon, Cassie made a poster on a big piece of cardboard to be tacked on a wall of the Meetcha Bar down the street.

ROOF RAISIN'

RENT RAISIN'

PARTY!

SAT. NITE 9 PM ONWARD

103 FROTT ST. (3rd FLOOR)

BRING YOUR RAISIN

ALL WELCOME (this ain't no church)

DISCO ELECTRONIC

ADMISSION $3.00

AND BRING YOUR OWN POWDER, JUICE, Etc.

The last line, Cassie conceded, was a halfway thing between saying no refreshments would be offered (untrue), and a suggestion that if people really had a preference as to drink and other things, they should bring their own so they'd be sure and get it. Cassie had been imbibing beer as she worked, and after an hour she was tired, but picked up at the boys' praise of her artwork. She had drawn a couple of nudes dancing, with real raisins glued on where the sex organs would have been. The nude figures were lanky and blue-colored.

"Really great!" Ben said. "Eye-*catching*!"

Cassie flopped on a bed on her back, smiling, and closed her eyes, her arms curled above her head. She looked lovely to Ralph, with her thighs bulging her jeans, shirt buttons straining over her breasts that were partly visible through the gaps.

Ralph was assigned to put the poster up, and went out with it, taking along also an old envelope in which Georgie had put six or more thumbtacks. For some reason (well, Ralph knew why), he was considered just a little more square than the others, more respectable even. Ralph didn't care much for that, and maybe it wouldn't last forever. So far he hadn't run up a bill with Ed Meecham, who owned the Meetcha, whereas the others had. Small bills, of course, because Ed didn't give credit higher than twenty dollars. Into this wooden-tabled, wooden-chaired establishment Ralph clumped in his cowboy boots with the poster in hand, and at once glanced around the walls, looking for a free and suitable place. The walls were already pretty much filled by art exhibition posters, announcements of sales of secondhand items, apartment-sharing opportunities, and cartoons of the patrons. Ralph greeted a couple of fellows hunched over beer or coffee at the tables, and made his way to Ed Meecham behind the bar at the back.

"Okay if I put this up, Ed?"

Ed, bald, with a mustache like a black and gray shaving brush, eyed the poster sharply as if examining it for porn—and maybe he was—then nodded consent. "If you find a spot, Ralph."

"Thanks, Ed." Ralph felt flattered because Ed had called him by name. Ed knew him, of course, but up to now hadn't called him anything. Funny how little things like that built up the ego, Ralph thought. That was what the group at the dump spent a lot of time talking about—ego—what you thought of *yourself*. It was important. Ralph's newfound confidence inspired him to tack, smoothly and with suitable speed, Cassie's poster over a small poster of graffiti which Ralph considered the clientele had laughed at long enough. Ralph waved good-bye and departed.

Back at the loft building, Ralph glanced at the mailbox before climbing the stairs. Two items. The box had a lock, but it had been broken. To Ralph's surprise, one envelope was addressed to him in his father's large yet angular hand with his genuine pen. His father didn't like ballpoints. Ralph climbed the stairs, reported his success with the poster-fixing, and went into the kitchen to look at his letter. Ben and Georgie were working with guitar and piano, talking also. They'd already had a practice session that day, and Ben wanted another, but there were still five minutes to read a letter, and maybe his father had even enclosed a check, Ralph thought as he picked open the envelope of sturdy white paper. No stamp on it. His father had delivered the letter. Ralph had noticed that at once downstairs, but now that fact—or something—made his fingers shake.

There was no check in the letter. It went, after the date which was Wednesday, yesterday:

Dear Ralph,

It is late in the evening but I feel inspired or compelled to write a few words to you by way of explaining my attitude, which I know you consider wrong, inhuman perhaps, or plain blind. So it may come as a relief to you to know that I've decided not to interfere or try to influence you from now on. Every human being has the right to make his own life. Birds must fly the nest. So did I when I left my parents exactly at your age, 20, and went to try my luck in Chicago and then in New York. You have the same right. And I realize that what seems to me wrong or unwise may be for you—right. At any rate, you are a man and you should be able to and be allowed to stand on your own feet.

I think this may help clear the atmosphere and enable us to have a better relationship, because God knows it cannot be pleasant for a son to sense "parental disapproval" all the time, even if for the most part you shrug it off.

However if you're sick, you know very well I'm here to look after you. You are not alone in the world, Ralph, just free. And my good wishes and love are with you.

Your dad, ever,

Steve

P.S. I know that the absence of your mother from the household has not helped, hasn't made you any happier or stronger. I am bitterly and personally sorry about that, and I am no happier for it either. We should both (you and I) realize that we are not the only father and son in the world who have had to experience the same thing.

Ralph felt shocked, in a strange and profound way. His father had cut him off. That P.S.—Well, they'd been over that, lots of times, in few words every time, but lots of times. That divorce had been his *mother's* fault, that "other man" and all that. His father had never wanted a divorce, in spite of Bert who had disappeared as his father had thought he would. Ralph knew his mother had also been disappointed in him, Ralph. But the divorce remarks in the letter weren't what upset Ralph. It was his father's washing his hands of him. And such a polite way of saying it: You have the same right. Ralph was still under twenty-one. Wasn't he still a minor? Well, no, if you could vote at eighteen, Ralph recalled.

"Love *letters*—in—the—sand—" Georgie came into the kitchen singing. "Somebody let you down?"

Ralph tried to get the frown off his face. "Na-ah. Letter from my dad. No dough.—Mister No-Dough."

"Well, you knew that." Georgie poured himself some cold coffee from the pot on the stove, and upended a cellophane bag of potato chips into his mouth, a bag nearly empty. "Let's go again, Ralphie? Another half hour or so. 'Airport Bird' now." Georgie gestured towards the living room.

Ralph got his clarinet from its place under the foot of one of the double beds, where he had put it while he tacked the poster.

He had to lift the bed to get it, rake the case out with his foot, but at least the instrument was always safe there, unstolen, unstepped on. The record-cutting would cost seventy-five dollars. They had a deal with Mike, the man in the Bronx. He distributed their records to cut-rate pop record shops which tried to push new groups, according to Mike. So far the Plastics hadn't had any revenue from that, but what they had created was *on record*, and there were two earlier records here at the dump. They practiced, Cassie included. It was after six, and the ceiling spotlights were on, three pink ones, a couple of blues, but mainly white ones. Someone had said such lights ran into big electricity bills, but the lights gave atmosphere, and after the music got going, who thought about an electricity bill? Ralph tried to play with especial care and exactitude, letting himself go only in the finale of "Fried Chicks," the song that would be number five, the last, on the record Sunday.

But Ralph's thoughts, most of his thoughts, were on his father and he couldn't shake them off. Amazing. He was upset. And ordinarily he would have said to his chums, "I'm uptight today, sort of thrown." But that evening he didn't say it, even in the break they took around nine in the kitchen, where Cassie was stirring up a tomato sauce for their spaghetti dinner. Ben lit a joint which they passed around. Georgie went out for lettuce and a bottle of Italian table wine, the kind that came in a big glass jug. No meat for the spaghetti sauce, Cassie announced, but it was going to taste good anyway. And his father thought they didn't eat properly, Ralph remembered.

Why not invite Steve to the party? If his father condescended to come, he could see that they ran a going household with clean walls, that they weren't a bunch of apes. Ralph knew his father thought they never knew what day of the week it was, that they lived off their parents—absolutely not true in the case of Georgie and Ben, who gave piano and guitar lessons—and that they never washed their clothes, whereas the tub had clothes soaking in it half the time, and Cassie was a great ironer.

"Hey, does anybody *mind*," Ralph began loudly, but the hi-fi was on, Ben had just said something funny, so everyone was laughing. Everyone now included two new people, a boy and girl who must have arrived with Georgie when he came back with lettuce and wine. Ralph tried again. "Hey, Cass! I feel like inviting my *father* Saturday night. Okay?"

Cassie, smiling, shrugged a little as usual. It looked like the movement she made when she was dancing. "*Why not?*"

Ralph smiled in a glow of contentment, even pride. Would his own parents, for instance, have opened their doors as freely to *his* chums of the dump? Good God, no! Who, between the two of them, was more charitable, Christian, tolerant, all that crap?

"That *crap!*" Ralph yelled. "Let's get rid of it! Let's conquer it with *love!*" No one was listening, no one heard, but that didn't matter. He had got his message out. "Across and *out!*" Ralph shouted, and plunged toward the telephone. Twenty to ten, if his watch was correct. Ralph dialed his father's number.

No one answered the telephone. This disappointed Ralph.

Throughout the evening, Ralph tried his father's number at half-hour intervals. By midnight, everyone at the dump, including three more arrivals, knew whom he was trying to reach and why, and Ben had said he would invite his uncle for Saturday. Ben's parents lived somewhere upstate, but he had an uncle in Brooklyn. At a little past 1 A.M. Ralph's father answered the telephone, and Ralph proceeded to invite him for Saturday night, any time after 9 P.M.

"Oh? A party. Well—y-yes, Ralph, thanks," his father said. "I'm glad you did call, because I was a little worried after I dropped that letter."

His father sounded unusually serious, even sad. "Oh, that's— Thanks, Dad, I was glad to get it really." The words came out of nowhere, and didn't mean anything, Ralph realized, but his tone was polite.

After they had hung up, Ralph had a strange feeling that the conversation hadn't really taken place, that he had imagined it. But his father's voice had said that he would come. Yes. Definitely.

The next two days till Saturday were enhanced by the coming party, in the way Ralph recalled that the approach of Christmas had made the days preceding magical, different, prettier, when he had been little. Ben had the brilliant idea of making potato soup their main dish, cheap and easy, and they would have thin slices of frankfurter floating in it, and a big bunch of parsley in the kitchen to garnish each bowl or paper cup or even plate of this thick soup, which Cassie promised to create. Plenty of garlic was to go into the soup, which would have a ham hock base. And Cassie and Georgie had also been busy with the decor. From a friend down the street she had acquired yards of old film reels, and these looked festive, twisted and strung from corner to corner of the room, and tied together in the center with somebody's long red scarf.

"Don't nobody strike a match!" Cassie said the evening of the party. "You know what they say about flaming cellophane!"

The potato soup, in two huge cauldrons (one borrowed from a girl who was coming to the party), steamed discreetly over low gas flames, the parsley stood ready, and there was one measly six-pack of beer in the fridge, two jugs of the Italian table wine, and six sticks of Italian bread. People were supposed to bring their own drink, after all. A shoe box labeled ALMS sat on the trestle work-table near the door, and Georgie voiced his disapproval of its being so near the door, because someone could depart hastily and be down the stairs with the box before anyone knew what had happened. But the box stayed there, because people were not to be admitted without their three dollars, and Ben and Cassie agreed that it would be silly to open the door and go off somewhere like the little bedroom to stick three dollars into the shoe box.

Stereo boomed and throbbed, and people trickled in. Coats and jackets even shoes got tossed in a heap on the double bed in the little bedroom, and then on the floor in the corner by the tres-

tle table. On the pushed-together double beds, Cassie had placed
a folded bridge table plus the ironing board to provide surfaces for
bowls of potato chips, pretzels, popcorn and olives.

Olives! Black and green olives. Ralph suddenly remembered
that he had bought them. A touch of elegance. He had spent about
ten dollars on them. Ralph, in a clean shirt, cleanish jeans, boots
which he had given a wipe, felt nervous, as if he alone were giving the party. He kept watching the door, expecting his father,
feeling relieved though a bit sweaty when each time the door
opened strange kids, or faces he barely recognized, came in. It was
nearly eleven. Had his father changed his mind?

> *You ain't forgotten* mee-*ah* . . .
> *You ain't forgotten mee-eee* . . .

sang the male voice on the blaring hi-fi.

Ralph tossed back a paper cupful of distasteful red wine. Why
was he drinking the stuff? He preferred beer any time.

Even Ben's uncle was here. Ralph saw him standing at the foot
of the beds, paper cup in hand, conspicuous because he wore a
tweed jacket with a white scarf at the neck in contrast to the blue
denim everywhere. Had Ralph met him before? Ralph made his
way toward Ben's uncle, stepping aside from or forging through
the hopping dancers.

"Hello!" Ralph yelled. "You're Ben's *uncle*!"

"Yes. Right!" said Ben's uncle with a smile. "Huey! That's my
name!"

Ralph wasn't sure he'd heard it aright. Huey? Louie? "*Ralph!*"
Ralph yelled, rocked back on his boot heels, and once more
glanced at the door.

It was impossible to talk, and so what? For a few moments,
Ralph and Huey shouted things at each other, then a fellow in
black leather and a cowboy hat, stoned to the gills, came up, to
Ralph's relief, and tried to start a conversation with Ben's uncle.

Ralph found himself laughing. Then Ralph looked again at the door, and there was his father!

Ralph saw Steve smile at a girl—who was she? long blonde hair and a black dress—who was asking him for the three dollars' admission fee. His father stuck a bill into the ALMS box, probably a ten, a fiver anyway. Ralph swallowed with difficulty, felt cold sober for an instant, then plunged toward his father, crashing through dancers.

"*Dad!*" Ralph and his father shook hands, each unable to hear what the other was saying.

His father gestured toward his shirt and tie apologetically, and Ralph thought he said something about having had to spend the evening with a business colleague. Ralph escorted his father around the edge of the dancers toward the kitchen, where if there was not a beer, there was at least instant coffee. Vaguely yet persistently, like a deep conviction, Ralph felt that *the kitchen*, the mere existence of a kitchen, would prove to his father that this was a household. But the kitchen was jammed with people, as if half the party had taken refuge in this appendix of the establishment to stand still and upright, even if they were packed as tightly as people on a subway train at rush hour.

"My *dad!*" Ralph yelled on a note of pride. "Is there a *beer*?"

"Beer, hah!" said a fellow with a little brown bottle in his hand, waggling the bottle upside down to show it was empty.

"Up yours!" Ralph retorted unheard, and lunged forward and downward, unsettling at least two standing girls, but the girls didn't mind, only giggled. Ralph was acutely aware of his father, standing more or less in the doorway, and aware also of people's surprised expressions upon seeing an older man among them. But Ralph found what he was after, Ben's precious beer cache behind the fridge, tepid, but still one small beer. Only one had been left there, and Ralph told himself to replace it tomorrow, otherwise Ben would be annoyed. He found an opener and got the top off. The paper cups were already gone.

"A beer!" said Ralph, proudly handing his father the bottle.

Then they were both in the big living room again, not quite together, because the dancers, the yelling people, somehow kept them apart, though Ralph pushed toward his father, who was now near the two-bed buffet spread. Someone—probably Georgie—had created a phallic symbol made of a banana plus a couple of oranges, which looked like a cannon on wheels or a sexual organ, whichever way you wanted to take it, underlaid and surrounded by purple grapes. This eye-catching display occupied the center of the gray-covered ironing board, and Ralph saw his father turn his eyes from it.

> . . . *yeeowr a* wing-*ding-ding* . . .
> *yeeowr a* wing-*ding-ding* . . .

the electronic voices were saying, not exactly human voices, but Ralph inevitably thought of those words when he heard this particular tape. Worse was to come on this tape, if by worse one meant porn. Ralph was fixated by his father's eyes, his expression. His father's eyes were wary, almost frightened, and he looked around, blinking a couple of times, then abruptly turned his head as if to try to change his view. These people, to his father, were the enemy, Ralph realized.

Damn that particular pair of faggots, smooching not for the first time as they danced in slow rhythm to music that was fast. Of course a lot of boy and girl couples were doing the same thing, but that would be okay from his father's point of view. Ralph heard a collective "*Oooh!*" and laughter, and saw a flame run up one of the film twists and burn itself out in a top corner, as the red scarf in the center fell and the other twists of film got yanked by, lost among, the dancers.

Ralph found Cassie and dragged her over to meet his father, intending to present her as their *housemother*—at least this respectable and maybe slightly funny term stuck in his head. Ralph hadn't reached his father, when somebody fell on the floor just in front of him and Cassie, causing another couple to fall also. The couple got up, but the one who had fallen first did not. He was a stranger to Ralph, in black trousers, red vest, white shirt with cuf-flinks, skinny and unconscious. A fellow in jeans dragged him by the heels, yelling for clearance, toward the trestle table, where there was a little clear space. Ralph pushed on with Cassie in hand.

"My father *Steve! Cassie!*" Ralph yelled.

Steve nodded and said, "Good evening!" loudly, but Cassie might as well not have heard it.

Cassie was tired, very tired, her eyes rolled toward the ceiling. She wore a fresh white shirt with big starched collar and cuffs, neat black trousers and stiletto heels, and she was standing up straight, too, but Ralph knew she was exhausted, and she'd plainly had a snort of something.

"Cassie *cooks for us all*!" Ralph shouted to his father, support-ing Cassie with a firm grip. "*She's tired from all the work today!*"

"Not tired!" Cassie said. "It's a rectangle! Not a square, a rec-tangle! Same as—"

While Cassie sought for a word, and Ralph's father tried to hear, Ralph shook Cassie's arm. It shook Cassie's whole body, but she kept her eyes fixed on the ceiling and continued:

". . . saw it yesterday too in the bathroom *basin*. It's every-where! Where I was washing my *hair* this afternoon!—It's a dim-diminishing TV screen, I swear to God! And it's a *window*! A window, too, Ralphie. Y'know what I mean? Outlined in *silver*!"

"Yep," Ralph said curtly, grinding his teeth for an instant. Cassie was in a trance. What had she had? She'd call it her mantra in a minute, the vision she'd had, or was having. "Okay, Cassie, very *good*!" Laughing, Ralph shook Cassie's arm again.

"And it's *heaving*," she assured Steve. "Going up and down in the basin, y'know?"

"The water, you mean," said Ralph. "It's going *down*, the water!"

"Up—*and* down!"

Smiling, Ralph steered Cassie back to the kitchen, away from his father, away and safe from the dancers who might bump her. Cassie, however, walked quite well on her own, she was just somewhere else now in her head. Ralph dragged deeply on a limp joint that someone extended, held the smoke in his lungs, swung around to go back to the living room, and banged his forehead against the door jamb.

> *Weedjie meenie you like mee-e . . .*
> *Weedjie weenie ooo-wee-ee mee-ee . . .*

Ralph saw his father and pushed toward him. At that instant, Ralph's energy gave out, maybe because he was thinking that his father had just nodded good-bye and was leaving. And Ralph had meant to introduce him to Ben and Georgie! Next to impossible in all this crowd!

Yes, Steve was gone. Over all the people, Ralph could just see the top of the tall door closing.

Well, that was that. Ralph's ears were now aching and ringing from the loud music, and he felt slightly deaf. He couldn't hear what someone was shouting at him, as he headed back for the kitchen. No, maybe there was more space in the little bedroom, and he could close the door on himself for a minute. But when Ralph pushed wider the slightly open door, he saw what looked like at least two fellows and a girl on the bed, wallowing and laughing. Ralph reeled back and closed the door.

Sometime later, Ralph awakened, jolted by a kick in his leg. A strange girl smiled down at him. Ralph was on the floor near the two pushed-together beds. The music still throbbed, and everything was the same as before. Ralph stood up, thought for a moment that the green-covered bed was rushing toward him with its now empty plates and bowls and its phallic display, but the bed stopped, and Ralph found himself quite upright. Ben was embracing Cassie tightly, swaying among the dancers.

So was Georgie embracing Cassie. She was a black and white–clad blonde-topped doll between them, and would have fallen without their support, Ralph could see. He felt superior (maybe that little nap or blackout had done him good), and he felt on a different and separate plane from the others.

"Better plane. Everything is planes," he murmured to himself. He wanted to say this to anyone near, but everyone looked quite occupied with other people. His *father*. Yes, for Christ's sake, his father had been *here*. Tonight. *This* party. And his father had left in not such a good mood. Ralph suddenly recalled his father's pale, shocked face as he had gone out the door. That hadn't been good.

Ralph felt like throwing up, surely due to the wine. Best to get to the bathroom, the toilet of course, and Ralph at once headed for the bathroom. The door was not locked, though a fellow and a girl were in there, leaning against the basin, and suddenly Ralph was angry and yelled for both of them to get out. He heard his own voice yelling, and kept on, until with startled faces they slowly made their way out, and then Ralph slid the bolt on the door. He did not have to throw up, though he recalled that this had been his intent.

"I am on a different plane," Ralph said aloud, in a calm voice. He felt quite well now. Purposeful. Full of energy. Serious. "A man of intent." He opened the medicine cabinet over the basin, and took down what he wanted, the communal safety razor. "A man of—intent."

The next several seconds represented a geographical trip to Ralph. He thought of a plane ride he had had with his family— mom and dad, yes—over the desert between Dallas–Fort Worth and Albuquerque. Purplish lake-like shapes down there, dried-up lakes or slightly filled ones, ravines twisting like snakes, dry maybe, down there. Little canyons. Beautiful colors, tan and green. And now red. Razor cut through the swollen rivers, and came out red. Now that was colorful! Amusing. Dangerous, maybe, but exciting. And absolutely painless. No pain at all.

Ralph woke up in a horizontal position, on his back, dry in the mouth. And when he tried to move his arms, he couldn't, and he thought for a moment that he was imprisoned somewhere. *Police*, maybe. Then he saw his hands except for fingers were heavily bandaged to halfway up his forearms, and they seemed to weigh a ton each. He could just move them by tugging backward. He was in a room with at least ten beds like his own, and there was a dim blue light over the door.

"Jesus, is this another *dream*?" Ralph said in a scared voice that cracked. He looked around again, wide-eyed.

Then he became aware of the smell: medicine, disinfectant. He was in a *hospital*. Definitely. What had happened? He tried to move his legs and was relieved to find that he could. Had there been a fight at the dump? Ralph couldn't remember any. *What* hospital was this? Where? Ralph felt groggy—they'd surely given him a sedative here—but he felt more angry than sleepy, and his anger grew as he looked around him, and found neither a lamp nor a button to press.

So he yelled. "*Hey!* . . . Where's anybody? . . . He-ey!"

A groan came from one of the beds in the room, an unintelligible voice from another. The door opened and a dimly white figure with a white cap came in noiselessly.

"Hey!" Ralph said, though more softly.

"You're to keep quiet, please," said the girl. She had a flashlight thin as a pencil.

"Where *is* this?"

She told him such-and-such hospital in some street on the East Side. And it was Sunday night, midnight, she replied in answer to his question.

The party had been Saturday night, Ralph was thinking. And today, yes, today they had been due in the Bronx. Where were his friends? "Got to call my friends," Ralph said to the nurse, twisting his neck under her fingers. She was trying to check his pulse, but Ralph had thought for a minute that she meant to throttle him.

"You can't call anyone at this hour. Two of your friends were here this afternoon. I had to tell them you were sleeping and couldn't be disturbed."

"Well—how long have I got to *be* here?"

"Probably two more days," the nurse whispered. "You lost a lot of blood. You were in a state of shock. You've had some transfusions—and you may need more. Now take this, please." She extended a glass of water in the hand that held the pencil flashlight between its fingers, and on her other palm lay a largish pink pill.

"What is—"

"Take it, please. You'll feel better."

Ralph gulped it down, wincing, and when he opened his eyes, the nurse was going out the door.

In the next seconds, things became a little clearer. He had cut his wrists. That he remembered now with a twinge of shame. Sort of stupid, maybe. It had caused a lot of trouble. Blood on the bathroom floor. All those people! And his father had come to the party! Yes, that was what had made Ralph so sad, disappointed, a little ashamed. But why *should* he feel ashamed? Ashamed of what? Ralph felt his heart beating faster, belligerently, defiantly. He and his chums had given a *party*, that was all.

The pill hit him like a zinging piece of music in his ears. Like electronic cymbals, with faint but deep drums in the background.

> . . . *and a zing-zing-zing* . . .
> *and a wing-ding-ding* . . .

and Ralph slept.

He got out Tuesday noonish. Ben and Cassie came to fetch him, and treated him to a taxi ride to the dump. The hospital had made a fuss about the bill which was over five hundred dollars, and Ralph had given them his father's name and address and telephone number. When they had telephoned his father (home number), his father hadn't been in, and it hadn't occurred to Ralph to give them his father's office number, which Ralph didn't know by heart, at least he hadn't at that moment. Ben and Cassie had beer at home, and Ben went out at once for pastrami sandwiches, which were available around the corner. Georgie was out giving a piano lesson. It was great to be home, and Cassie was an angel, sympathetic, gentle, making him put his feet up, removing his shoes for him and putting pillows behind his head.

"You weren't the only one, Ralphie dear," Cassie said. "Two fellows passed out and didn't wake up till Sunday *afternoon*, and we thought we'd never get them out. But we took in three hundred and sixty-two *dollars!* Can you imagine?"

That sounded good, but it was for the rent, not his hospital bill, and the hospital had given Ralph a piece of paper that looked like a prison sentence or an extremely nasty threat to say the least, and it had a deadline for payment which Ralph had forgotten, but it was a matter of days and he had to see his father.

Ralph's father answered the telephone at a few minutes before eight that evening. Ralph had slept and felt better, braced for cool-ness on the part of his father, braced for his father even to say, "To be honest, Ralph, I don't ever want to see you again. You're a grown man now, etc." Or "My eyes were opened at that party."

But to his surprise, his father sounded calm and gentle. Yes, Ralph could come over, even this evening, if he wanted to, but not after ten, please.

Ralph shaved and washed as best he could. His wrists were still bandaged, of course, but the bandages were lighter. Ralph chose a big loose plastic jacket, hoping that his father might not see the bandages.

"Good luck, Ralphie," Cassie said, kissing him on the cheek. "We're glad you're still with us, and we can cut that record any old time."

"Take it easy now," Ben said. "Don't collapse anywhere."

Their words reminded Ralph of the faint pink stains in the corners of their bathroom floor. That floor must have been a mess, and his chums hadn't got the stains entirely removed as yet. Ralph caught a bus, found a seat, and tried to breathe in a slow Zen way.

His father had a white bandage all across his nose and onto his cheeks in the form of adhesive tape. Steve nodded, holding the door open. "Come in, Ralph."

Ralph went in. "What happened?"

"Something very stupid.—Funny." In the living room now, his father looked at Ralph, smiling. Again he wore house shoes and had been reading a book. "Had a slight accident—on the way home from that party. Very stupid accident. I turned too close on a left turn—hit another car nearly head-on. Third Avenue. Completely my fault. And my nose hit the windshield. Broken nose." His father laughed. His shoulders moved, but the laugh was silent.

"I'm sorry. The police—" Ralph at once thought of a drunken-driving charge, but how could Steve have been drunk?

"Oh! Well, yes, they gave me a test for alcohol and found I was well under the limit. Plain carelessness on my part, I said . . . Like a beer, Ralph?" Without waiting for an answer, Steve went off to the kitchen to get one.

Ralph felt shocked. His father in a dumb accident like that! And sober! Ralph understood: his father had been totally shook up by that party, just by what he had seen there. Ralph took the beer can from his father. "Thanks dad."

"And that?" His father had caught sight of the bandage on Ralph's right wrist, and at once looked at the other wrist, whose bandage was not entirely concealed by the loose blue plastic sleeve.

"Yeah, well—little accident at my place too. Nothing serious." Ralph sipped from the hole in the can, and felt his face grow warm. If it wasn't serious, why else was he here? He was here because of a five-hundred-dollar hospital bill. Ralph found himself looking into his father's eyes, aware of his father's firm mouth. His father knew what those bandages were for.

"Night of the party?" Steve asked, reaching for his matches.

"Yes," said Ralph.

"They put you in a hospital, I suppose. I tried to phone you yesterday. Got some kind of silly answer there. Man's voice."

Ralph swallowed dryly, and sipped more beer. "Nobody told me about that."

"Couldn't be that you need money for the hospital bill."

"Yeah, that's exactly it. That's true, Dad . . . And they were pretty nasty at the hospital. Insistent, I mean." And the cut wrists, the hospital bill had been his own fault, Ralph realized. *Unnecessary*. Ralph's gaze dropped to the level of his father's white coat sweater, to its brown leather buttons. His father's broken nose had been an accident, too, hadn't it? Really unnecessary. "I was upset—" Ralph shrugged, still unable to look his father in the eyes. Hadn't his father been upset too? Didn't everybody get upset now and then?

"You'll get the money," said his father finally, in a rather tense voice, as if he were paying off a blackmailer whom he didn't quite dare to treat rudely.

Or so Ralph felt. Ralph felt this even more, when his father added:

"After all, you're still my son." He walked to the secretaire bookcase where he kept his checkbook. "How much is it, Ralph?"

"It's a little over five hundred."

"I'll write this for not over six hundred. You can fill out the rest." His father wrote the check without sitting down.

"Thanks . . . I'm sorry, dad," Ralph said as he took the check from his father's hand.

"Shall I say it's the last? I wish it were."

"I swear I'll—"

"I despise your life," his father interrupted, "to be perfectly truthful."

Now Ralph stared into his father's blue eyes as if hypnotized by them. The white bandage across his father's nose and face, which might have been funny if they had both been in a different mood, now made Ralph think of a gas mask, or some kind of battle gear, not funny at all. And Ralph felt defeated.

"I've tried to—appreciate your way of life, to understand it, anyway."

Ralph said nothing. He knew his father had tried. One of his wrists was pulsing, and he glanced at its bandage to see if any blood had come through. None had, so far. Ralph took an awkward step backward, as if to leave. "Yeah, I know . . . I'm sorry, Dad."

His father nodded, but it wasn't an affirmative nod, rather a hopeless, resigned and rather tired nod. "Don't come back again—if you can help it."

Ralph bit his underlip, wanting to speak, finding no words. He resented being treated like a bum, fairly told not to come back for a handout. Now he stood like a dolt, wordless, unable even to get his anger together, and he did feel anger. Yes. Ralph started to shout "Yes!" like a big affirmative, a big okay for himself, but his lips barely opened. Then he turned and strode towards the door, opened it and went out, and closed the door firmly but he didn't bang it.

The battle wasn't over, Ralph knew.

The Dream
of the Emma C

The nineteen-year-old Sam, youngest of the crew, was at the wheel when he caught sight of a white fleck in the blue water, about half a mile ahead and a bit to port. A lone gull, he thought, bobbing on the summer sea, all by itself. The *Emma C* was headed north in Cape Cod Bay, and the Cape shore with its clusters of white houses marking the towns was quite visible on Sam's right. The mackerel haul had been miserable early this morning, and Captain Bif Haskins had decided they should try again at another spot before heading for home. The rest of the crew, four men plus Bif, were having a second breakfast of coffee and doughnuts in the galley now.

When Sam looked again at the white gull, it looked round, like a beach ball. It wasn't a gull. Sam had good eyesight, and he concentrated his gaze. It was a *swimmer!* And way out here, at least two miles from shore! Was the fellow maybe dead? Just floating?

"*Hey!*" Sam yelled, at the same time turning the wheel so the *Emma C* would be headed straight for the white dot. "Hey, Louie!—*Johnny!*"

A heavy tread clunked on the deck, then Chuck appeared at the port door of the wheelhouse. "What's up?"

"Somebody's floating out there. Look!"

Within seconds, all of them were looking. Bif got his binoculars from a little locker behind the wheel. The face under the white cap was pronounced that of a girl.

"A *girl?*"

The binoculars were passed around.

"I can see her *eyes!*"

"She's not moving. If she was dead, her eyes'd be open too!"

"Got a blue bathing suit on!" Chuck reported.

Sam grabbed a quick look through the glasses which he held with one hand. "She's an exhausted swimmer. Get a blanket ready!"

Louie, the stocky half-Portuguese, lowered the Jacob's ladder on Captain Bif's orders. The ladder trailed in the sea. Now they

were quite close. The girl was simply floating, making no movement with her arms or legs, as if she were too tired for any effort.
But her eyes were open, a little. Louie was first down the ladder.
Sam had cut the motor. Behind Louie went Johnny, a tallish fellow a little older than Sam.

Louie groped, wet to his thighs, and caught the girl's right arm
at the elbow. They all heard her groan slightly. She was definitely
alive, but so spent that her head nodded forward as Louie lifted her
by both her arms. And Johnny tugged at Louie. Willing hands
caught the girl's hands, then her waist, her feet, and four pairs of
hands lowered her gently onto the rough olive-green blanket that
someone had spread on the deck.

She was pale, just a little pink on shoulders and arms, not very
tall, with a full breast, a smallish waist from which sprang rounded
hips like those of a mermaid, but this was no mermaid. She had
small, graceful feet, and legs, and the rest.

"Tea! Hot tea!" said Captain Bif. "Then we'd better radio to
shore."

"Coffee's quicker, Bif!" Chuck went off to get some.

Sam was pulling back her white cap, ever so gently so as not
to tug at her hair. She was very blonde. Her lips were pale and
bluish, her tongue bright pink, running its tip along the edge of
her white teeth.

"Ain't she *pretty*!" someone whispered in a tone of awe.

"Coffee, ma'am?" Chuck held the thick white cup to her lips.
He knelt, as did Louie who supported her with the blanket around
her shoulders.

"Um-m," she murmured, and took a tiny sip.

"Where you from? . . . Are you cold? . . . How'd you get way
out here?" The questions came fast.

The girl's blue eyes had barely opened. "A bet—"

"Where'd you think you were swimming to?"

"Stow it, all of you!" Sam said as if he were the captain. "She needs a bunk to rest in. She can have mine. Give me a hand, Louie?" Sam was ready to carry her in the blanket.

"*My* bunk!" Chuck said. "Mine's got a *sheet* since this morning."

Every bunk was offered—there were only four tucked away under the forward deck—but Chuck's with the sheet was agreed upon. Chuck beamed as if he had won a bride, and followed Louie and Sam as they carried the girl toward the cabin. Chuck glanced over his shoulder as if to say to the three remaining men, including the captain, "Keep your distance!"

The low-ceilinged cabin held two bunks on either side, one above the other. The crew sometimes snoozed in shifts, but they were almost never out all night. Once in a while, a man treated himself to a sheet from home to put between the blankets, and now Chuck happened to be sporting a sheet, which he considered a piece of luck. He carefully tucked the girl's feet in, and made sure her shoulders were covered, because her skin was cool.

"Like the sleepin' beauty," Chuck said softly. "Isn't she?"

"Oughtn't we to take that wet suit off, Chuck?" Sam asked.

Chuck frowned, thinking. "Um—yeah, but we oughta leave that to her—in a while. Don't you think so? . . . Are you gettin' warmer, miss?"

The girl's eyes were open again. Her lips parted slightly, but she said nothing.

Sam went off and returned with a corked wine bottle which he wrapped in a towel. "Hot water from the stove," he said to Chuck, and placed the bottle carefully at the girl's feet, inside the blanket but outside the sheet.

Louie had departed, summoned by Bif. Filip, a boy of twenty, ugly and timid, peered curiously down the hatch at the girl in the lower starboard bunk.

"Let's let her be for a while," Chuck said. Sam was standing near him, and Chuck poked him in the ribs with an elbow, so hard that Sam winced. "And no funny business, fella. Leave her alone."

Sam glowered at the older man. "Funny business from *me*?"

The *Emma C* chugged northward in Massachusetts Bay but more slowly than before, moved in an almost dreamy way, as if the girl's presence had cast a spell not only over the six men, but the engine. Captain Bif was at the wheel, nervously chewing a cigar that had gone out, gazing ahead of him at familiar water and at the fading Cape on his right. He had radioed Provincetown, giving a description of the girl, blonde and about twenty, saying she was too tired to speak now, but she did not seem to be injured and would probably be all right. Judging from what the Provincetown operator said, such a girl had not been reported missing as yet. Now where was he heading? They had the right to try their luck anywhere along here, closer to shore, and farther north, to lower their nets, make a sweep and fill the hold, or try to, before turning back for Wellfleet, their home port. But Bif realized he didn't give a damn if they caught any more fish today or not. Neither did the crew, he knew. Where was the girl from? What was her name? She certainly was beautiful! Fantastic to pull something like *that* out of the sea! It was like a tall story, a legend that was amusing to listen to, but not to be believed. He and his men would treat her right. It was a time for all of them to be gentlemen. "Gentlemen," Captain Bif murmured to himself, with a certain satisfaction. Yes, he'd see to that. "Hey, *Sam*!" Bif called loudly over his shoulder.

Sam, organizing nets on the after deck, dropped his work and went to the wheelhouse.

"Keep her steady—as she goes," said Bif.

"Yessir." Sam took over the wheel. After a minute or so, he slightly decreased their speed. Today was a special day. Sam didn't want to look at another dead or dying fish today. Sam had done two years of college, which had included six months on the training ship *Westward* that operated out of Woods Hole, Massachusetts, whereby he had gained credits in nautical and marine science. Sam intended to be an oceanographer. His job on the *Emma C* was a one-month hitch during summer vacation. On the *Westward*, Sam had cruised the Caribbean and the Florida coasts, they had seen phosphorescent jellyfish at night, lovely porpoise leaping in schools, but somehow nothing so strange, startling and beautiful as this calm girl that the sea had presented to them out of nowhere.

Chuck was standing by the cabin hatch as Bif approached with an air of intending to enter. "She's okay, Bif. Sleeping now."

"Good. Thought I'd have a shave—and I can be quiet about it. Tell Filip to bring me a pan of hot water, would you, Chuck?"

Bif usually didn't bother shaving on board. Chuck slid open the hatches a little, saw that the girl looked asleep, and touched his lips with a forefinger to indicate to Bif to be quiet. Then Chuck looked around for Filip and found him sweeping little dead fish on the after deck into a heap. He gave Bif's order, and admonished Filip to be quiet when he entered the cabin, because the girl was sleeping. On second thoughts, Chuck decided to take the pan from Filip himself when he brought it. Filip trotted off, smiling. True there was a mirror on the wall between the bunks, but couldn't Bif have shaved somewhere in the galley?

Then a voice yelled, "Damn you to *hell*, Filip!"

There was a thud, a tinny clatter, and Chuck saw Filip reel backward out of the galley and fall, and his head hit the bulwark. Louie stood over him with a clenched fist, then picked up the pan and went into the galley with it. Filip sat up, bleeding from his head. Blood rapidly soaked the back of his denim shirt.

Chuck took the boy's arm, and helped him to his feet.

From the port door of the wheelhouse, Sam glanced aft and realized what had happened. He had also heard some of the conversation. Both had wanted to take the hot water to Bif in the cabin. Smiling, Sam steered the boat a little to starboard, toward the open Atlantic. They were passing Race Point and the tip of Cape Cod to their starboard.

Louie brought the pan of hot water, and stared at the sleeping

girl until Bif told him to leave. Then Chuck reported Filip's accident to Bif, and said that Filip's head would need stitches. Bif
cursed gently.

"I'll see to it," Bif said, knowing he was the best man for
stitching, because he'd done it many times before. "Make Filip lie
down somewhere—not here—till I finish my shave."

Chuck made Filip lie down on the deck with his head out of
the sun. He had a nearly three-inch gash. Captain Bif arrived with
a half bottle of whiskey, a bottle of surgical spirits, and his kit of
gauze, adhesive tape, needle and scissors. He gave Filip a slug of
whiskey for morale, because the boy was almost weeping, and
when no one was looking Bif took a snort himself. Bif was rather
strict about drinking on board: a little wine or beer was permissi-
ble, but no hard stuff, whatever the weather.

Then the girl came awake, and there was a big to-do in the
galley about what to give her to eat.

"Soup," said Johnny, as there was a lot of vegetable soup left
over from yesterday's lunch, but someone remarked that Johnny
had thrown some fish fillets into it, like a dummox, and the soup
at present wouldn't be fit for a dog. "If you don't like my cooking—" Johnny began, balling a fist at Chuck who had called him
a dummox. This was a standing joke or threat: nobody wanted to
cook on the Emma C, so anyone who criticized the food was apt
to be appointed cook on the spot.

Chuck had clenched his fists too. "I just meant—fishy soup,
lousy soup is not appropriate for her! Scrambled eggs are more like
it!" Then Chuck's right fist shot forward as if released by a spring,
and hit Johnny in the solar plexus.

Johnny gasped, and a second later swung a right to Chuck's jaw.
Chuck staggered back and tripped, which was a good thing, as he
fell on deck instead of over the low bulwark into the sea. Chuck
shook his head and got up, thrust off Bif, and hit Johnny again under
his ribs with a left, followed by a right to the jaw that floored him.
Both men were big and evenly matched. Johnny did not get up.

"You guys better *stop* this!" Bif said. "That's enough! Understand? I'm giving orders here . . . We've got frozen steaks, haven't we? You make her a steak, Chuck. You feel up to it?"

Chuck stood tall, though his lip was bleeding. "I feel fine, Cap'n!" He went to the galley, stepping over Johnny as if Johnny were no more than a coiled rope.

Filip winced as Bif stuck a bandage on his clumsily shaved head with adhesive tape. Filip knew he was low man on the totem pole on the *Emma C*, a kid not even tall enough to impress anybody. But Louie wasn't any taller, just heavier, and Filip vowed his vengeance.

Captain Bif ordered Louie to clean the galley floor with a bucket and rag on his hands and knees by way of punishment for his attack on Filip, and Louie started his work. Louie was curious about the girl. Had she taken off her wet bathing suit? What could he possibly do to serve her? So he said to Chuck, as Chuck added some home fried potatoes to the steak plate and set a glass of milk on the tray, "I'll be glad to take that in to her, Chuck—sir."

Chuck gave a laugh. "I bet you would, fella! I'll do it. Get on with your job here." Chuck dipped half a dishtowel into the pot of hot water on the stove, wiped his lip and his hands, and picked up the tray. "Gangway!" he said, stepping on deck. The cabin hatch was closed, and he tapped with his foot. "Hello, miss! Can I—" Chuck scowled off Johnny, who was on his feet now, but holding the left side of his jaw as if it hurt. Johnny was ready to open the sliding hatch doors.

"Um-m—what?" came from within, and at a nod from Chuck, Johnny slid back the hatches.

Chuck went down the steps with his tray.

The girl was sitting up with the sheet pulled nearly to her shoulders, and Chuck saw at once that she had removed her blue bathing suit. In fact it lay on the floor beside the bunk. "Excuse me, ma'am. A bite to eat. You feeling better?"

She smiled at him. "Yes, sure . . . I don't think I'm hurt."

Chuck looked at her, remembering her smooth, pale body, unblemished. "Not a scratch, far as I know. Can you manage this?" He was ready to set the tray on her thighs, then it occurred to him that the sheet would fall from her shoulders, and he had a brilliant idea. "Hold this for a minute!" He set the tray on her lap, then knelt and pulled out a drawer from the side of the bunk. In this he had at least one clean shirt besides woolen socks and various underpants and T-shirts. He found the red-and-white checked flannel shirt that he wanted. "This. It's warm. You want to keep warm."

The girl extended an arm, and Chuck handed the shirt to her and at once turned his back. This caused him to notice Johnny and also Bif looking down through the open hatch. "Well, don't stand there *gawking*!" Chuck shouted, and advanced to the foot of the steps, blocking their view. There was even Louie peeking between Bif and Johnny!

"Thought there might be something else she needs," Johnny said. "Ketchup?"

Too annoyed to reply, Chuck turned his back on them. The girl was buttoning his big shirt over her breasts, and then she picked up knife and fork. She poked a piece of steak into her mouth, and smiled at Chuck, chewing with an appetite.

"Salt, miss? Is that all right?" Chuck had salted the steak.

"It's fine. Good, really."

Chuck glanced up, and saw a single figure, Louie, slip away. Chuck reached up and slammed the hatch doors firmly. "Will you tell me your name?"

"Natalie."

Natalie. It made Chuck think of things that came from the sea, like pearls and pretty corals, pink and red. He realized that he didn't want to ask her where she lived. Wouldn't it be fantastic if she could stay always in his bunk here, smiling at him, and he could wait on her hand and foot? "You're getting some color back in your cheeks."

She nodded, and sipped from the glass of milk.

"Would it annoy you, Natalie, if I shaved here? It's the only mirror on board—and I really need a shave."

The girl said it wouldn't annoy her, and Chuck opened the hatch and yelled, "Galley!"

Filip with bandaged head was first to arrive.

"Pan of hot water for shavin', Filip. Can you manage that?"

Filip gazed past Chuck at the girl. "Sure. Right away." He went off.

Chuck got his razor from the drawer, and whetted it on the leather strap that hung by the mirror. Then he heard a yelp from on deck, the snarl of an angry voice, and Bif's roar of reprimand.

"God's *sake*!" Bif said.

"*He's* not tellin' me what to do! *That* son of a bitch!"

Chuck climbed partway up the steps, opened the hatch doors and looked out. Louie was lying on the port deck outside the galley. Bif was feeling his pulse, and Filip stood with feet apart and a belaying pin in his right hand.

Louie was dead. Chuck could tell that from the way Bif straightened up from the fallen figure, from the way he rubbed his chin. Chuck quietly shut the cabin hatches. Louie must have asked Filip to let him carry the hot water. Something like that. And Filip had got his own back at Louie for causing the cut on his head. There'd be a burial at sea now. Wouldn't there be?

The girl had closed her eyes again. She had long golden lashes. Was she maybe twenty? Or even younger? Her delicate hands and slender wrists rested outside the covers, beside the tray. She had eaten nearly all the steak.

Filip with shaking hands brought a pan of steaming water a minute later. Chuck took it through the hatch and asked no questions, set the pan on a step and closed the hatch doors at once.

At the helm of the *Emma C*, Sam Wicker had composed a poem. He had made three drafts of it, writing on the ruled scrap paper that lay on the shelf before the wheel, and it had taken him some time.

> *I watched for leaping fish*
> *And troubled waters, signaling*
> *Action and the lowering of nets,*
> *The whirl of winches, and flapping death.*
> *Instead there floated tranquil*
> *On the sea's blue face*
> *A lovelier prize.*
> *We hauled it up gently*
> *Like coral that might break,*
> *In awe-struck silence beheld you,*
> *A beautiful girl, alive and perfect,*
> *Born of the sea!*
> *Need we, need I search further?*
> *Our prize is here, and as she sleeps*
> *A paradisic peace prevails.*

And Sam had just copied out the last line, when Louie's dying scream rent the air. Sam had been about to yell out himself for relief at the wheel, and now he watched in blinking astonishment the scene on the port deck. Louie was being covered with a tarpaulin. Had Filip done that? Sam knew about Filip's cracked head. "Johnny!" Sam called, and when Johnny swaggered up, frowning, Sam nodded toward the wheel. "Take over, would you? I've been here a long time."

Slowly, saying nothing, Johnny stepped into the wheelhouse.

The *Emma C* moved gently northeastward, at creeping speed. Ordinarily Captain Bif would have given orders who was to man the helm, or would have taken the wheel himself, but today was a different day indeed. Sam kept silent and watched. Chuck, with a puffy lip and jaw but freshly shaved, stood on the deck in earnest conversation with Bif. Filip leaned against the superstructure near them, and the patch on his head glared white in the sunshine. Filip was from the gutter, Sam thought. Like Louie. Louie had been a little better, with a family in Truro, but Filip was rather like a street urchin. Funny to think of Filip standing trial for murder or manslaughter, and this was what Captain Bif and Chuck were dealing with now.

". . . accident," Bif was saying. "Slipped and hit his head, you know? Sure enough he *did* die from a concussion—that blow with the belaying pin . . ." Then Bif saw Sam and beckoned to him.

They went into the galley, Bif opened a locker, and pulled out a full bottle of whiskey. They all had a neat drink. Sam grimaced, but finished his.

"You're to say nothing, Sam, understand?" said Bif. "Unless asked. And then you say Louie tripped in some rope and fell and hit his head."

"Are we heading back for Wellfleet tonight?" Sam asked.

"Tonight? . . . Tonight," Bif repeated dreamily, and poured another drink for himself, frowning.

Sam fingered his poem, which was folded in the back pocket of his dungarees. "The girl's all right?" he asked both Chuck and Bif.

Chuck looked challengingly at him. "Sure, she's fine. Why shouldn't she be?"

It was past three, and they'd all forgotten lunch. Sam shook his head at the offer of another drink, and went out on deck. He pulled his poem out, glanced at the open page, then made his way forward to the cabin and knocked so gently on the hatch doors, it might not have awakened the girl, if she had been asleep.

"Yes? Come in?" the girl's voice said.

Smiling with sudden relief, Sam slid open the doors. Sunlight slanted down just above the girl's head, lighting her blonde hair as if she wore a halo. Her lips and cheeks were pink now with a natural color. "I came to ask how you are—and if I can do anything for you."

"Thanks. I feel much better. I'm—"

"Well—what're *you* doing here?" Chuck seized Sam's arm from behind.

"Hey, cut it *out*, Chuck!"

"Better leave, Sammy boy." Chuck pushed past Sam and went down a couple of steps.

"I found this girl!" Sam said. "I've got a poem to give her."

"A poem!" Chuck smiled, and waved Sam back.

To Sam, Chuck looked insane. In defense, Sam made a fist of his right hand. "Really, Chuck, I don't know why—"

Chuck jumped on deck, and a blow in the left side of Sam's ribs cut his words off. Sam let go with his fist against Chuck's chest, barely shaking the heavier man. Then Chuck shoved Sam with a foot, and Sam fell on the deck.

The girl said something in a tone of protest, and Chuck interrupted with, "I don't want those apes coming in here!"

Sam got to his feet a little breathless, furious. Apes? What was on *Chuck's* mind? "If you try anything—with *that* girl—"

Chuck closed the hatch doors in Sam's face.

Trembling, Sam folded his poem and stuck it back in his pocket. He went to Captain Bif, who was still drinking in the galley, sitting at the table, and said in a voice so hoarse, it didn't sound like his own, "Chuck's up to something in the cabin, I think, sir. Maybe you'd better go see."

"Wh–at?" said Bif incredulously, not getting up.

"I can't do anything. He's *over* me." Sam meant Chuck had higher rank, was next below Bif.

Captain Bif went out, past Louie's wrapped body, and Sam stood on the deck, sneakered feet braced, watching. Bif knocked and shouted. The cabin was some four yards distant from Sam.

Chuck opened the hatch a little, and Bif said, "Are you all right there, Chuck?" and Chuck replied something that included ". . . protecting this girl . . ."

Sam's anger mounted. Was Chuck telling the truth? Chuck was a tough customer, nearly thirty, with a scar in one eyebrow and a naked woman tattooed on his right forearm. And could Chuck write a poem? Sam spat bitterly over the side, and looked again toward the cabin. Bif must have given Chuck some order, because Chuck was climbing the steps, coming on deck. Sam walked past Chuck without looking at him to the prow, pulled his ballpoint pen out, and wrote in a small hand above the poem:

I am the one who saw you in the water. I wrote this for you. With all my love, Sam

And bitter tears stung his eyes for a moment. Sam glanced around, and saw no one except Bif, who was steering. The cabin was close. Sam tapped quickly on the hatch door, and said, " 'Scuse me, miss! Can I hand you something?" He heard a soft reply that he did not understand, but there was no time to lose, so he opened the hatch doors, fairly slid down the steps, and extended his folded paper to the girl in the lower starboard bunk. "Take this, please!" He stuck it into her hand, and as he scrambled up the steps, he saw Chuck approaching on the port deck.

"Well, well! Peeping *Tom*!" Chuck said, and dashed for the cabin hatch as if to see if Sam had murdered the girl or done her some other damage.

Sam waited tensely to see if the swine Chuck was going to make the girl give up the poem.

"It's just a piece of paper!" Sam heard the girl say. "I want to read it!"

Sam drew a breath and smiled with satisfaction as if he had bashed Chuck to the deck! He walked slowly aft, feeling happy. And there was Johnny, lowering buckets over the side, rinsing. Johnny was apparently sprucing up their toilet facilities, such as they were. Sam wanted to laugh, but he only grinned, through nervously set teeth. Did the girl like his poem? Where were they heading? And why? Captain Bif at the wheel was still chewing his old unlit cigar. The captain had a wife in Wellfleet, Sam knew. What was Captain Bif thinking about now? Bif had told Sam that he had radioed P'town about the girl. And surely the girl would tell them her name and where she lived. Had she already told Chuck?

Suddenly hungry, Sam stepped into the galley, over the back of Filip who was scrubbing away slowly at the floor. Sam cut a hunk of the orange cheese they called rat cheese, and stood munching it. The old linoleum floor of the galley had never looked so clean. Blood had appeared in Filip's white bandage, and as Sam gazed at him, Filip slumped over in a faint and dropped his scrub brush. Sam stretched him out, and put a towel moistened with cold water over his forehead. Filip's face was pale.

"You'll be okay," Sam said. "You've done enough. The floor looks great."

In the cabin, Chuck had ascertained that the girl's family name was Anderson, and that she lived in Cambridge. Her father was a history professor. She had been on a camping trip with some friends, and she had taken a swim around nine that morning, intending to swim to a certain little cape or projection (Chuck thought he knew where she meant), but she had deliberately swum out farther to sea, aiming for somewhere else, and then she had become very tired.

"I had a quarrel—with someone. Then a kind of bet with someone else—a girl."

Chuck thought he understood. Maybe she had quarreled over a boy, some worthless kid. Chuck resented that possibility, and in fact did not wish to ask details. He didn't want to imagine her attracted to anyone. "You're much too . . ." He hesitated a long while. ". . . valuable to risk your life in a silly way like that."

The girl laughed a little, amused. "Can I get up? I'm feeling much better now."

"You can do anything you *wish*—Natalie." Chuck got up from where he had been sitting, on the opposite lower bunk, and again pulled out his clothes drawer. Dungarees. There was a pair, reasonably clean. "May I offer you these, ma'am?—I'll wait outside while you put them on." Chuck went up on deck.

At that moment, Captain Bif gave a shout—his customary "*Hey!*" which could mean anything. Chuck didn't respond; there were other men on board.

Sam left Filip and went to answer. The captain wanted to see Chuck. Sam, finding Chuck on deck by the cabin, told him this.

"Tell Bif he can come to see me," said Chuck.

Sam relayed this message to Bif.

With a look of annoyance, Bif motioned for Sam to take the wheel, which Sam did.

"Did you find out her name?" Bif asked Chuck.

"Yessir. Natalie Anderson."

"And where does she live?"

"Cambridge."

"Um—I'd better call shore now and tell 'em."

"She doesn't care, Bif. I mean—she's not in a hurry."

"No? You asked her?"

Chuck hadn't. He didn't reply.

Bif went to the wheelhouse. Sam was steering. Bif started to use the radio-telephone, and found it dead. "What's the matter here, Sam?"

"Sir?"

"Radio's out." Bif looked at the back of the radio. The aerial was in place. But someone had removed an essential part, Bif knew, and maybe had it in his pocket now, or had thrown it over the side. "Do you know who touched this?"

"No, sir," said Sam, strongly suspecting Johnny.

"Damn nuisance," Bif murmured, and went out, toward the cabin.

Chuck saw him and said, "She's putting on some clothes now, Bif."

Bif snorted. "Well, ask her if she's finished yet."

Chuck knocked. "Are you finished dressing, ma'am?" he called to the closed hatch doors.

"Yes, you can come down."

The girl stood barefoot in Chuck's big dungarees, which she had rolled at the cuffs. She held the waist up with one hand.

"Got a belt—somewhere," said Chuck, and started rummaging in his drawer again. "Try this, Natalie." He handed her a brown leather belt. "You might have to tie it."

"Radio's dead," Bif said to Chuck, who looked only mildly surprised and not much interested. "We radioed shore that we picked a girl up, miss—but not your name. Won't your family be worried?"

The girl smiled her easy smile, which lit up her blue eyes. "My family?—They just think I'm on a camping trip. As long as you said you picked a girl *up*—What's the worry?"

Bif nodded, thinking that it wouldn't be long before the Coast Guard sent out a boat looking for the *Emma C*, and they were still headed away from home.

Chuck watched with fascination as the girl threaded the long belt through the loops of his dungarees, and tied it loosely in a way that left both ends hanging to one side. He was hoping the girl would hold out, that she'd decide she never wanted to go back on shore, that she'd stay—at least a week with them, even longer. Chuck envisaged the *Emma C* putting in for fresh food and water at any old port, while Natalie stayed below in the cabin out of sight.

"I'm not in a hurry to get back," the girl said finally.

Chuck glowed with satisfaction. His very words to Bif!

"I'd love to see the rest of the ship," she added.

Bif nodded in a puzzled way. "All right—Natalie."

"Socks!" Once more the drawer, and Chuck produced heavy white socks with a red stripe in the cuff.

The girl slipped these on quickly. "Marvelous!"

They all went up on deck. The girl lifted her face to the sun and smiled, looked above her at a gliding gull, at the horizon. Johnny stared with parted lips as she approached him.

Sam saw her and gripped the wheel hard in astonishment. Now she was walking toward the prow. Sam stared at her, wondering if she had his poem in a pocket of those trousers, thinking what a splendid figurehead she would make for the *Emma C*, looking just like this, leaning forward with the wind blowing her blonde hair back! Except that she deserved a better ship. What had Bif been thinking about while he was steering? They were way north, leaving Massachusetts Bay and entering the Atlantic, to eastward. It would take them all night to get back to Wellfleet, even if they put about now.

The girl turned and leaned back against the prow. She looked directly at Sam, and his heart jumped.

Sam raised his right hand in something between a wave and a salute, and suddenly grinned back at her.

Johnny came into the wheelhouse, and Sam left the helm before Johnny could say anything, so Johnny had to take it. Sam went down to the girl. The sun was setting.

"You're feeling better?" Sam asked.

She nodded. "Oh, sure!"

Sam kept a distance from her, partly out of courtesy, partly so he could better see her whole figure. "Did you—I'm the—"

"What?"

"I'm the one who wrote that lousy poem . . . You read it?"

"I don't think it's lousy."

Sam sighed, aching.

"Can you show me around the ship?"

"Certainly can!"

They began to walk aft on the starboard deck. Sam at once got a whiff of fish from the hold. He thought of the mackerel lying on salted ice below their feet now. That catch might have to be chucked. And why hadn't somebody thought to put Louie in the hold?

"That's the galley," Sam said, gesturing. "Cleaner than usual today, I have to admit. I think that's in your honor." He saw Filip still lying on the worn, shiny linoleum.

"Somebody's sleeping there?" she asked.

"Y-yes, ma'am," Sam said, aware of footsteps behind him.

It was Chuck behind him, with a grin that was merely bared teeth. "Well, Sam?"

"So—Chuck." Sam kept his cool. "Would you like to join us on a tour of the ship?"

Chuck followed them like a heavy, ugly shadow. Sam glanced at the girl for comfort, for alliance, but she was looking straight ahead, her gaze a bit lifted, as if unaware of Chuck's attitude. Her feet in the big white socks made no sound on the deck, and Sam could almost believe she didn't exist, except that when he glanced at her, the mere corner of her eye jolted him into reality. Sam heard Bif give an order for Johnny to put about. The port and starboard lights had come on. Filip's blood was still on the deck, but the girl didn't look down.

Then on the port deck, she stopped suddenly. She had seen the tarpaulin-wrapped form of Louie. The rope circle was smaller at his ankles. It was unmistakably a human form. "*This?*" she said, looking with wide blue eyes at Sam, then at Chuck.

Chuck cleared his throat and said, "Sacks.—Extra burlap sacks for fish. Have to keep 'em dry."

Sam walked on slowly with the girl, wishing he had thought to say that.

Now they were at the cabin hatch, and Chuck stopped, but the girl did not want to go in. She said she felt quite well now, and wanted to stay out in the air. Captain Bif spoke to Sam and also to Filip, who was now sitting on a bench in the galley: they were to prepare supper, a good supper as they'd all more or less missed lunch. Then the captain produced some red wine. It was homemade by the local Portuguese, not notably good, but not mouth-puckering either.

Sam slipped out the starboard galley door, and went forward to the cabin. From the drawer he shared with Johnny, Sam dragged out an orange waterproof jacket with a cozy lining, and dashed up the steps again and closed the hatches. He presented the jacket to the girl. "Getting cooler," Sam said.

She put it on. "Thank you, Sam. Just what I needed!"

Sam smiled, and without a glance at the other men, returned to his cooking. It was getting dark now. The *Emma C*'s white steaming light atop the mast shed a lovely glow over the ship, nearly as pretty as moonlight. And a moon would be coming up, Sam knew, nearly full. Someone, probably Johnny, had switched on a transistor to guitar music. Ordinarily Captain Bif forbade transistors except for news, but Bif was in a good mood tonight. Sam heard laughter, and occasionally the girl's soft voice, because the others fell silent when she spoke.

"Hey, the catch is starting to *stink*!" Chuck yelled out, and the others laughed, even Natalie.

Then Sam heard the planks over the hold being tossed aside on deck. Mackerel and the occasional pilchard arced over the bulwarks, over the stern.

"Pity the gulls're all asleep!" someone said.

Sam put frozen broccoli on to boil, and sipped his red wine. He could hear the captain laughing—a rare thing, Sam thought, with a half-a-hold catch going overboard. When Sam called everyone to table, the moon was up, and he had a glimpse of the girl leaning gracefully against the superstructure with her stemmed glass of wine—the only stemmed glass on board—and it seemed to Sam that she looked directly at him for a couple of seconds.

Johnny had lashed the helm. There was no other vessel in sight, and the Cape lights lay far ahead, somewhere, as yet invisible. Four sat at the table, including Natalie, who had been provided with a pillow for the hard bench and another pillow to lean back against. Sam was happy to stand and serve, and Captain Bif, with new found sprightliness, remained on his feet also, and peered out from time to time to see if another boat might be in the neighborhood.

"Natalie . . . Natalie . . ." But no one wanted to know her last name. No one asked where she lived. There were only questions like, "What is your favourite color? . . . What size shoe do you wear?" Were some of these idiots going to try to buy shoes for her, Sam wondered. But he also took note of her size: seven, sometimes seven and a half. No one asked her address. And there was much hearty laughter, at nothing. They were eating lamb chops, the best fare the freezer had afforded this evening. Natalie said the meal was delicious. Sam had discovered a jar of mint jelly to go with the lamb chops. And then ice cream. And more wine.

Johnny was a bit drunk, and sang "Moon River," addressing Natalie, but in a comical way addressing Chuck also, the man he had fought with that day.

> "... wherever you're going
> I'm going—with you-u ..."

Chuck smiled contemptuously and told him to shut up.

After supper, they went on deck in the moonlight, and the jettisoning of fish continued. The girl declined the offer of a cigarette from Johnny. She and two or three fellows were on the starboard deck where the moon shone brightest. Would he ever forget her face, Sam thought, as she stood leaning against the superstructure, hands behind her, in his orange jacket? The curve of her cheek, pale like the round moon? Sam wished another poem would spring full-blown to his mind, so he could write it out and give it to her, now.

More guffaws as Johnny fell into the stinking hold! Johnny pronounced the hold empty, and Chuck and Bif pulled him out. Sam went into the galley to help Filip, who was clearing away. They began to wash dishes.

On deck, the girl yawned like a child, and seeing this Captain Bif and Chuck both informed her that she was sleepy, that she'd had a long hard day.

"You'll sleep by yourself in the cabin," Chuck said. "And I'll be your guard." Chuck was weaving on his feet, from drink and fatigue. He had bumped his swollen lip, the skin had split, and it was bleeding a little.

"And I'll kiss her good night," said Johnny, approaching with a wobbling attempt at a bow.

Natalie laughed, turned slightly from Johnny, and at that moment Chuck swung a fist that caught Johnny squarely in the chest. Johnny went straight backward over the bulwark into the sea, and Chuck's feet slid forward, and he landed on his rump on the deck.

"What the hell *next* on this *boat!*" Bif bawled. "Na-ow—where in God's name's a *rope?*"

Natalie saw a rope first, the length that trailed from the tied feet of Louie, lifted it, and Bif hurled it over the side.

"Man overboard!" Bif yelled. "Turn about!"

Sam heard this and raced to the wheel. Johnny caught the rope after a minute or so, and was hauled gasping and spitting over a bulwark. He lay on the deck, mumbling still about kissing Natalie good night. Louie's shoes had become exposed, and the girl saw beyond a doubt what the tarpaulin contained. Chuck took her hand firmly, and led her to the cabin. The cabin light was on. Chuck took a blanket from another bunk and added this to the blanket she had, and tucked her feet.

"You'll be safe as a—as a bug in a rug," he assured her. He pulled two other blankets from the other bunks, and went on deck with them. Here he announced that no one was sleeping in the cabin that night except Natalie.

Bif laughed, as if Chuck's giving such an order amused him.

But no one protested. Filip wanted a sweater, and Chuck entered the cabin with a torch, as quietly as possible, got a sweater and jackets and oil slickers for warmth, and tossed them out on deck. Then he sat on deck with his back against the low cabin. Filip curled up on the galley floor, and Bif against the superstructure out of the wind. Sam was to steer for an hour or so, then awaken Bif. Sam lashed the wheel, leaned tiredly against the back wall of the wheelhouse, and smoked a rare cigarette, dreaming.

And *was* it a dream, Sam thought. His head was still buzzing from wine. If so, they were all dreaming it. Or was it only he, dreaming about all of them?

The captain offered to take over around 4 A.M. and Sam wrapped himself in a blanket and collapsed, face to the super-structure. Chuck was sleeping with his head between his knees, determined to sit up beside the cabin.

Around 6:30, Sam made coffee. The Cape showed fuzzily on the port side, but Wellfleet was a couple of hours away. The *Emma C* was still not doing her full speed. No one mentioned lowering the nets, trying for another catch. They were going to give up the girl, deliver her, in a little while. Johnny sipped black coffee and didn't want anything to eat. He cast dreary glances at the shore. It seemed to Sam that everyone's eyes were sad that morning. Chuck had finally stretched out with his back against the cabin below the hatch doors, and as others awakened, so did Chuck.

Sam wanted to go to Bif and say, "Let's put in for food and fuel and take off again!" But he couldn't give such an order. Instead, he poured two mugs of coffee and brought them on a tray to Chuck. "One for Natalie," Sam said.

Chuck stood up, folded his blanket, and fortified himself with a swallow of coffee. Then he rapped on the cabin hatch.

Sam lingered, not trying to look into the cabin, but listening for the girl's voice. She said, "Good morning, Chuck. Where are we now?" Sam walked on toward the galley.

A few minutes later, a Coast Guard launch slid near enough to hail them. "*Emma C!*—What's the matter with your *radio?*"

"Conked out!" Johnny replied before anyone else could.

"You got the Anderson girl?"

This time Bif replied. "Yep . . . Didn't know her name when we radioed you."

The man with the bullhorn said: "Heading for Wellfleet?"

"Yep!" Bif replied. "All's well."

The *Emma C* plowed on. Towards ten o'clock they were rounding the sandy spit that protected Wellfleet Harbor, and the wharves came into view. The girl was on deck in Chuck's dungarees, socks and shirt, and some five men on the dock stared and smiled and commented.

". . . swimming and we picked her up!" Bif replied curtly to a question.

"That the Anderson girl? . . . Why didn't you radio?"

Bif didn't reply. He was going to ignore or stave off the queries. The girl was safe, wasn't she? Unhurt.

Sam had a secondhand car on shore. So had Chuck, who did not live in Wellfleet. Sam was about to ask Natalie if he could drive her anywhere, even to Cambridge, when he heard the wharf fellows saying, ". . . police . . . Coast Guard . . ." and someone ran off to the wharf telephone booth, no doubt to notify these groups.

"Didn't you have your radio on, Bif, you—"

Bif didn't answer. But on the wharf he spoke with a police officer who had driven up in a patrol car. Bif was talking about their casualty, Louie Galganes, whose body they had on board. He had died as a result of a fall on deck, a head concussion. The officer said he would have to see Louie's work papers.

"From the looks of your crew, you had a rough trip, Bif," a wharf man said.

Another twenty-four hours on the *Emma C*, Bif was thinking, and he might not have had any crew at all.

Chuck held Natalie's hand as she stepped from the rocking boat onto the wharf. Two other men on the wharf were ready to assist. Natalie staggered a little and recovered, smiling. Three fellows stared at her, then a policeman spoke to her and began writing in a notebook. Chuck stood near, attentive.

"Your family's been really worried, miss. We'll phone them again to say that you're really here." Seeing that his fellow officer was busy with the tarpaulin bundle on the *Emma C*'s port deck, the officer went to the patrol car and spoke over the radio telephone.

"Chuck, you've been very nice to me. Thank you." The girl looked shy, a little awkward. She pulled a sock up higher. "Captain Bif—" She waited until he had removed his unlighted cigar and thrown it down. "I want to say thanks to all of you for saving me . . . And you for finding me, Sam, and for the poem."

Sam was biting the tip of his tongue, staring at her as if sheer concentration could create a miracle, that she'd stay, that he'd have the courage to—to do what? If he asked her for a date next Saturday night, would she say yes? "A p-pleasure," he said finally.

The police officers were ready to take her in their car. "Nothing else with you, miss?"

Natalie lifted her hand, in which she carried her rolled up blue swimsuit. "No." She turned to Chuck. "I can return your clothes, if I know where to reach you—if I see you again. You can find my address in the phone book under Anderson—Herbert."

Chuck squirmed as if in pain. "Oh, I don't mind. I mean, you can keep the clothes. I just want to keep you—for my dream."

"For your what?"

"For my dream. Like a dream. *My* dream."

Sam heard this, with the taste of blood in his mouth, and realized that the girl must have left his orange jacket in the cabin. He could have given her *that*. Now he'd never wear that jacket again, just keep it. And damn fool Chuck, not to see her again! And yet, maybe that was what they all wanted, just this fantastic experience, this dream. Sam looked intently at Natalie as she waved to the crew, then got into the police car. All the crew, Filip, Johnny, and Chuck and Bif were staring at the girl in the same way. Then Sam blinked, and took his eyes away from the departing black car.

A police car was an ugly object.

Old Folks
at Home

"Well," Lois said finally, "let's do it." Her expression as she looked at her husband was serious, a little worried, but she spoke with conviction.

"Okay," said Herbert, tensely.

They were going to adopt an elderly couple to live with them. More than elderly, old probably. It was not a hasty decision on the part of the McIntyres. They had been thinking about it for several weeks. They had no children themselves, and didn't want any. Herbert was a strategy analyst at a government-sponsored institution called Bayswater, some four miles from where they lived, and Lois was an historian, specializing in European history of the seventeenth and eighteenth centuries. Thirty-three years old now, she had three books and a score of articles to her credit. She and Herbert could afford a pleasant two-story house in Connecticut with a glass-enclosed sunroom that was Herbert's workroom and also their main library, handsome grounds and a part-time gardener all year round to look after their lawn and trees, bushes and flowers. They knew people in the neighborhood, friends and acquaintances, who had children—young children and teenagers—and the McIntyres felt a little guilty about not fulfilling their duty in this department; and besides that, they had seen an old people's nursing home at first hand a few months ago, when Eustace Vickers, a retired inventor attached to Bayswater, had passed away. The McIntyres, along with a few of Herbert's colleagues, had paid a visit every few days to Eustace, who had been popular and active until his stroke.

One of the nurses at the home had told Lois and Herbert that lots of families in the region took in old people for a week at a time, especially in winter or at the Christmas season, to give them a change, "a taste of family life for a few days," and they came back much cheered and improved. "Some people are kind enough to adopt an old person—even a couple—to live with them in their homes," the nurse had said.

Lois remembered her shudder at the thought, then, with a

twinge of guilt. Old people didn't live forever. She and Herbert might be in the same boat one day, objects of semi-charity, really, dependent on the whim of nurses for basic physical needs. And old people loved to be helpful around the house, if they possibly could be, the nurse had said.

"We'll have to go—and look," Herbert said to Lois, then broke out in a grin suddenly. "Something like shopping for an orphan child, eh?"

Lois laughed too. To laugh was a relief after the earnest conversation of the past minutes. "Are you joking? Orphanages give people the children the *orphanages* choose to give. What kind of a child do you think we'd rate, Herb? White? High I.Q.? Good health? I doubt it."

"I doubt it too. We don't go to church."

"And we don't vote, because we don't know which party to vote for."

"That's because you're an historian. And I'm a policy analyzer. Oh yes, and I don't sleep at regular hours and sometimes switch on foreign news at four in the morning. But—you really mean this, Lois?"

"I said I did."

So Lois rang up the Hilltop Home and asked to speak to the superintendent. She was not sure of his or her title. A man's voice came on, and Lois explained her and her husband's intentions in prepared words. "I was told such arrangements were made sometimes—for six months, for instance." These last words had come out of nowhere, as if by themselves.

The man on the telephone gave the shortest of laughs. "Well—yes, it would be possible—and a great help usually for all concerned. Would you and your husband like to come and see us, Mrs. McIntyre?"

Lois and Herbert drove to the Hilltop Home just before seven that evening. They were received by a young nurse in blue and white uniform, who sat with them in a waiting room for a few

minutes and told them that the ambulant guests were having their
dinner in the refectory, and that she had spoken to three or four
couples about the McIntyres' offer, and two of the couples had
been interested, and two hadn't.

"These senior citizens don't always know what's good for
them," the nurse said, smiling. "How long did you and your husband plan on, Mrs. McIntyre?"

"Well—doesn't it depend on whether *they're* happy?" Lois
asked.

The nurse pondered with a slight frown, and Lois felt that she
wasn't thinking about her question, but was turning over a for-
mularized response. "I asked because we usually consider these
arrangements permanent, unless of course the single guest or the
couple wishes to return to the Hilltop."

Lois felt a cold shock, and supposed that Herbert did too, and
she did not look at him. "Has that happened? They want to come
back?"

"Not often!" The nurse's laugh sounded merry and practiced.

They were introduced to Boris and Edith Basinsky by the
nurse in blue and white. This was in the "TV room," which was a
big long room with two television sets offering different programs.
Boris Basinsky had Parkinson's disease, the nurse volunteered
within Mr. Basinsky's hearing. His face was rather gray, but he
smiled, and extended a shaking hand to Herbert, who shook it
firmly. His wife, Edith, appeared older than he and rather thin,
though her blue eyes looked at the McIntyres brightly. The TV
noise conflicted with the words the McIntyres were trying to
exchange with the Basinskys, such as, "We live nearby . . . we're
thinking . . ." and the Basinskys' "Yes, Nurse Phyllis told us about
you today. . . ."

Then the Forsters, Mamie and Albert. Mamie had broken her
hip a year ago, but could walk now with a cane. Her husband was
a tall and lanky type, rather deaf and wearing a hearing aid whose
cord disappeared down the open collar of his shirt. His health was

quite good, said Nurse Phyllis, except for a recent stroke which made it difficult for him to walk, but he did walk, with a cane also.

"The Forsters have one son, but he lives in California and—isn't in a good position to take them on. Same with the two or three grandchildren," said Nurse Phyllis. "Mamie loves to knit. And you know a lot about *gardening*, don't you, Mamie?"

Mamie's eyes drank in the McIntyres as she nodded.

Lois felt suddenly overwhelmed, somehow drowned by gray heads all around her, wrinkled faces tipped back in laughter at the events on the TV screen. She clutched Herbert's tweed jacket sleeve.

That night around midnight, they decided on the Forsters. Later, they were to ask themselves, had they decided on the Forsters because their name sounded more ordinary, more "Anglo-Saxon"? Mightn't the Basinskys have been an easier pair, even if the man had Parkinson's, which required the occasional enema, Nurse Phyllis had warned?

A few days later, on a Sunday, Mamie and Albert Forster were installed in the McIntyre house. In the preceding week, a middle-aged woman from the Hilltop Home had come to inspect the house and the room the Forsters would have, and seemed genuinely pleased with the standard of comfort the McIntyres could offer. The Forsters took the room the McIntyres called their guest room, the prettier of the two extra rooms upstairs, with its two windows giving on the front lawn. It had a double bed, which the McIntyres thought the Forsters wouldn't object to, though they didn't consult the Forsters about it. Lois had cleared the guest room closet completely, and also the chest of drawers. She had brought an armchair from the other twin-bed spare room, which meant two comfortable armchairs for the Forsters. The bathroom was just across the hall, the main bathroom with a tub in it, though downstairs there was also a shower with basin and toilet. This move took place around 5 P.M. Lois's and Herbert's neighbors the Mitchells, who lived about a mile away, had asked them for drinks, which usually meant dinner, but Herbert had declined on Saturday on the telephone, and had explained why. Then Pete Mitchell had said, "I understand—but how about our dropping in on you tomorrow around seven? For half an hour?"

"Sure." Herbert had smiled, realizing that the Mitchells were simply curious about the elderly pair. Pete Mitchell was a history professor at a local college. The Mitchells and the McIntyres often got together to compare notes for their work.

And here they were, Pete and Ruth Mitchell, Pete standing in the living room with his scotch on the rocks, and Ruth with a Dubonnet and soda in an armchair, both smiling.

"Seriously," Pete said, "how long is this going to last? Did you have to sign anything?" Pete spoke softly, as if the Forsters, way upstairs and in a remote corner, might hear them.

"Well—paper of agreement—responsibility, yes. I read it over, no mention of—time limit for either of us, perpetuity or anything like that."

Ruth Mitchell laughed. "Perpetuity!"

"Where's Lois?" Pete asked.

"Oh, she's—" At that moment, Herbert saw her entering the living room, brushing her hair to one side with a hand, and it struck him that she looked tired. "Everything okay, darling?"

"Hel-lo, Ruth and Pete!" Lois said. "Yes, everything's all right. I was just helping them unpack, hanging things and putting stuff in the medicine cabinet in the bathroom. I'd forgotten to clear a shelf there."

"Lots of pills, I suppose," said Pete, his eyes still bright with curiosity. "But you said they were both ambulant at least."

"Oh sure," said Lois. "In fact I asked them to come down and join us. They might like—Oh, there's some white wine in the fridge, isn't there, Herb? Tonic too."

"Can they get down the stairs all right?" asked Herbert, suddenly recalling their rather slow progress up the stairs. Herbert went off toward the stairway.

Lois followed him.

At that moment, Mamie Forster was descending the stairs one at a time, with a hand touching the wall, and her husband, also with his cane, was just behind her. As Herbert dashed up to lend an arm to Mamie, Albert caught his heel, lurched forward and bumped his wife who went tumbling toward Herbert. Albert regained his balance with his cane, Herbert seized Mamie's right arm, but this did not prevent her from swinging forward and striking Lois who had started up the stairs at a fast pace. It was Lois who fell backward, landing on the floor and bumping her head against the wall. Mamie cried out with pain.

"My arm!" she said.

But Herbert had her, she hadn't fallen, and he released her arm and looked to his wife. Lois was getting to her feet, rubbing her head, putting on a smile.

"I'm quite okay, Herb. Don't worry."

"Good idea—" Albert Forster was saying as he shuffled toward the living room.

"What?" Herbert hovered near Mamie, who was walking all right, but rubbing her arm.

"Good idea to put a *handrail* on those stairs!" Albert had a habit of shouting, perhaps because he did not move his lips much when he spoke, and therefore what he said was not clear.

Lois introduced Mamie and Albert Forster to Pete and Ruth, who got up from her armchair to offer it to one or the other of them. There were pleasant murmurs from the Mitchells, who hoped the Forsters would enjoy their new surroundings. The Mitchells' eyes surveyed both the Forsters, Mamie's round gray head with its quite thin hair all fluffed up and curled evidently by a professional hairdresser to make it seem more abundant, the pale pink apron that she wore over her cotton dress, her tan house slippers with limp red pompoms. Albert wore plaid house slippers, creaseless brown corduroy trousers, an old coat sweater over a flannel shirt. His expression was slightly frowning and aggressively inquisitive, as if consciously or unconsciously he had decided to hang on to an attitude of a more vigorous prime.

They wanted the television on. There was a program at 7:30 that they always watched at the Hilltop.

"You don't like television?" asked Mamie of Lois, who had just turned the set on. Mamie was seated now, still rubbing her right elbow.

"Oh, of course!" said Lois. "Why not?" she added gaily.

"We were—we were just wondering—since it's there, why isn't it *on*?" said Albert out of his slightly parted but hardly moving lips. If he had chewed tobacco, one would have thought that he was trying to hold some juice inside his lower lip.

As Lois thought this, Albert drooled a little saliva and caught it on the back of his hand. His pale blue eyes, now wide, had fixed on the television screen. Herbert came in with a tray that held a glass of white wine for Albert, tomato juice for Mamie, and a bowl of cashew nuts.

"Could you turn up the *sound*, Mis'r McIntyre?" asked Albert.

"This all right?" asked Herbert, having turned it up.

Albert first laughed at something on the screen—it was a sit-com and someone had slipped and fallen on a kitchen floor—and glanced at his wife to see if she was also amused. Smiling emptily, rubbing her elbow as if she had forgotten to stop, eyes on the screen, Mamie did not look at Albert. "More—*louder*, please, if y'don't mind," said Albert.

With a quick smile at Pete Mitchell, who was also smiling, Herbert put it up even louder, which precluded conversation. Herbert caught his wife's eye and jerked his head toward the sun-room. The four adjourned, bringing their drinks, grinning.

"Whew!" said Ruth.

Pete laughed loudly, as Herbert closed the door to the living room. "Another TV set next, Herb. For them up in their room."

Lois knew Pete was right. The Forsters could take the living room set, Lois was thinking. Herbert had a TV set here in his workroom. She was about to say something to this effect, when she heard, barely, a call from Mamie. The TV drama was over and its theme music boomed. Through the glass door, she saw Mamie looking at her, calling again. When Lois went into the living room, Mamie said:

"We're used to eating at seven. Even earlier. What time do you people eat supper?"

Lois nodded—it was a bore to try to shout over the blaring TV—raised a forefinger to indicate that she would be right on the job, and went off to the kitchen. She was going to broil lamb chops for dinner, but the Forsters were in too much of a hurry for that.

After a few minutes, Herbert went looking for Lois, and found her spooning scrambled eggs onto warmed plates on the stove. She had made toast, and there were also slices of cold boiled ham on a separate plate. This was to go on trays of the kind that stood up on the floor.

"Help me with one of these?" Lois asked.

"The Mitchells think we're nuts. They say it's going to get worse—a lot worse. And then what do we do?"

"Maybe it won't get *worse*," Lois said.

Herbert wanted to pause a moment before taking the tray in. "You think after we tuck them in bed we could go over to the Mitchells'? They've asked us for dinner. You think it's safe—to leave them?"

Lois hesitated, knowing Herbert knew it wasn't safe. "No."

THE LIVING ROOM television set was brought up to the Forsters' room. TV was the Forsters' main diversion or occupation, even their only one, from what Lois could see. It was on from morning till night, and Lois sometimes sneaked into their bedroom at eleven o'clock or later to switch it off, partly to save electricity, but mainly because the noise of it was maddening, and her and Herbert's bedroom was adjacent on the same side of the hall. Lois took a small flashlight into their bedroom to do this. The Forsters' teeth stood in two glasses on their night table, usually, though once Lois had seen a pair in a glass on the shelf in the bathroom, out of which she and Herbert had moved their toothbrushes, shampoos and shaving articles to the smaller bathroom downstairs. The teeth gave Lois an unpleasant shock, and so they did when she switched off the loud TV every night, even though she did not shine the light on them: she simply knew they were there, one pair, anyway, and maybe the second pair was in the big bathroom. She marveled that anyone could fall asleep with the TV's bursts of canned laughter, marveled also that the sudden silence never woke the Forsters up. Mamie and Albert had said they would be more comfortable in separate beds, so Lois and Herbert had made the exchange between the two upstairs rooms, and the Forsters now had the twin beds.

A handrail had been installed on the stairway, a slender black iron rail, rather pretty and Spanish-looking. But now the Forsters seldom came downstairs, and Lois served their meals to them on trays. They loved the TV, they said, because it was in color, and those at the Hilltop hadn't been. Lois took on the tray-carrying, thinking it was what was called women's work, though Herbert fetched and carried some of the time too.

"Certainly a bore," Herbert said, scowling one morning in his pajamas and dressing gown, about to take up the heavy tray of boiled eggs and teapot and toast. "But it's better than having them fall down the stairs and break a leg, isn't it?"

"Frankly, what's the difference if one of them did have a leg broken now?" Lois replied, and giggled nervously.

Lois's work suffered. She had to slow up on a long article she was writing for an historical quarterly, and the deadline made her anxious. She worked downstairs in a small study off the living room and on the other side of the living room from Herbert's workroom. Three or four times a day she was summoned by a shout from Mamie or Albert—they wanted more hot water for their tea (four o'clock ritual), because it was too strong, or Albert had mislaid his glasses, and could Lois find them, because Mamie couldn't. Sometimes Lois and Herbert had to be out of the house at the same time, Lois at the local library and Herbert at Bayswater. Lois had not the same joy as in former days on returning to her home: it wasn't a haven any longer that belonged to her and Herbert, because the Forsters were upstairs and might at any moment yell for something. Albert smoked an occasional cigar, not a big fat one, but a brand that smelled bitter and nasty to Lois, and she could smell it even downstairs when he lit up. He had burnt two holes in the brown and yellow cover on his bed, much to Lois's annoyance, as it was a handwoven blanket from Santa Fe. Lois had warned him and Mamie that letting ash drop could be dangerous. She hadn't been able to tell, from Albert's excuses, whether he had been asleep or merely careless.

Once, on returning from the library with some borrowed books and a folder of notes, Lois had been called upstairs by Mamie. Mamie was dressed, but lying on her bed, propped against pillows. The TV was not as loud as usual, and Albert appeared to be dozing on the other twin bed.

"Can't find my *teet*!" Mamie said petulantly, tears started to her eyes, and Lois saw from her downturned mouth, her little clamped jaw, that she was indeed toothless just now.

"Well—that should be easy." Lois went into the bathroom, but a glance revealed that no teeth or toothglass stood on the shelf above the basin. She even looked on the floor, then returned to the Forsters' bedroom and looked around. "Did you have them out—in bed?"

Mamie hadn't, and it was her lowers, not her uppers, and she was tired of looking. Lois looked under the bed, around the TV, the tops of the bookcases, the seats of the armchairs. Mamie assured Lois they were not in the pockets of her apron, but Lois felt the pockets anyway. Was old Albert playing a silly trick, playing at being asleep now? Lois realized that she didn't really know these old people.

"You didn't flush them down the toilet by accident?"

"No! And I'm tired of looking," said Mamie. "I'm tired!"

"Were you downstairs?"

"No!"

Lois sighed, and went downstairs. She needed a cup of strong coffee. While she was making this, she noticed that the lid was off the cake tin, that a good bit of the pound cake was gone. Lois didn't care about the cake, but it was a clue: the teeth might be downstairs. Lois knew that Mamie—maybe both of them—came downstairs sometimes when she and Herbert were out. The big square ashtray on the coffee table would be turned a little so that it looked like a diamond shape, which Lois detested, or Herbert's leather chair would be pulled out from his desk, instead of shoved close as he always left it, as if Mamie or Albert had tried the chair. Why couldn't the Forsters be equally mobile for their meals? Now with her coffee mug in hand, Lois looked over her kitchen—for teeth. She looked in her own study, where nothing seemed out of place, then went through the living room, then into Herbert's workroom. His chair was as he would have left it, but still she looked. They'll turn up, she thought, if they weren't somehow down the toilet. Finally, Lois sat down on the sofa with the rest of her coffee, and leaned back, trying to relax.

"My God!" she said, sitting up, setting the mug down on the coffee table. She had nearly spilled what was in the mug.

There were the teeth—lowers, Lois assumed—on the edge of the shelf of the coffee table that was otherwise filled with magazines. The denture looked shockingly narrow, like the lower jaw of a little rabbit. Lois took a breath. She would have to handle them. She went to the kitchen for a paper towel.

HERBERT LAUGHED LIKE A FOOL at the teeth story. They told it to their friends. They still had their friends, no change there. After two months, the McIntyres had had two or three rather noisy and late dinner parties at their house. With their TV going, the Forsters pre-

sumably heard nothing; at any rate, they didn't complain or make a
remark, and the McIntyres' friends seemed to be able to forget
there was an elderly pair upstairs, though everyone knew it. Lois
did notice that she and Herbert couldn't or didn't invite their New
York friends for the weekend any longer, realizing that their friends
wouldn't want to share the upstairs bathroom or the Forsters' TV
racket. Christopher Forster, the son in California, had written the
McIntyres a letter in longhand. The letter read as if it had been
prompted by the Hilltop Home: it was courteous, expressed gratitude, and he hoped that Mom and Dad were pleased with their
new home.

> I would take them on but my wife and me haven't got too
> much extra space here, just one room as spare that
> our own children and families use when they visit us . . .
> Will try to get the grandchildren to write but the whole
> family is not much for writing . . .

The letterhead stated the name and address of a drycleaning
shop of which Christopher Forster was not the manager. Albert
Forster, Lois remembered, had been a salesman of some kind.

Albert started wetting the bed, and Lois acquired a rubber
sheet. Albert complained of backache from "the damp," so Lois
offered him the double bed in the spare room, while she aired the
twin-bed mattress for a couple of days. She telephoned the Hilltop Home to ask if there were pills that Albert might take, and had
he had this complaint before? They said no, and asked if Albert was
happy. Lois went to see the Hilltop Home doctor in attendance,
and got some pills from him, but he doubted the complete efficacy
of the pills, he said, if the subject was not even aware of his damp-
ness until he woke up in the morning.

The second teeth story was not so funny, though both Herbert and Lois laughed at first. Mamie reported that she had
dropped her teeth—again the lowers—down the heating vent in

the floor of the bathroom. The teeth were not visible down there in the blackness, even when Herbert and Lois shone a flashlight. All they saw was a little dark gray lint or dust.

"You're sure?" Herbert asked Mamie, who was watching them.

"Dropped 'em *bot'* but only one fell t'rough!" said Mamie.

"Damned grill's so narrow," Herbert said.

"So are her teeth," said Lois.

Herbert got the grill off with a screwdriver. He rolled up his sleeves, poked gently at first in the fluffy dust, then with equal delicacy explored more deeply with a bottlebrush, not wanting to send the denture falling all the way down, if he could help it. At last he and Lois had to conclude that the teeth must have fallen all the way down, and the heating tube, rather square, curved about a yard down. Had the teeth fallen all the way into the furnace below? Herbert went down alone to the cellar, and looked with a feeling of hopelessness at the big square, rivet-secured funnel that went off the furnace and branched into six tubes that brought the heat to various rooms. Which one even belonged to the upstairs bathroom? Was it worth it to tear the whole furnace apart? Certainly not. The furnace was working as usual, and maybe the teeth had burned up. Herbert went downstairs and undertook to explain the situation to Mamie.

"We'll see that you get another set, Mamie. Might even fit better. Didn't you say these hurt and that's why—" He paused at Mamie's tragic expression. Her eyes could get a crumpled look that touched him, or disturbed him, even though he thought Mamie was usually putting on an act.

However, between him and Lois, she was consoled. She could eat "easy things" while the dental work was done. Lois at once seized on the idea of taking Mamie back to the Hilltop Home, where they might well have a dentist in residence, or an office there where dentists could work, but if they had, the Hilltop Home denied it on the telephone to Lois. This left her and Herbert to take Mamie to their own dentist in Hartford, twenty-three miles away, and the trips seemed endless, though Mamie enjoyed the rides. There was a cast of lower gums to be made, and of the upper denture for the bite, and just when Herbert and Lois, who took turns, had thought that the job was done in pretty good time, came the "fittings."

"The lowers always present more difficulties than the uppers," Dr. Feldman told them regretfully. "And my client here is pretty fussy."

It was plain to the McIntyres that Mamie was putting on an act about the lowers hurting or not fitting, so she could be taken for rides back and forth. Every two weeks, Mamie wanted her hair cut and waved at a beauty salon in Hartford, which she thought better than the one in the town near where the McIntyres lived. Social Security and the pension sent on by the Hilltop helped more than fifty percent with the Forsters' expenses, but bills of the hairdresser and also the dentist the McIntyres paid. Ruth and Pete Mitchell commiserated with the McIntyres by telephone or in person (at the same time laughing their heads off), as if the McIntyres were being afflicted with the plagues of Job. In Herbert's opinion, they were. Herbert became red in the face with repressed wrath, with frustration from losing work time, but he couldn't countenance Lois losing more of her time than he did, so he did his half of hauling Mamie back and forth, and both the McIntyres took books to read in the dentist's waiting room. Twice they took Albert along, as he wanted to go, but once he peed in the waiting room before Herbert could point out the nearby toilet (Albert's deafness made him slow to understand what people were saying), so Lois and Herbert flatly refused to take him along again, saying sympathetically but really quite grimly that he shouldn't risk having to go to the toilet again in a hurry, if he happened to be in a public place. Albert snatched out his hearing aid while Lois was speaking about this. It was Albert's way of switching off.

That was in mid-May. The McIntyres had intended to fly out

to Santa Barbara, where Herbert's parents had a house plus a guest house in the garden, and to rent a car there and drive up to Canada. Every other summer they visited the older McIntyres, and it had always been fun. Now that was impossible. It was impossible to think of Mamie and Albert running the house, difficult but maybe not impossible to engage the services of someone who would look after them and sleep in, full time. When they had taken on the Forsters, Lois was sure they had been more able to get about. Mamie had talked of working in the garden of the Hilltop Home, but Lois had not been able to interest Mamie in doing anything in their garden in April, even the lightest of work, such as sitting and watching. She said something to this effect to Herbert.

"I know, and it's going to get worse, not better," he replied.

"What do you mean exactly?"

"This bed-wetting—Kids'll grow out of it. Kids grow other teeth if them lose 'em." Herbert laughed madly for an instant. "But these two'll just get more decrepit." He pronounced the last word with bitter amusement and looked Lois in the eyes. "Have you noticed the way Albert bangs his cane now—instead of just tapping it? They're not *satisfied* with us. And they're in the saddle! We can't even have a vacation this summer—unless we can possibly shove 'em back in the Hilltop for a month or so. You think it's worth a try?"

"Yes!" Lois' heart gave a leap. "Maybe. What a good idea, Herb!"

"Let's have a drink on it!" They were standing in the kitchen, about to have their own dinner, the Forsters having been served earlier upstairs. Herbert made Lois a scotch, and replenished his own glass. "And speaking of shoving," he went on, pronouncing his words very clearly as he did when he had something to say that passionately interested him, "Dr. Feldman said today that there was absolutely nothing the matter with Mamie's lowers, no sign of gum irritation, and he could hardly pull 'em off her jaw himself, they fitted so well. Ha!—Ha-ha-ha-a!" Herbert fell about the kitchen laughing. He had lost three hours taking Mamie to the dentist that afternoon. "The goddamn last time—*today!* I was saving it to tell you." Herbert lifted his glass and drank.

When Lois rang the Hilltop the next morning, she was told that their accommodations were more than filled, some people were four in a room or booked for that, because so many other people were placing their elderly relatives in the Hilltop in order to be free for vacations themselves. Somehow Lois didn't believe the mechanical-sounding voice. But what could she do about it? She didn't believe that *so* many people lived with their parents or grandparents these days. Yet if they didn't, what did people do with them? Lois had a vision of a tribe shoving its elders off a cliff, and she shook her head to get the thought out, and stood up from the telephone. Lois did not tell Herbert.

Unfortunately, Herbert, who fetched the tray down at lunchtime, shouted to the Forsters that they would be going back to the Hilltop for two months that summer. He turned the TV down and repeated it with a big smile. "Another nice change of *scene*. You can see some of your old friends again—visit with them." He looked at both of them, and saw at once that the idea did not appeal.

Mamie exchanged a look with her husband. They were lying on their respective beds, shoes off, propped facing the TV screen. "No particular friends *there*," said Mamie.

In her sharp eyes Herbert saw a blood-chilling hostility. Mamie knew also that she wasn't going to be driven to the Hartford dentist or hairdresser again. Herbert did not mention this conversation to Lois. But Lois told Herbert during their lunch that the Hilltop Home had no room this summer. She hadn't wanted to disturb Herbert with the bad news while he had been working that morning.

"Well, that cooks it," Herbert said. "Damn, I'd like to get away this summer. Even for *two* weeks."

"Well, you can. I'll—"

Herbert shook his head bitterly, slowly. "We might do it in shifts? No, darling."

Then they heard Albert's cane—it made a different sound from Mamie's—tapping down the stairs. Then another cane. Both the Forsters were coming down. Most unusual. Lois and Herbert braced themselves as if for enemy attack.

"We don't want to go to the Hilltop this summer," said Mamie. "You—"

"No!" said Albert with a bang of his cane from his standing position.

"You agreed to let us *live* with you." Mamie had her squinty, pity-poor-me face on again, while Albert's eyes were suspicious, his lower lip twisted with inquiry.

"Well," said Lois with an embarrassed, retreating feeling that she hated, "the Hilltop is filled up, so you needn't worry. Everything's all right."

"But you *tried*," said Mamie.

"We're trying—to have a little *vacation*," said Herbert loudly for the deaf Albert's benefit, and he felt like socking the old bed-wetting bastard and knocking him down, old as he was. How dare that recipient of charity glare at him as if he were a crook, or someone who meant to do him harm?

"We don't understand," said Albert. "Are you trying—"

"You're staying *here*," Lois interrupted, forcing a huge smile to calm the atmosphere, if she could.

But Mamie began again, and Herbert was livid. They both spoke at once, Albert joined in, and in the Babel-like roar, Lois heard her husband assuring the Forsters grimly that they were *staying*, and heard the Forsters saying that the McIntyres had gone back on their word to them and the Hilltop. The phrase ". . . not *fair*" came again and again from the mouths of Mamie and Albert, until Herbert uttered a dreadful curse and turned his back. Then there was a sudden silence which fairly made Lois's ears ring, and thank God Albert decided to turn and leave the kitchen, but in the living room he paused, and Lois saw that he had begun to pee. *Is that deliberate?* Lois wondered as she rushed toward him to steer him toward the downstairs bathroom which was to the right of the kitchen door around a partition of bookshelves. She and Albert were on the way, but by the time they got there, Albert was finished, and the pale green carpet quite splotched between kitchen and the bathroom door which she had not even opened. She jerked her hand away from his coat-sweatered arm, disgusted that she had even touched him.

She went back to her husband, past Mamie. "My God," she said to Herbert.

Herbert stood like a fortress with feet apart, arms folded, eyebrows lowered. He said to his wife, "We'll make it." Then he sprang into action, grabbed a floor rag from a cupboard under the sink, wet it, and tackled the splotches on their carpet.

Albert was on his slow way upstairs, Mamie started to follow him, but paused to present her stricken face to Lois once more. Herbert was stooped and scrubbing, and didn't see it. Lois turned away and faced the stove. When Lois looked again, Mamie was creeping toward the stairs.

As Herbert rinsed and re-rinsed the floor cloth, a task he would not let Lois take over, he muttered plans. He would speak with the Hilltop Home in person, inform them that since he and Lois worked at home and needed a certain amount of solitude and silence, they could not and should not have to spend more money for a full-time servant to take meals upstairs, plus changing bed linen every day. When they had taken on the Forsters, they had both been continent and more able to look after themselves, as far as the McIntyres had known.

Herbert went to the Hilltop Home that afternoon around three, without having made an appointment. He was in an aggressive enough mood to insist on seeing the right person, and he had thought it best not to make an appointment. Finally, he was shown into the office of one Stephen Culwart, superintendent, a slender, balding man, who told him calmly that the Forsters could not be taken back into the Hilltop, because there was no room. Mr McIntyre could get in touch with the Forsters' son, of course, and another home might be found, but the problem was no longer the responsibility of the Hilltop Home. Herbert went away frustrated, and a bit tired, though he knew the tiredness was only mental and that he'd best shake it off.

Lois had been writing in her study off the living room, with her door closed, when she heard a crash of breaking glass. She went into the living room and found Mamie in a trembling state near the bookshelf partition outside the kitchen door. Mamie said she had been downstairs and had wanted to use the downstairs toilet, and had bumped the vase at the end of one of the bookshelves by accident. Mamie's manner was one of curiously mixed aggression and apology. Not for the first time, Mamie gave Lois the creeps.

"And I'd like to have some knitting," Mamie said quaveringly.

"Knitting?" Lois pressed the side of the pencil in her hand with her thumb, not hard enough to break it. She herself felt shattered at the sight of the blue and white glass shards near her feet. She had loved that Chinese vase, which had belonged to her mother—not a museum piece, perhaps, that vase, but still special and valuable. The point was, Mamie had done it on purpose. "What kind of knitting? You mean—wool for knitting?"

"Ye-es! Several colors. And *needles*," Mamie said almost tearfully, like a pitiable pauper begging for alms.

Lois nodded. "Very well."

Mamie made her slow, waddling way toward the stairs. Gay music came from the TV set above, an afternoon serial's theme music.

Lois swept up the vase, which was too much in pieces—or she thought so now—to be mended. Nevertheless, she kept the pieces, in a plastic bag, and then Herbert came in and told her his lack of success.

"I think we'd better see a lawyer," Herbert said. "I don't know what else to do."

Lois tried to calm him with a cup of tea in the kitchen. They could get in touch with the son again, Lois said. A lawyer would be expensive and maybe not even successful. "But they know something's up," Lois said as she sipped her tea.

"How so? . . . What do you mean?"

"I feel it. In the atmosphere." Lois didn't tell him about the vase, and hoped that he would not soon notice it.

Lois wrote to Christopher Forster. Mamie knitted, and Albert peed. Lois and their once-a-week cleaning girl, Rita, a plump half–Puerto Rican girl who was cheerful and an angel, rinsed the sheets and hung them on the garden line. Mamie presented Lois with a round knitted doily which was rather pretty but of a dark purple color that Lois didn't care for, or was she simply all round turned off of Mamie? Lois praised Mamie for her work, said she loved the doily, and put it in the center of the coffee table. Mamie did not seem gratified by Lois's words, strangely, but put on her wrinkled frown. After that, Mamie began turning out messes of mixed colors, dropped stitches, in articles presumably meant to be more doilies, or teapot cozies, even socks. The madness of these items made Lois and Herbert more uneasy. Now it was mid-June. Christopher had replied that his house situation was more strained than ever, because his own four-year-old grandson was spending the summer with him and his wife, as his parents were probably going to get a divorce, so the last thing he could do just now was take on his father and Mamie. Herbert invested in an hour's consultation with a lawyer, who suggested that the McIntyres might take up the situation with Medicare, combined with cooperation from Christopher Forster, or Herbert might look for another rest home for the elderly, where the problem might be difficult for him, because he was not a blood relation, and would have to explain that he had taken on responsibility for the Forsters from the Hilltop Home.

Herbert and Lois's neighbors rallied round with moral support and invitations to break their monotony, but none offered to put the Forsters up for even a week. Lois mentioned this to Herbert, jokingly, and both of them smiled at the idea: that was too much to expect even from the best of friends, and the fact that such an offer had not been forthcoming from the Mitchells or their other good friends the Lowenhooks did not diminish the McIntyres' esteem for their friends. The fact was that the Forsters were, combined, a pain, a cross, albatrosses. And now the Forsters were waging a subtle war. Things got broken. Lois no long cared what happened to Albert's mattress, or the carpet upstairs for that matter, as she had crossed them off. She did not suggest taking Albert's trousers to the cleaners, because she didn't care what their condition was. Let them stew in their own juice was a phrase that crossed her mind, but she never said it aloud. Lois was worried that Herbert might crack up. They had both reached the point, by early August, at which they could no longer laugh, even cynically.

"Let's rent a couple of studios—office rooms to work in, Lois," Herbert said one evening. "I've been looking around. There're two free in the same building on Barington Street in Hartford. Four hundred dollars a month—each. It's worth it, to me at least and I'm sure to you. You've really had the worst of it." Herbert's eyes were pinkish from fatigue, but he was able to smile.

Lois thought it a wonderful idea. Eight hundred dollars a month seemed not outrageous to pay for peace of mind, for the ability to concentrate. "I can make them a box lunch with thermoses . . ."

Herbert laughed, and tears of relief made his eyes shine. "And I'll be your chauffeur for our nine-to-five jobs. Think of it— *solitude*—in our own little cells!"

Lois and Herbert installed themselves the following Monday in the Hartford office rooms. They took typewriters, business files, letters, books, and Lois her manuscript-in-progress. When Lois had told Mamie about the move the weekend before, Mamie had asked who was going to serve their meals, and then Lois had explained that she would be here to serve their breakfast and dinner, and for lunch they'd have—a picnic, a surprise, with a thermos of hot soup, another of hot tea.

"Teatime . . ." Albert had begun vaguely, with an accusing eye fixed on Lois.

"Anyway, it's *done*," Lois had said, meaning it, because she and Herbert had signed a six-month agreement.

Mamie and Albert soured still more against the McIntyres. Albert's bed was wet every evening when the McIntyres came home between six and seven, and changing it was Lois's duty before preparing dinner. Herbert insisted on rinsing the sheet or sheets himself and hanging them either on the garden line or on the cellar line if it looked like rain.

"Moving out of your own house for those so-and-sos," Pete Mitchell said one evening when he and Ruth came for drinks. "That's a bit much, isn't it?"

"But we can work," Herbert replied. "It *is* better. Isn't it, Lois?"

"It really is. It's obvious," Lois said to the Mitchells, but she could see that they didn't believe her, that they thought she was merely trying hard. Lois was aware that she and Herbert had been to the Mitchells' house perhaps only once for dinner since the Forsters' arrival six months ago, because they, she and Herbert, felt too uneasy to leave the Forsters alone from eight in the evening till maybe after midnight. But wasn't that a little silly? After all, now the Forsters were alone in the house from before nine until around six in the evening. So Lois and Herbert accepted a dinner invitation, so often extended by the Mitchells, and the Mitchells were delighted. It was for next Saturday.

When the McIntyres returned from the Mitchells' the following Saturday night, or rather Sunday morning at nearly 1 A.M., all was well in their house. Only the living room light was on, as they had left it, the TV murmured in the Forsters' room as usual, and the Forsters' light was off. Herbert went into their room, switched off the TV, and tiptoed out with their dinner tray. He was feeling pleasantly mellow, as was Lois, because the Mitchells had given them a good dinner with wine, and the Lowenhooks had been there too.

Herbert and Lois had a nightcap in the kitchen while Lois washed up the Forsters' dinner dishes. They were making it, weren't they? In spite of the jokes tonight from the Lowenhooks. What had they said? *What if Mamie and Albert outlive you both?* Herbert and Lois managed to laugh heartily in their kitchen that night.

On Sunday, Mamie asked Lois where they had been last evening, though Lois had left the Mitchells' name and telephone number with the Forsters. The phone had rung "a dozen times," said Mamie, and she had not been able to answer it quickly enough before it stopped ringing, and neither had Albert been able to reach the phone in the McIntyres' bedroom in time, though he had tried when Mamie got tired of trying.

Lois didn't believe her. How could they hear a ring with their TV on so loud? "Funny it hasn't rung at all today."

One evening in the next week, when Lois and Herbert came home together from their offices, they found a large pot of dwarf rhododendrons upset on the living room floor, though the pot was not broken. No one could have knocked over such a big pot by merely bumping into it, and they both knew this but didn't say it. Herbert got to work with broom and scoop and righted the pot, leaving Lois to admire the new item in the living room, a vaguely hexagonal knitted thing—if it was a doily, it was pretty big, nearly a yard in diameter—which lay over one arm of the sofa. Its colors were turquoise, dark red, and white, and its surface undulated.

"Peace offering?" asked Herbert with a smirk.

It was on a Friday in early autumn, around seven, when the McIntyres drove home, that they saw smoke coming out of one of the Forsters' room windows. The window was open very little at the top, but the smoke looked thick and in earnest.

"F' God's sake!" said Herbert, jumping out of the car, then stopping, as if for a few seconds he didn't know what to do.

Lois had got out on the passenger side. Higher than the poplars the gray smoke rose, curling upward. Lois also felt curiously paralyzed. Then she thought of an unfinished article, the first four chapters of a book she was not working on now, but would soon, which were in the downstairs front room, below the Forsters' room, and a need for action took hold of her. She flung her handbag onto the front seat of the car. "Got to get our *things* out!"

Herbert knew what she meant by things. When he opened the front door, the smell of smoke made him step back, then he took a breath and plunged forward. He knew that leaving the door open, creating a draft, was the worst thing to do, but he didn't close the door. He ran to the right toward his workroom, then realized that Lois was in the house too, so he turned back and joined her in her study, flung open a window, and tossed outside to the grass the papers and folders and boxes that she handed to him. This was achieved in seconds, then they dashed across the living room to Herbert's workroom, which was comparatively free of smoke, though its door was open. Herbert opened a French window, and out onto the lawn went his boxes and files, his spare portable typewriter, reference books, current reading, and nearly half of a fourteen-volume encyclopaedia. Lois, helping him, finally paused for breath, her mouth wide open.

"And—upstairs!" she said, gasping. "Fire department? Not too late, is it?"

"Let the goddamn thing burn!"

"The Forsters—"

Herbert nodded quickly. He looked dazed. He glanced around in the sunroom to see if he had forgotten anything, then snatched his letter-opener from his desk and pocketed it, and slid open a drawer. "Traveler's checks," he murmured, and pocketed these too.

"Don't forget the house is insured," Herbert said to Lois with a smile. "We'll make it. And it's *worth* it!"

"You don't think—upstairs—"

Herbert, after a nervous sigh, crossed the living room to the stairs. Smoke was rolling down like a gray avalanche. He ran back to Lois, holding part of his unbuttoned jacket over his face. "Out! *Out*, darling!"

When they were both on the lawn, the window top of the Forsters' room broke through in flames that curled upward toward the roof. Without a word, Lois and Herbert gathered the items they had tossed onto the lawn. They stowed their possessions away rather neatly, in spite of their haste, on the back seat and in the boot of the car.

"*They* could've rung the fire department, don't you think?" Herbert said with a glance up at the flaming window.

Lois knew, and Herbert knew, that she had written FIRE DEPT. and the number on the upstairs telephone in her and Herbert's bedroom, in case anything did happen. But now the Forsters were certainly overcome by smoke. Or were they possibly *outdoors*, hidden in the dusk behind the hedges and the poplars, watching the house burn? Ready to join them—now? Lois hoped not. And she didn't think so. The Forsters were up there, already dead. "Where're we going?" she asked as Herbert turned the car onto the road, not in the Hartford direction. But she knew. "The Mitchells'?"

"Yes, sure. We'll telephone from there. The fire department. If some neighbor hasn't already done it. The Mitchells'll put us up for the night. Don't worry, darling." Herbert's hands were tense on the wheel, but he drove smoothly and carefully.

And what would the Mitchells say? *Good*, probably, Lois thought.

When in Rome

Isabella had soaped her face, her neck, and was beginning to relax in the spray of deliciously warm water on her body when suddenly—there he was again! An ugly grinning face peered at her not a meter from her own face, with one big fist gripping an iron bar, so he could raise himself to her level.

"Swine!" Isabella said between her teeth, ducking at the same time.

"Slut!" came his retort. "Ha, ha!"

This must have been the third intrusion by the same creep! Isabella, still stooped, got out of the shower and reached for the plastic bottle of yellow shampoo, shot some into a bowl which held a cake of soap (she removed the soap), let some hot shower water run into the bowl and agitated the water until the suds rose, thick and sweet-smelling. She set the bowl within easy reach on the rim of the tub, and climbed back under the shower, breathing harder with her fury.

Just let him try it again! Defiantly erect, she soaped her face-cloth, washed her thighs. The square recessed window was just to the left of her head, and there was a square emptiness, stone-lined, between the blue-and-white tiled bathroom walls and the great iron bars, each as thick as her wrist, on the street side.

"Signora?" came the mocking voice again.

Isabella reached for the bowl. Now he had both hands on the bars, and his face was between them, unshaven, his black eyes intense, his loose mouth smiling. Isabella flung the suds, holding the bowl with fingers spread wide on its underside.

"Oof!" The head disappeared.

A direct hit! The suds had caught him between the eyes, and she thought she heard some of the suds hit the pavement. Isabella smiled and finished her shower.

She was not looking forward to the evening—dinner at home with the First Secretary of the Danish Embassy with his girlfriend; but she had had worse evenings in the past, and there were worse to come in Vienna in the last week of this month, May, when her husband Filippo had to attend some kind of human-rights-and-pollution conference that was going to last five days. Isabella didn't care for the Viennese—she considered the women bores with nothing on their minds but clothes, who was wearing what, and how much did it cost.

"I think I prefer the green silk tonight," Isabella said to her maid, Elisabetta, when she went into her bedroom, big bathtowel around her, and saw the new black dress laid out on her bed. "I changed my mind," Isabella added, because she remembered that she had chosen the black that afternoon. Hadn't she? Isabella felt a little vague.

"And which shoes, signora?"

Isabella told her.

A quarter to eight now. The guests—two men, Filippo had said, besides the Danish secretary, who was called Osterberg or Ottenberg, were not due until eight, which meant eight-thirty or later. Isabella wanted to go out on the street, to drink an espresso standing up at the bar, like any other ordinary Roman citizen, and she also wanted to see if the Peeping Tom was still hanging around. In fact, there were two of them, the second a weedy type of about thirty who wore a limp raincoat and dark glasses. He was a "feeler," the kind who pushed his hand against a woman's bottom. He had done it to Isabella once or twice while she was waiting for the porter to open the door. Isabella had to wait for the porter unless she chose to carry around a key as long as a man's foot for the big outside doors. The feeler looked a bit cleaner than her bathroom snoop, but he also seemed creepier and he never smiled.

"Going out for a cafè," Isabella said to Elisabetta.

"You prefer to go out?" Elisabetta said, meaning that she could make a cafè, if the signora wanted. Elisabetta was forty-odd, her hair in a neat bun. Her husband had died a year ago, and she was still in a state of semi-mourning.

Isabella flung a cape over her shoulders, barely nodded, and left. She crossed the cobbled court, whose stones slanted gently toward a center drain, and was met at the door by one of the three porters who kept a round-the-clock guard on the palazzo, which was occupied by six affluent tenants. This porter was Franco. He lifted the heavy crossbar and opened the big doors enough for her to pass through.

Isabella was out on the street. Freedom! She stood tall and breathed. An adolescent boy cycled past, whistling. An old woman in black waddled by slowly, burdened with a shopping bag that showed onions and spaghetti on top, carelessly wrapped in newspaper. Someone's radio blared jazz through an open window. The air promised a hot summer.

Isabella looked around, but didn't see either of her nuisances, and was aware of feeling slightly disappointed. However, there was the bar-café across the street and a bit to the right. Isabella entered, conscious that her fine clothes and well-groomed hair set her apart from the usual patrons here. She put on a warm smile for the young barman, who knew her by now.

"Signora! *Buona sera!* A fine day, no? What is your wish?"

"Un espress', per piacere."

Isabella realized that she was known in the neighborhood as the wife of a government official who was reasonably important for his age, which was still under forty, aware that she was considered rather rich, and pretty too. The latter, people could see. And what else, Isabella wondered as she sipped her espresso. She and Filippo had a fourteen-year-old daughter in school in Switzerland now. Susanna.

Isabella wrote to her faithfully once a week, as Susanna did to her. How was Susanna going to shape up? Would she even *like* her daughter by the time she was eighteen or twenty-two? Was Susanna going to lose her passion for horses and horseback riding (Isabella hoped so) and go for something more intellectual such as geology and anthropology, which she had shown an interest in last year? Or was she going to go the usual way—get married at twenty before she'd finished university, trade on her good looks and marry "the right kind of man" before she had found out what life was all about? What *was* life all about?

Isabella looked around her, as if to find out. Isabella had had two years of university in Milan, had come from a rather intellectual family, and didn't consider herself just another dumb wife. Filippo was good-looking and had a promising career ahead of him. But then Filippo's *father* was important in a government ministry, and had money. The only trouble was that the wife of a man in diplomatic service had to be a clotheshorse, had to keep her mouth shut when she would like to open it, had to be polite and gracious to people whom she detested or was bored by. There were times when Isabella wanted to kick it all, to go slumming, simply to laugh.

She tossed off the last of her coffee, left a five-hundred-lire note, and turned around, not yet leaving the security of the bar's counter. She surveyed the scene. Two tables were occupied by couples who might be lovers. A blind beggar with a white cane was on his way in.

And here came her dark-eyed Peeping Tom! Isabella was aware that her eyes lit up as if she beheld her lover walking in.

He grinned. He sauntered, swaggered slightly as he headed for the bar to a place at a little distance from her. He looked her up and down, like a man sizing up a pick-up before deciding yes or no.

Isabella lifted her head and walked out of the bar-cafè.

He followed. "You are beautiful, signora," he said. "I should know, don't you think so?"

"You can keep your filthy ideas to yourself!" Isabella replied as she crossed the street.

"My beautiful lady-love—the wife of my dreams!"

Isabella noticed that his eyes looked pink. Good! She pressed the bell for the porter. An approaching figure on her left caught her eye. The bottom-pincher, the gooser, the real oddball! Raincoat again, no glasses today, a faint smile. Isabella turned to face him, with her back to the big doors.

"Oh, how I would like to . . ." the feeler murmured as he passed her, so close she imagined she could feel the warmth of his breath against her cheek, and at the same time he slapped her hip with his left hand. He had a pockmark or two, and big cheekbones that stuck out gauntly. Disgusting type! And a disgusting phrase he had used!

From across the street, Peeping Tom was watching, Isabella saw; he was chuckling silently, rocking back on his heels.

Franco opened the doors. What if she told Filippo about those two? But of course she had, Isabella remembered, a month or so ago, yes. "How would *you* like it if a psychopath stared at you nearly every time you took a shower?" Isabella had said to Filippo, and he had broken out in one of his rare laughs. "If it were a *woman* maybe, yes, I might like it!" he said, then he had said that she shouldn't take it so seriously, that he would speak to the porters, or something like that.

Isabella had the feeling that she didn't really wake up until after the dinner party, when the coffee was served in the living room. The taste of the coffee reminded her of the bar that afternoon, of the dark-haired Peeping Tom with the pink eyes walking into the bar and having the nerve to speak to her *again*!

"We shall be in Vienna too, at the end of the month," said the girlfriend of the Danish First Secretary.

Isabella rather liked her. Her name was Gudrun. She looked healthy, honest, unsnobbish. But Isabella had nothing to say except, "Good. We shall be looking forward," one of the phrases that came out of her automatically after fifteen years of being the wife-of-a-government-employee. There were moments, hours, when she felt bored to the point of going insane. Like now. She felt on the brink of doing something shocking, such as standing up and screaming, or announcing that she wanted to go out for a walk

(yes, and have another espresso in the same crummy bar), of shouting that she was bored with them *all*, even Filippo, slumped with
legs crossed in an armchair now, wearing his neat, new dinner suit
with a ruffled shirt, deep in conversation with the three other
men. Filippo was long and lean like a fashion model, his black hair
beginning to gray at the temples in a distinguished way. Women
liked his looks, Isabella knew. His good looks, however, didn't
make him a ball of fire as a lover. Did the women know that,
Isabella wondered.

Before going to bed that night, Isabella had to check the shopping list with Luigi the cook for tomorrow's dinner party, because
Luigi would be up early to buy fresh fish. Hadn't the signora suggested fish? And Luigi recommended young lamb instead of
tournedos for the main course, if he dared say so.

Filippo paid her a compliment as he was undressing. "Osterberg thought you were charming."

They both slept in the same big bed, but it was so wide that
Filippo could switch his reading-light on and read his papers and
briefings till all hours, as he often did, without disturbing Isabella.

A couple of evenings later Isabella was showering just before
7 P.M. when the same dark-haired creep sprang up at her bathroom
window, leering a "Hello, beautiful! Getting ready for me?"

Isabella was not in a mood for repartee. She got out of the
shower.

"Ah, signora, such beauty should not be hidden! Don't try—"

"I've told the *police* about you!" Isabella yelled back at him, and
switched off the bathroom light.

Isabella spoke to Filippo that evening as soon as he came in.
"Something's got to be done—opaque glass put in the window—"

"You said that would make the bathroom look ugly."

"I don't care! It's revolting! I've told the porters—Giorgio,
anyway. He doesn't do a damned thing, that's plain!—Filippo?"

"Yes, my dear. Come on, can't we talk about this later? I've got to change my shirt, at least, because we're due—already." He looked at his watch.

Isabella was dressed. "I want your tear-gas gun. You remember you showed it to me. Where is it?"

Filippo sighed. "Top drawer, left side of my desk."

Isabella went to the desk in Filippo's study. The tear-gas gun looked like a fountain pen, only a bit thicker. Isabella smiled as she placed her thumb on the firing end of it and imagined her counterattack.

"Be careful how you use that tear gas," Filippo said as they were leaving the house. "I don't want you to get into trouble with the police just because of a—"

"*Me* in trouble with the police! Whose side are you on?" Isabella laughed, and felt much better now that she was armed.

The next afternoon around five, Isabella went out, paid a visit to the pharmacy where she bought tissues and a bottle of new eau de cologne which the chemist suggested, and whose packaging amused her. Then she strolled toward the bar-cafè, keeping an eye out for her snoops as she went. She was bareheaded, had a bit of rouge on her lips, and she wore a new summer frock. She looked pretty and was aware of it. And across the street, walking past her very door now, went the raincoated creep in dark glasses again—and he didn't notice her. Isabella felt slightly disappointed. She went into the bar and ordered an espresso, lit a rare cigarette.

The barman chatted. "Wasn't it a nice day? And the signora is looking especially well today."

Isabella barely heard him, but she replied politely. When she opened her handbag to pay for her espresso, she touched the tear-gas gun, picked it up, dropped it, before reaching for her purse.

"*Grazie*, signora!"

She had tipped generously as usual.

Just as she turned to the door, the bathroom peeper—her special persecutor—entered, and had the audacity to smile broadly and nod, as if they were dear friends. Isabella lifted her head higher as if with disdain, and at the same time gave him an appraising glance, which just might have been mistaken for an invitation, Isabella knew. She had meant it that way. The creep hadn't quite the boldness to say anything to her inside the cafè, but he did follow her out of the door. Isabella avoided looking directly at him. Even his shoes were unshined. What could he do for a living, she wondered.

Isabella pretended, at her door, to be groping for her key. She picked up the tear-gas gun, pushed off its safety, and held it with her thumb against its top.

Then he said, with such mirth in his voice that he could hardly get the words out, "Bellissima signora, when are you going to let me—"

Isabella lifted the big fountain pen and pushed its firing button, maneuvering it so that its spray caught both his eyes at short range.

"Ow!—Ooh-h!" He coughed, then groaned, down on one knee now, with a hand across his eyes.

Even Isabella could smell the stuff, and blinked, her eyes watering. A man on the pavement had noticed the Peeping Tom struggling to get up, but was not running to help him, merely walking toward him. And now a porter opened the big wooden doors, and Isabella ducked into her own courtyard. "Thank you, Giorgio."

The next morning she and Filippo set out for Vienna. This excursion was one Isabella dreaded. Vienna would be dead after 11:30 at night—not even an interesting coffee house would be open. Awful! But the fact that she had fired a shot in self-defense— in attack—buoyed Isabella's morale.

And to crown her satisfaction she had the pleasure of seeing Peeping Tom in dark glasses as she and Filippo were getting into the chauffeured government car to be driven to the airport. The figure in dark glasses had stopped on the pavement some ten meters away to gaze at the luggage being put into the limousine by the liveried driver.

Isabella hoped his eyes were killing him. She had noted there was a box of four cartridges for the tear-gas gun in the same drawer. She intended to keep her gadget well charged. Surely the fellow wasn't going to come back for more! She might try it also on the feeler in the dirty raincoat. Yes, there was one who didn't mind approaching damned close!

"Why're you dawdling, Isabella? Forget something?" Filippo asked, holding the car door for her.

Isabella hadn't realized that she had been standing on the pavement, relishing the fact that the creep could see her about to get into the protective armor of the shiny car, about to go hundreds of kilometers away from him. "I'm ready," she said, and got in. She was not going to say to Filippo, "There's my Peeping Tom." She liked the idea of her secret war with him. Maybe his eyes were permanently damaged. She hoped so.

This minor coup made Vienna seem better. Isabella missed Elisabetta—some women whose husbands were in government service traveled with their maids, but Filippo was against this, just now. "Wait a couple of years till I get a promotion," Filippo had said. Years. Isabella didn't care for the word year or years. Could she stand it? At the stuffy dinner parties where the Austrians spoke bad French or worse Italian, Isabella carried her tear-gas gun in her handbag, even in her small evening bag at the big gala at the Staatsoper. *The Flying Dutchman.* Isabella sat with legs crossed, feet crossed also with tension, and dreamed of resuming her attack when she got back to Rome.

Then on the last evening Filippo had an "all-night meeting" with four men of the human rights committee, or whatever they called it. Isabella expected him back at the hotel about three in the morning at the latest, but he did not get back till 7:30, looking exhausted and even a bit drunk. His arrival had awakened her, though he had tried to come in quietly with his own key.

"Nothing at all," he said unnecessarily and a little vaguely. "Got to take a shower—then a little sleep. No appointment till— eleven this morning and it won't matter if I'm late." He ran the shower.

Then Isabella remembered the girl he had been talking to that evening, as he smoked a fine cigar—at least, Isabella had heard Filippo call it "a fine cigar"—a smiling, blonde Austrian girl, smiling in the special way women had when they wanted to say, "Anything you do is all right with me. I'm yours, you understand? At least for tonight."

Isabella sighed, turned over in bed, tried to sleep again, but she felt tense with rage, and knew she would not sleep before it was time for breakfast, time to get up. Damn it! She knew Filippo had been at the girl's apartment or in her hotel room, knew that if she took the trouble to sniff his shirt, even the shoulders of his dinner jacket, she would smell the girl's perfume—and the idea of doing that revolted her. Well, she herself had had two, no, three lovers during her married life with Filippo, but they had been so brief, those affairs! And so discreet! Not one servant had known.

Isabella also suspected Filippo of having a girlfriend in Rome, Sibilla, a rather gypsy-like brunette, and if Filippo was "discreet," it was because he was only lukewarm about her. This blonde tonight was more Filippo's type, Isabella knew. She heard Filippo hit the twin bed that was pushed close to her bed. He would sleep like a log, then get up in three hours looking amazingly fresh.

When Isabella and Filippo got back to Rome, Signor Sore-Eyes was on hand the very first evening, when Isabella stood under the shower about 7:30 in the evening. Now that was fidelity for you! Isabella ducked, giggling. Her giggle was audible.

And Sore-Eyes' response came instantly: "Ah, the lady of my heart is pleased! She laughs!" He had dropped to his feet, out of sight, but his voice came clearly through the stone recess. "Come, let me see more. *More!*" Hands grasped the bars; the grinning face appeared, black eyes shining and looking not at all damaged.

"Get lost!" she shouted, and stepped out of the shower and began to dry herself, standing near the wall, out of his view.

But the other nut, the feeler, seemed to have left the neighborhood. At least Isabella did not see him during three or four days after her return from Vienna. Nearly every day she had an espresso at the bar-cafè across the street, and sometimes twice a day she took taxis to the Via Veneto area, where a few of her friends lived, or to the Via Condotti for shopping. Shiny-Eyes remained faithful, however, not always in view when she came out of her big doors, but more often than not.

Isabella fancied—she liked to fancy—that he was in love with her, even though his silly remarks were intended either to make her laugh or, she had to admit it, to insult and shock her. It was this line of thinking, however, which caused Isabella to see the Peeping Tom as a rival, and which gave her an idea. What Filippo needed was a good jolt!

"Would you like to come for after-dinner coffee tonight?" Isabella murmured to Shiny-Eyes one day, interrupting his own stream of vulgarity, as she stood not yet pushing the bell of her house.

The man's mouth fell open, revealing more of his stained teeth.

"Ghiardini," she said, giving her last name. "Ten-thirty." She had pushed the bell by now and the doors were opening. "Wear some better clothes," she whispered.

That evening Isabella dressed with a little more interest in her appearance. She and Filippo had to go out first to a "buffet cocktail" at the Hotel Eliseo. Isabella was not even interested in what country was host to the affair. Then she and Filippo departed at 10:15 in their own government car, to be followed by two other groups of Americans, Italians, and a couple of Germans. Isabella and Filippo were earlier than the rest, and of course Luigi and Elisabetta already had the long bar-table well equipped with bottles, glasses, and ice, and platters of little sausages stuck with toothpicks. Why hadn't she told Shiny-Eyes eleven o'clock?

But Shiny-Eyes did the right thing, and arrived just after eleven. Isabella's heart gave a dip as he entered through the living room door, which had been opened by Luigi. The room was already crowded with guests, most of them standing up with drinks, chattering away, quite occupied, and giving Shiny-Eyes not a glance. Luigi was seeing to his drink. At least he was wearing a dark suit, a limp but white shirt, and a tie.

Isabella chatted with a large American and his wife. Isabella hated speaking English, but she could hold her own in it. Filippo, Isabella saw, had left his quartet of diplomats and was now concentrating on two pretty women; he was standing before them while they sat on the sofa, as if mesmerizing them by his tall elegant presence, his stream of bilge. The women were German, secretaries or girl friends. Isabella almost sneered.

Shiny-Eyes was nursing his scotch against the wall by the bar-table, and Isabella drifted over on the pretense of replenishing her champagne. She glanced at him, and he came closer. To Isabella he seemed the only vital person in the room. She had no intention of speaking to him, even of looking directly at him, and concentrated on pouring champagne from a small bottle.

"Good evening, signora," he said in English.

"Good evening. And what is your name?" she asked in Italian.

"Ugo."

Isabella turned gracefully on her heel and walked away. For the next minutes she was a dutiful hostess, circulating, chatting, making sure that everyone had what he or she wanted. People were relaxing, laughing more loudly. Even as she spoke to someone, Isabella looked in Ugo's direction and saw him in the act of pocketing a small Etruscan statue. Isabella drifted slowly but directly across the room toward Ugo.

"You put that back!" she said between her teeth, and left him.

Ugo put it back, flustered, but not seriously.

Filippo had caught the end of this, Isabella speaking to Ugo.

Filippo rose to find a new drink, got it, and approached Isabella. "Who's the dark type over there? Do you know him?"

Isabella shrugged. "Someone's bodyguard, perhaps?"

The evening ended quietly, Ugo slipped out unnoticed even by Isabella. When Isabella turned back to the living room expecting to see Filippo, she found the room empty. "Filippo?" she called, thinking he might be in the bedroom.

Filippo had evidently gone out with some of the guests, and Isabella was sure he was going to see one of the blondes tonight. Isabella helped herself to a last champagne, something she rarely did. She was not satisfied with the evening after all.

When she awakened the next morning, at the knock of Elisabetta with the breakfast tray, Filippo was not beside her in bed. Elisabetta, of course, made no comment. While Isabella was still drinking cafè latte, Filippo arrived. All-night talk with the Americans, he explained, and now he had to change his clothes.

"Is the blonde in the blue dress American? I thought she and the other blonde were Germans," Isabella said.

Now the row was on. So what, was Filippo's attitude.

"What kind of life is it for *me*?" Isabella screamed. "Am I nothing but an *object*? Just some female figure in the house—always here, to say *buona sera*—and smile!"

"Where would I be without you? Every man in government service needs a wife," replied Filippo, using the last of his patience. "And you're a very good hostess, Isabella, really!"

Isabella roared like a lioness. "Hostess! I detest the word! And your girl friends—*in* this house—"

"Never!" Filippo replied proudly.

"Two of them! How many have you now?"

"Am I the only man in Rome with a mistress or two?" He had recovered his cool and intended to stand up for his rights. After all, he was supporting Isabella and in fine style, and their daughter, Susanna, too. "If you don't like it—" But Filippo stopped.

More than ever, that day, Isabella wanted to see Ugo. She went out around noon, and stopped for an americano at the little bar-cafè. This time she sat at a table. Ugo came in when she had nearly finished her drink. Faithful, he was. Or psychic. Maybe both. Without looking at him, she knew that he had seen her.

She left some money on the table and walked out. Ugo followed. She walked in an opposite direction from the palazzo across the street, knowing that he knew she expected him to follow her.

When they were safely around another corner, Isabella turned. "You did quite well last night, except for the attempted—"

"Ah, sorry, signora!" he interrupted, grinning.

"What are you by profession—if I dare to ask?"

"Journalist, sometimes. Photographer. You know, a freelance."

"Would you like to make some money?"

He wriggled, and grinned more widely. "To spend on you, signora, yes."

"Never mind the rubbish." He really was an untidy specimen, back in his old shoes again, dirty sweater under his jacket, and when had he last had a bath? Isabella looked around to see if anyone might be observing them. "Would you be interested in kidnapping a rich man?"

Ugo hesitated only two seconds. "Why not?" His black eyebrows had gone up. "Tell me. Who?"

"My husband. You will need a friend with a gun and a car."

Ugo indulged in another grin, but his attitude was attentive.

Isabella had thought out her plans that morning. She told Ugo that she and Filippo wanted to buy a house outside of Rome, and she had the names of a few real estate agents. She could make an appointment with one for Friday morning, for instance, at nine o'clock. Isabella said she would make herself "indisposed" that morning, so Filippo would have to go alone. But Ugo must be at the palazzo with a car a little before nine.

"I must make the hour the same, otherwise Filippo will suspect me," Isabella explained. "These agents are always a little late. You should be ten minutes early. I'll see that Filippo is ready."

Isabella continued, and walked slowly, since she felt it made them less conspicuous than if they stood still. If Ugo and his friend could camp out somewhere overnight with Filippo, until she had time to get a message from them and get the money from the government? If Ugo could communicate by telephone or entrust someone to deliver a written message? Either way was easy, Ugo said. He might have to hit Filippo on the head, Isabella said, but Ugo was not to hurt him seriously. Ugo understood.

After some haggling, a ransom sum was agreed for the kidnapping on Friday morning. Tomorrow was Thursday, and if Ugo had spoken to his friend and all was well, he was to give Isabella a nod, merely, tomorrow afternoon about five when she would go out for an espresso.

Isabella was so exhilarated she went that afternoon to see her friend Margherita, who lived off the Via Veneto. Margherita asked her if she had found a new lover. Isabella laughed.

"No, but I think Filippo has," Isabella replied.

Filippo also noticed, by Thursday afternoon, that she was in a merry mood. Filippo was home Thursday evening after their dinner out at a restaurant where they had been two at a table of twenty. Isabella took off her shoes and waltzed in the living room. Filippo was aware of his early date with the real estate agents, and cursed it. It was already after midnight.

The next morning Elisabetta awakened them with the breakfast tray at 8:30, and Isabella complained of a headache.

"No use in my going if you're not going," Filippo said.

"You can at least tell if the house is possible—or houses," she replied sleepily. "Don't let them down or they won't make a date with us again."

Filippo got dressed.

Isabella heard the faint ring of the street-door bell. Filippo went out. By this time he was in the living room or the kitchen in quest of more coffee. It was two minutes to nine. Isabella at once got up, flung on a blouse, slacks and sandals, ready to meet the real estate agents who she supposed would be twenty minutes late, at least.

They were. Elisabetta announced them. Two gentlemen. The porter had let them into the court. All seemed to be going well, which was to say Filippo was not in view.

"But I thought my husband had already left with you!" She explained that her husband had left the house half an hour ago. "I'm afraid I must ask you to excuse me. I have a migraine today."

The agency men expressed disappointment, but left in good humor finally, because the Ghiardinis were potentially good clients, and Isabella promised to telephone them in the near future.

Isabella went out for a pre-lunch cinzano, and felt reassured by the absence of Ugo. She was about to answer a letter from Susanna which had come that morning when the telephone rang. It was Filippo's colleague Vincenzo, and where was Filippo? Filippo was supposed to have arrived at noon at Vincenzo's office for a talk before they went out to lunch with a man who Vincenzo said was "important."

"This morning was a little strange," Isabella said casually, with a smile in her voice, "because Filippo went off with some estate agents at nine, I thought, then—"

"Then?"

"Well, I don't know. I haven't heard from him since," Isabella replied, thinking she had said quite enough. "I don't know anything about his appointments today."

Isabella went out to mail her letter to Susanna around four. Susanna had fallen from her horse taking a low jump, in which the horse had fallen too. A miracle Susanna hadn't broken a bone! Susanna needed not only new riding breeches but a book of photographs of German cathedrals which the class was going to visit this summer, so Isabella had sent her a check on their Swiss bank.

As soon as Isabella had got back home and closed her door, the telephone rang.

"Signora Ghiardini—" It sounded like Ugo speaking through a handkerchief. "We have your husband. Do not try to find out where he is. One hundred million lire we want. Do you understand?"

"*Where* is he?" Isabella demanded, putting on an act as if Elisabetta or someone else were listening; but no one was, unless Luigi had picked up the living room extension phone. It was Elisabetta's afternoon off.

"Get the money by tomorrow noon. Do not inform the police. This evening at seven a messenger will tell you where to deliver the money." Ugo hung up.

That sounded all right! Just what Isabella had expected. Now she had to get busy, especially with Caccia-Lunghi, Filippo's boss, higher than Vincenzo in the Bureau of Public Welfare and Environment. But first she went into her bathroom, where she was sure Ugo would not be peering in, washed her face and made herself up again to give herself confidence. She would soon be putting a lot of money into Ugo's pocket and the pocket of his friend— whoever was helping him.

Isabella now envisaged Ugo her slave for a long time to come. She would have the power of betraying him if he got out of hand, and if Ugo chose to betray *her*, she would simply deny it, and between the two of them she had no doubt which one the police would choose to believe: her.

"Vincenzo!" Isabella said in a hectic voice into the telephone (she had decided after all to ring Vincenzo first). "Filippo has been kidnapped! That's why he didn't turn up this morning! I've just had a message from the kidnappers. They're asking for a hundred million lire by tomorrow noon!"

She and Filippo, of course, had not that much money in the bank, she went on, and wasn't it the responsibility of the government, since Filippo was a government employee, an official?

Vincenzo sighed audibly. "The government has had enough of such things. You'd better try Filippo's father, Isabella."

"But he's so stubborn!—The kidnapper said something about throwing Filippo in a *river*!"

"They all say that. Try the father, my dear."

So Isabella did. It was nearly 6 P.M. before she could reach him, because he had been "in conference." Isabella first asked, "Has Filippo spoken to you today?" He had not. Then she explained that Filippo had been kidnapped, and that his captors wanted a hundred million lire by tomorrow noon.

"What? Kidnapped—and they want it from me? Why *me*?" the old man spluttered. "The government—Filippo's in the government!"

"I've asked Vincenzo Carda." Isabella told him about her rejection in a tearful voice, prolonging her story so that Filippo's predicament would have time to sink in.

"*Va bene, va bene.*" Pietro Ghiardini sounded defeated. "I can contribute seventy-five million, not more. What a business! You'd think Italy . . ." He went on, though he sounded on the brink of a heart attack.

Isabella expressed gratitude, but she was disappointed. She would have to come up with the rest out of their bank account—unless of course she could make a deal with Ugo. Old Pietro promised that the money would be delivered by 10:30 the following morning.

If she and Filippo were due to go anywhere tonight, Isabella didn't give a damn, and she told Luigi to turn away people who might arrive at the door with the excuse that there was a crisis tonight—and they could interpret that as they wished, Isabella thought. Luigi was understanding, and most concerned, as was Elisabetta.

Ugo was prompt with another telephone call at seven, and though Isabella was alone in her bedroom, she played her part as though someone were listening, though no one could have been unless Luigi had picked up the living room telephone. Isabella's voice betrayed anxiety, anger, and fear of what might happen to her husband. Ugo spoke briefly. She was to meet him in a tiny square which Isabella had never heard of—she scribbled the name down—at noon tomorrow, with a hundred million lire in old bills in twenty-thousand and fifty-thousand denominations in a shopping bag or basket, and then Filippo would be released at once on the edge of Rome. Ugo did not say where.

"Come *alone*. Filippo is well," Ugo said. "Good-bye, signora."

Vincenzo telephoned just afterward. Isabella told Vincenzo what she had to do, said that Filippo's father had come up with seventy-five million and could the government provide the rest? Vincenzo said no, and wished Isabella and Filippo the best of luck.

And that was that. So early the next morning Isabella went to their bank and withdrew twenty-five million lire from their savings, which left so little that she had to sign a check on their Swiss bank for a transfer when she got home. At half past ten a chauffeur in uniform and puttees, with a bulge under his tunic that must have been a gun, arrived with a briefcase under each arm. Isabella took him into the bedroom for the transfer of money from the briefcases into the shopping bag—a black plastic bag belonging to Elisabetta. Isabella didn't feel like counting through all the soiled banknotes.

"You're sure it's exact?" she asked.

The calm and polite chauffeur said it was. He loaded the shopping bag for her, then took his leave with the briefcases.

Isabella ordered a taxi for 11:15, because she had no idea how long it might take her to get to the little square, especially if they ran into a traffic jam somewhere. Elisabetta was worried, and asked for the tenth time, "Can't I come with you—just sit in the taxi, signora?"

"They will think you are a man in disguise with a gun," Isabella replied, though she intended to get out of the taxi a couple of streets away from the square, and dismiss the taxi.

The taxi arrived. Isabella said she should be back before one o'clock. She had looked up the square on her map of Rome, and had the map with her in case the taxi driver was vague.

"What a place!" said the driver. "I don't know it at all. Evidently you don't either."

"The mother of an old servant of mine lives there. I'm taking her some clothing," Isabella said by way of explaining the bulging but not very heavy shopping bag.

The driver let her out. Isabella had said she was uncertain of the house number, but could find out by asking neighbors. Now she was on her own, with a fortune in her right hand.

There was the little square, and there was Ugo, five minutes early, like herself, reading a newspaper on a bench. Isabella entered the little square slowly. It had a few ill-tended trees, a ground of square stones laid like a pavement. One old woman sat knitting on the only sunlit bench. It was a working-class neighborhood, or one mainly of old people, it seemed. Ugo got up and walked toward her.

"Giorno, signora," he said casually, with a polite nod, as if greeting an old acquaintance, and by his own walking led her toward the street pavement. "You're all right?"

"Yes. And—"

"He's quite all right.—Thank you for this." He glanced at her shopping bag. "Soon as we see everything's in order, we'll let Filippo—loose." His smile was reassuring.

"Where are we—"

"Just here," Ugo interrupted, pushing her to the left, toward the street, and a parked car's door suddenly swung open beside her. The push had not been a hard one, only rude and sudden enough to fluster Isabella for a moment. The man in the driver's seat had turned half around and had a pistol pointed at her, held low on the back of the front seat.

"Just be quiet, Signora Isabella, and there will be no trouble at all—nobody hurt at all," the man with the gun said.

Ugo got in beside her in the back and slammed the door shut. The car started off.

It had not even occurred to Isabella to scream, she realized. She had a glimpse of a man with a briefcase under his arm, walking only two meters away on the pavement, his eyes straight ahead. They were soon out in the country. There were a few houses, but mostly it was fields and trees. The man driving the car wore a hat.

"Isn't it necessary that I *join* Filippo, Ugo?" she asked.

Ugo laughed, then asked the man driving to pull in at a roadside bar-restaurant. Here Ugo got out, saying he would be just a minute. He had looked into the shopping bag long enough to see that it contained money and was not partly stuffed with newspaper. The man driving turned around in his seat.

"The signora will please be quiet," he said. "Everything is all right." He had the horrible accent of a Milan tough, attempting to be soothing to an unpredictable woman who might go off in a scream louder than a police siren. In his nervousness he was chewing gum.

"Where are you taking me?"

Ugo was coming back.

Isabella soon found out. They pulled in at a farmhouse whose occupants had evidently recently left—there were clothes on the line, dishes in the sink—but the only people now in the house seemed to be Isabella, Ugo, and his driver chum whom Ugo called Eddie. Isabella looked at an ashtray, recognizing Filippo's Turkish cigarette stubs, noticed also the pack empty and uncrumpled on the floor.

"Filippo has been released, signora," Ugo said. "He has money for a taxi and soon you should be able to phone him at home.— Sit down. Would you like a coffee?"

"Take me back to Rome!" Isabella shouted. But she knew. They had kidnapped *her*. "If you think there is any *more* money coming, you are quite mistaken, Ugo—*and you!*" she added to the smiling driver, an old slob now helping himself to whiskey.

"There is always more money," Ugo said calmly.

"Swine!" Isabella said. "I should have known from the time you first stared into my bathroom! That's your real occupation, you creep!" A fear of assault crossed her mind, but only swiftly. Her rage was stronger just now. "After I tried to—to give you a break, turn a little money your way! *Look* at all that money!"

Eddie was now sitting on the floor counting it, like a child with an absorbing new toy or game, except that a big cigar stuck out of his mouth.

"Sit down, signora. All will be well when we telephone your husband."

Isabella sat down on a sagging sofa. There was mud on the heels of her shoes from the filthy courtyard she had just walked across. Ugo brought some warmed-over coffee. Isabella learned that still another chum of Ugo's had driven Filippo in another car and dropped him somewhere to make his own way home.

"He is quite all right, signora," Ugo assured her, bringing a plate of awful-looking sliced lamb and hunks of cheese. The other man was on his feet, and brought a basket of bread and a bottle of inferior wine. The men were hungry. Isabella took nothing, refusing even whiskey and wine. When the men had finished eating, Ugo sent Eddie off in the car to telephone Filippo from somewhere. The farmhouse had no telephone. How Isabella wished she had brought her tear-gas gun! But she had thought she would be among friends today.

Ugo sipped coffee, smoked a cigarette, and tried to assuage Isabella's anger. "By tonight, by tomorrow morning you will be back home, signora. No harm done! A room to yourself here! Even though the bed may not be as comfortable as the one you're used to."

Isabella refused to answer him, and bit her lip, thinking that she had got herself into an awful mess, had cost herself and Filippo twenty-five million lire, and might cost them another fifty million (or whatever she was worth) because Filippo's father might decide not to come up with the money to ransom her.

Eddie came back with an air of disappointment and reported in his disgusting slang that Signor Ghiardini had told him to go stuff himself.

"What?" Ugo jumped up from his chair. "We'll try again. We'll threaten—didn't you threaten—"

Eddie nodded. "He said . . ." Again the revolting phrase.

"We'll see how it goes tonight—around seven or so," said Ugo.

"How much are you asking?" Isabella was unable to repress the question any longer. Her voice had gone shrill.

"Fifty million, signora," replied Ugo.

"We simply haven't got it—not after *this*!" Isabella gestured toward the shopping bag, now in a corner of the room.

"Ha, ha," Ugo laughed softly. "The Ghiardinis haven't got another fifty million? Or the government? Or Papa Ghiardini?"

The other man announced that he was going to take a nap in the other room. Ugo turned on the radio to some pop music. Isabella remained seated on the uncomfortable sofa. She had declined to remove her coat. Ugo paced about, thinking, talking a little to himself, half drunk with the realization of all the money in the corner of the room. The gun lay on the center table near the radio. She looked at it with an idea of grabbing it and turning it on Ugo, but she knew she could probably not keep both men at bay if Eddie woke up.

When Eddie did wake up and returned to the room, Ugo announced that he was going to try to telephone Filippo, while Eddie kept watch on Isabella. "No funny business," said Ugo like an army officer, before going out.

It was just after six.

Eddie tried to engage her in a conversation about revolution-ary tactics, about Ugo's having been a journalist once, a photographer also (Isabella could imagine what kind of photographer). Isabella was angry and bored, and hated herself for replying even slightly to Eddie's moronic ramblings. He was talking about making a down payment on a house with the money he had gained from Filippo's abduction. Ugo would also start leading a more decent life, which was what he deserved, said Eddie.

"He deserves to be behind bars for the protection of the *public*!" Isabella shot back.

The car had returned. Ugo entered with his slack mouth even slacker, a look of puzzlement on his brow. "Gotta let her go, he may have traced the call," Ugo said to Eddie, and snapped his fingers for action.

Eddie at once went for the shopping bag and carried it out to the car.

"Your husband says you can go to hell," said Ugo. "He will not pay one lira."

It suddenly sank into Isabella. She stood up, feeling scared, feeling naked somehow, even though she still wore her coat over her dress. "He is joking. He'll—" But somehow she knew Filippo wouldn't. "Where're you taking me now?"

Ugo laughed. He laughed heartily, rocking back as he always did, laughing at Isabella and also at himself. "So I have lost fifty million! A pity, eh? Big pity. But the joke is on *you*! Hah! Ha, ha, ha!—Come on, Signora Isabella, what've you got in your purse? Let's see." He took her purse rudely from her hands.

Isabella knew she had about twenty thousand in her billfold. This Ugo laid with a large gesture on the center table, then turned off the radio.

"Let's go," he said, indicating the door, smiling. Eddie had started the car. Ugo's happy mood seemed to be contagious. Eddie began laughing too at Ugo's comments. *The lady was worth nothing!* That was the idea. *La donna niente*, they sang.

"You won't get away with this for long, you piece of filth!" Isabella said to Ugo.

More laughter.

"Here! Fine!" yelled Ugo who was with Isabella in the back seat again, and Eddie pulled the car over to the edge of the road.

Where were they? Isabella had thought they were heading for Rome, but wasn't sure. Yes. She saw some high-rise apartment buildings. A truck went by, close, as she got out with Ugo, half pulled by him.

"Shoes, signora! Ha, ha!" He pushed her against the car and bent to take off her pumps. She kicked him, but he only laughed. She swung her handbag, catching him on the head with it, and nearly fell herself as he snatched off her second shoe. Ugo jumped, with the shoes in his hand, back into the car which roared off.

To be shoeless in silk stockings was a nasty shock. Isabella began walking—toward Rome. She could see lights coming on here and there in the twilight dimness. She'd hitch a ride to the next roadside bar and telephone for a taxi, she thought, pay the taxi when she got home. A large truck passed her by as if blind to her frantic waving. So did a car with a single man in it. Isabella was ready to hitch a lift with anyone!

She walked on, realizing that her stockings were now torn and open at the bottom, and when she stopped to pick something out of one foot, she saw blood. It was more than fifteen minutes later when Isabella made her painful way to a restaurant on the opposite side of the road, where she begged the use of the telephone.

Isabella did not at all like the smile of the young waiter who looked her up and down and was plainly surmising what must have happened to her: a boy friend had chucked her out of his car. Isabella telephoned a taxi company's number which the waiter provided. There would be at least ten minutes to wait, she was told, so she stood by the coat rack at the front of the place, feeling miserable and ashamed with her dirty feet and torn stockings. Passing waiters glanced at her. She had to explain to the proprietor—a stuffy type—that she was waiting for a taxi.

The taxi arrived, Isabella gave her address, and the driver

looked dubious, so Isabella had to explain that her husband would pay the fare at the other end. She was almost in tears.

Isabella fell against the porter's bell, as if it were home, itself. Giorgio opened the doors. Filippo came across the court, scowling.

"The taxi——" Isabella said.

Filippo was reaching into a pocket. "As if I had anything left!"

Isabella took the last excruciating steps across the courtyard to the door out of which Elisabetta was now running to help her.

Elisabetta made tea for her. Isabella sat in the tub, soaking her feet, washing off the filth of Ugo and his ugly chum. She applied surgical spirits to the soles of her feet, then put on clean white woolen booties and a dressing gown. She cast one furious glance at the bathroom window, sure Ugo would never come back.

As soon as she came out of her bathroom, Filippo said, "I suppose you remember—tonight we have the Greek consul coming to dinner with his wife. And two other men. Six in all. I was going to receive them alone—make some excuse." His tone was icy.

Isabella did remember, but had somehow thought all that would be canceled. Nothing was canceled. She could see it now: life would go on as usual, not a single date would be canceled. They were poorer. That was all. Isabella rested in her bed, with some newspapers and magazines, then got up and began to dress. Filippo came in, not even knocking first.

"Wear the peach-colored dress tonight—not that one," he said. "The Greeks need cheering up."

Isabella began removing the dark blue dress she had put on.

"I know you arranged all this," Filippo continued. "They were ready to kill me, those hoodlums—or at least they acted like it. My father is furious! What stupid arrangements!—I can also make some arrangements. Wait and see!"

Isabella said nothing. And *her* future arrangements? Well, she might make some too. She gave Filippo a look. Then she gritted her teeth as she squeezed her swollen feet into "the right shoes" for the evening. When she got up, she had to walk with a limp.

Blow It

The two other young and unmarried men in the office considered Harry Rowe lucky, very. Harry had two pretty girls in love with him. Sometimes one girl or the other picked him up at his midtown Manhattan office, because Harry often had to stay a half hour or more after the usual quitting time at five or five-thirty, and one girl, Connie, could leave her office rather easily at five. The other girl, Lesley, was a fashion model with irregular hours, but she had been to his office a few times. That was how the firm of five men knew about Harry's girls. Otherwise Harry would have kept his mouth shut, not introduced them to—well, everybody, because someone would have been bound to blabble to one girl about the other girl. Harry did not mind, however, that Dick Hanson knew the situation. Dick was a thirty-five-year-old married man who could be trusted to be discreet, because he must have had experiences along the same lines, and even now had a girlfriend, Harry knew. Dick was a senior partner in the accounting firm of Raymond and Hanson.

Harry really didn't know which girl he preferred, and wanted to give himself time to consider, to choose. These days, Harry thought, lots of girls didn't care about marriage, didn't believe in it, especially at the age of twenty-three, as these girls were. But both Lesley and Connie were quite interested in marriage. They had not proposed to him, but he could tell. This further boosted Harry's ego, because he saw himself as a good catch. What man wouldn't, under such circumstances? That meant, he was earning well (true), and would go on to bigger and better, and also he wasn't bad looking, if he did say so himself (and he did), and he took the trouble to dress in a way that girls liked, always a clean shirt, not always a tie if the occasion didn't demand it, good shoes informal or not, far-out shirts sometimes, safari trousers or shorts maybe on the weekends when he loafed around with Lesley on Saturday and Connie on Sunday, for instance. Harry was a lawyer as well as a Certified Public Accountant.

Lesley Marker, a photographers' model, made even better

money than Harry. She had dark brown, straight hair, shining brown eyes, and the loveliest complexion Harry had ever seen, not to mention a divine body, not even too thin, as a lot of models were, or so Harry had always heard. Lesley had a standing date with her parents and grandmother for Sunday lunch, so this ruled out Lesley for Sundays, but there was Friday night and Saturdays. There were of course seven nights in the week, and Lesley could spend the night at his apartment, or he at hers, if she did not have to get up very early. Lesley was always cheerful, it wasn't even an act with her. It was marvelous and refreshing to Harry. She had a sense of humor in bed. She was a delight.

Connie Jaeger was different, more mysterious, less open, and certainly she had more moods than Lesley. Harry had to be careful with Connie, subtle, understanding of her moods, which she did not always explain in words. She was an editor in a publishing house. Sometimes she wrote short stories, and showed them to Harry. Two or three she had sold to little magazines. Connie often gave Harry the impression that she was brooding, thinking of things she would not disclose to him. Yet she loved him or was in love with him, of that Harry was sure. Connie was more interesting than Lesley, Harry would have had to admit, if anyone asked him.

Harry had a walk-up apartment on Jane Street, on the fourth floor. It was an old house, but the plumbing worked, the kitchen and bath were nicely painted, and he had a terrace with a roof garden of sorts: the garden was some three yards square, its earth contained within a wooden frame, and the watering drained into a corner hole on the terrace. Harry had acquired deck chairs, metal chairs and a round table. He and Lesley or Connie could lunch or dine out here, and the girls could take naked sunbaths, if they wished, as in a certain corner no one could see them. Lesley did that more often than Connie, who had done it only once, and then not naked entirely. He had met both girls around the same time, about four months ago. Which did he like better? Or love more?

Harry could not tell as yet, but he had realized weeks ago that his other girlfriends, two or three, had simply faded away. Harry hadn't rung them up for dates, didn't care to see them. He was in love with two girls at the same time, he supposed. He had heard of it before, and somehow never believed it was possible. He supposed also that Lesley and Connie might think he had other girlfriends, and for all Harry knew, both the girls might be going to bed with other men now and then too. But considering the time they both gave Harry, they hadn't a lot of time, or many nights, for other fellows.

Meanwhile Harry was careful to keep the girls apart, very good about changing his bedsheets, which were drip-dry and which he could hang on a line on his terrace. He was also careful to keep out of sight Lesley's shampoo and Connie's cologne. Twice he had found one of Connie's little crescent-shaped yellow combs in the bed when he changed it, had stuck them in a pocket of one of his raincoats and returned them the next time he saw Connie. He was not going to be tripped up by the usual, the cliché of a hairpin or something like that on the night table.

"I'd love to live in the country," Connie said one night around eleven, lying in his bed naked and smoking a cigarette, with the sheet pulled up to her waist. "Not too far from New York, of course."

"I too," said Harry. He meant it. He was in pajama pants, barefoot, slumped in an armchair with his hands behind his head. A vision of a country house, maybe in Connecticut, maybe Westchester if he could afford it, came into his eyes: white maybe, a bit of lawn, old trees. And with Connie. Yes, Connie. She wanted it. Lesley would always have to spend her nights in New York, Harry thought, because of having to get up so often at six and seven in the morning for the photographers. On the other hand, how long did a model's career last? Harry was ashamed of his thoughts. He and Connie had just spent a wonderful hour in bed. How dare he think of Lesley now! But he did think of Lesley, and he was thinking of her. Would he have to give up those enchanting brown eyes, that smile, that straight brown hair (always with an excellent cut, of course) that looked freshly washed every time he saw it? Yes, he would have to give it up, if he married Connie and slept in Connecticut every night.

"What're you thinking about?" Connie smiled, sleepy looking. Her full lips were lovely without rouge, as they were now.

"Us," said Harry. It was a Sunday night. He had been in the same bed with Lesley last night, and she had left this morning for her Sunday parental lunch.

"Let's do something about it," Connie said in her soft but very definite voice, and put out her cigarette. She held the sheet against her breasts, but one breast was exposed.

Harry stared at the one breast, stupidly. What was he going to do? Stall both girls indefinitely? Enjoy them both and not get married? How long could that go on until one or the other got fed up? Two more months? One month? Some girls moved fast, others hung on. Connie was the patient type, but too intelligent to waste a lot of time. Lesley would fly even sooner, Harry believed, if she thought he was being evasive on the subject of marriage. Lesley would leave him with a smile and without a scene. In that way, the two girls were the same: neither was going to wait forever. Why couldn't a man have two wives?

Lesley, on the following Tuesday evening, brought him flowers, in a pot. "A Japanese something or other. Geranium, I think they said. Anyway the studio would just've thrown it away."

They both went out on the terrace and chose a spot for the new orange-colored plant. Harry had a climbing rose, a large pot of parsley from which he took sprigs when he needed them. He pinched off some now. Harry had bought halibut steaks for their dinner. Lesley was fond of fish. After dinner they watched a television program as they lay on Harry's bed, holding hands. The program became boring, lovemaking more interesting. *Lesley*. Lesley was the girl he wanted, Harry thought. Why should he doubt it?

Why debate? She was every bit as pretty as Connie. And Lesley was more cheerful, better balanced. Wouldn't Connie's moods get in the way sometimes, make things difficult—because Harry didn't know how to pull Connie out of them, her silences sometimes, as if she were brooding on something far away, or maybe deep inside her, but she would never enlighten him, therefore he never knew what to say or do.

Around midnight Harry and Lesley went out to a disco three streets away, a modest place as discos went, where the music didn't break your eardrums. Harry had a beer, Lesley a tonic without the gin.

"It's almost as if we're married," Lesley said in a moment when the music was not so loud. She smiled her fresh smile, the corners of her lips went up like a child's. "You're the kind of man I could live with. There are very few."

"Easygoing, eh? No demands," Harry replied in a mocking tone, but his heart was thumping with pride. A couple of fellows at the table on their right were looking at Lesley with envy, even though they had their girls with them.

Harry put Lesley into a taxi a few minutes later. She had to be up by 7:30, and her make-up kit was at her apartment. As he walked back to Jane Street, Harry found himself thinking of Connie. Connie *was* as beautiful as Lesley, if one wanted to think about beauty. Connie didn't earn her living by it, as it happened, as Lesley did. Connie had admirers too, whom she brushed off like gnats, because she preferred him. Harry had seen this. Could he really abandon *Connie*? It was unthinkable! Was he drunk? On two gin-and-tonics before dinner and one beer? Two beers counting the one with dinner? Of course he wasn't drunk. He just couldn't come to a decision. Twenty past midnight now. He was tired. That was logical. People couldn't think after a sixteen-hour day. Could they? Think tomorrow, Harry told himself.

When he got home, the telephone was ringing. Harry ran for it. "Hello?"

"Hello, darling. I just wanted to say good night," Connie said in a quiet, sleepy voice. She always sounded young on the telephone, like a child of twelve sometimes.

"Thanks, my love. You all right?"

"Sure. Reading a manuscript—which is putting me to sleep." Here she sounded as if she were stretching in bed. "Where were you?"

"Out buying cigarettes and milk."

"When do we see each other? Friday? I forgot."

"Friday. Sure." Was she deliberately avoiding Saturday, Lesley's night? Had Connie done this before? Harry couldn't remember. "Come to my place Friday? I'll be home by six-thirty anyway."

The next day, Wednesday, Dick Hanson buzzed Harry's office around ten and said, "Got a little news that might interest you, Harry. Can I come in for a minute?"

"I would be honored," said Harry.

Dick came in smiling, with a couple of photographs in his hand, a manila envelope, a couple of typewritten pages. "House for sale in my neck of the woods," said Dick, after closing Harry's door. "We know the owners, their name is Buck. Anyway, look. See if it interests you."

Harry looked at the two photographs of a Westchester house—white, with a lawn, with grown-up trees, and it looked to him like his dream house, the one that came into his head when he was with Connie or Lesley. Dick explained that the Bucks didn't want to put it with an agent if they could avoid it, that they wanted to sell it quickly at a fair price, because Nelson Buck's company was transferring him to California on short notice, and they had to buy a house in California.

"Ninety thousand dollars," Dick said, "and I can tell you it'd go for a hundred and fifty thousand via an agent. It's five miles from where we live. Think about it, Harry, before it's too late—meaning in the next two or three days. I could see that you get good mortgage terms, because I know the town bank people . . . What do you think?"

Harry had been speechless for several seconds. Could he? Dare he?

Dick Hanson's reddish brown eyes looked down affectionately at Harry, eagerly. Harry had the feeling he stood on the edge of a swimming pool or a diving board, hesitating.

"Handsome, isn't it? Helen and I know the house well, because we're good friends with the Bucks. This is on the up and up. And . . . well, the general impression is that you're going to get married soon. I hope I'm not jumping the gun by saying that." Dick looked as if he were doing anything but talking out of turn, as if Harry were already due for congratulations. "Which girl is it going to be—you lucky swine," Dick drawled with good humor. "You look like the cat—who just swallowed the bird."

Harry was thinking, *I dunno which girl*. But he kept a smug silence, as if he did know.

"You're interested?" Dick asked.

"Sure I'm interested," Harry replied. He held a photograph in each hand.

"Think it over for a couple of days. Take the photos. I brought the envelope. Show them—you know." Dick meant to one of the girls, Harry knew. "It'd be great to be neighbors, Harry. I mean that. We could have fun up there—besides a little useful business on weekends, maybe."

Around three, Dick sent a memo in a sealed envelope to Harry with more information on mortgage terms, and Dick added that Harry couldn't go wrong on this house purchase, even if he didn't intend to get married in the immediate future. An 1850s house in superb condition, three bedrooms, two baths, and the value could only go up.

That afternoon Harry seized ten or fifteen minutes, did some figuring on his computer, and also in his own head with pencil and paper. He could swing the Westchester house, all right. But he wouldn't want to move there alone. Could Lesley live there with him and still commute? At very early hours sometimes? She might not consider a country house worth it. Could Connie? Yes, more easily. She didn't have to get to work till nine-thirty or even ten. But a man didn't choose a wife for her ease of commuting. That was absurd.

Harry's thoughts drifted back to a perfect weekend (Sunday noon till Monday morning), when he and Connie had painted his kitchen bright orange. Wonderful! Connie in already paint-spattered jeans, on the ladder, alternating with him on the ladder—drinking beer, laughing, making love. God! He could see Connie more easily in the Westchester house than Lesley.

By five o'clock, Harry had come to at least one decision. He would take a look at the house, and right away, if possible. He rang Dick's office, caught Dick in the middle of a talk with Raymond, but Harry was able to say, "I'd love to *see* the house. Can I maybe drive up with you this evening?"

"Absolutely! Stay overnight with us? See it in the morning too?—I'll give Helen a blast. She'll be pleased, Harry."

So at 6 P.M. Harry walked with Dick to his garage, and got into Dick's car. It was a pleasant drive of less than forty minutes, Dick in cheerful mood, and not trying to query Harry again about which girl it might be. Dick talked about the easy driving, the easy route he was taking. Harry was thinking that he would have to acquire a car too. But that would still be within his financial pos-sibilities. His parents in Florida would give him a car as a wedding present, Harry was sure, if he dropped a hint. No problem there.

"You seem to have pre-marital tension," Dick remarked.

"No. Ha-ha." Harry supposed he had been silent for several minutes.

They went to the Bucks' house first, because it was on the way, and because Dick wanted Harry to see the place and sleep on it. Dick said he had not bothered telephoning Julie Buck, because he knew the Bucks so well, and Julie was quite informal.

Julie welcomed them with a smile on the white front porch.

Harry and Dick went into a large hall which had a polished wooden staircase, carpeted, three handsome rooms going off the hall, one being the library. Julie said she was packing up the books, and there were cartons of books on the floor, some of the shelves empty. The Bucks' ten-year-old son, in blue jeans with holes in the knees, followed them around, tossing his football in his hands and eyeing Harry with curiosity.

"Very good apple trees. You'll have to give the apples away to the neighbors, they're so many," Julie said as they gazed from a second-story window.

The lawn sloped beautifully downward from the back of the house. Julie said something about a brook in the hollow beyond, which marked property boundary. The upstairs bedrooms were square and generous, the two baths not the last word in modernity but somehow just right for the country. The upstairs hall had a window front and back of the house. Harry was sold, though he didn't at once say so.

"I like it. But I've got to think, you know," Harry said. "A couple of days, Dick said I had."

"Oh, of course. You ought to look at some other houses too," said Julie. "Of course we love this one. And we'd like to think of a friend of the Hansons taking it over."

Julie insisted on giving them a scotch before they left. Dick and Harry drank theirs standing up in the living room, which had a fireplace. The scotch was neat and tasted lovely. Wouldn't it be great to be master of such a house, Harry was thinking. And which girl would be mistress? He had a vision of Lesley walking through the door from the hall, bearing a tray of something, smiling her divine smile. And almost immediately he saw Connie strolling through, blonde, calm and gentle, lifting her blue eyes to meet his.

Good Christ!

That night, after roast beef, cheese and wine at the Hansons', Harry hoped he would have a dream that might enlighten him about Connie and Lesley. Connie or Lesley. He did not dream at all, or if he did, he did not remember any dream. He awakened to blue-flowered wallpaper, maple furniture, sunlight streaming into his room, and thought, *this* was the kind of life he wanted. Fresh air, no city grit.

Dick and Harry departed at 8:30 with well-wishes from Helen, who hoped as much as Dick that Harry would opt for the Bucks' house. In the early morning, Harry fell more deeply in love with the white house which could, with a word and a check, be his. One solution was, Harry thought, to speak to both girls and ask them straight out if they would like such a house, in such a location, and—either Lesley or Connie might say no. Maybe for different reasons. Lesley might find it impossible with her present work. Connie might prefer a house in Long Island. Harry hated feeling vague, but what else could he do? How else could he feel?

When Harry tried to get down to it, asking the question, in the next days, he found that he couldn't. He spent one night at Connie's manuscript-and-book-cluttered apartment, and couldn't get the question out. That was Thursday night. Was he really hanging onto Lesley, therefore, because he preferred Lesley? But the same thing happened with Lesley during a hasty Friday lunch. Harry was rather obliged to give an answer to Dick that day. The Bucks were leaving Tuesday, and Monday was the date for putting the house on the market, before their departure for California. Harry had considered looking at other houses in the area, but the low price of the Bucks' house made the effort appear absurd. From a glance at newspaper ads, Harry saw that the Bucks' property was a bargain, with its acreage. Harry pulled himself together at the end of the lunch with Lesley, and said:

"I've seen a house—"

Lesley looked at him over her coffee cup. "Yes? What house?"

"House for sale, Westchester. In the area where Dick Hanson lives. You know, Dick in my office. You've met him."

They went on from there. Harry told her about spending the night at Dick's, that the house was a bargain and about thirty-five minutes from Manhattan, a railway station two miles away, a bus also.

Lesley looked dubious, or hesitant. She was concerned about the commuting angle. They didn't even mention marriage, maybe because Lesley took that for granted, Harry thought.

"The problem is, it's such a bargain, they want an answer now, or it'll be put with an agent Monday at a higher price. The house."

Lesley said she'd love to see the place, anyway, since Harry seemed to like it so much, and maybe they could go up tomorrow? Saturday? Harry said he was sure he could arrange that, either through Dick or the Bucks who would probably not mind at all picking them up at the railway station or the bus stop. That afternoon, Harry spoke with Dick Hanson about a Saturday afternoon appointment with the Bucks. Dick said he would ring Norman Buck at his New York office and fix it. By 4:30 that afternoon, Harry had a date with Norman, who would meet the train that left from Grand Central and got in at Gresham, Westchester, at 3:30.

Harry had a date that evening with Connie, who was to come to his apartment. Harry did some shopping in his neighborhood, having decided to speak to Connie at home and not in a restaurant. He was so nervous, a bottle of red wine slipped from his hands and broke on the kitchen floor, before Connie arrived. Fortunately he had another bottle in his rack, and it was so warm Connie might prefer beer, but the wine had been a good one.

He had come to a desperate but at the same time not very clear conclusion that afternoon just before leaving the office: he would invite *both* girls to see the Westchester house. He could at least see which girl liked the house better. Maybe there would be a scene, maybe there wouldn't be. Maybe they'd both say no. At least it would clear the atmosphere. Harry had not been able to concentrate during the afternoon, and had scraped through the minimum of work that he should have done. He had reasoned: if he showed the house to the girls one at a time, what then? Suppose both Lesley and Connie liked the house equally? Would he have come to any decision about Connie or Lesley even then? No. He somehow had to confront both of them, and himself, with the Westchester house at the same time. Since the girls had never met, this presented a different problem: introduce them at Grand Central, and they would all ride up on the same train? This seemed unthinkable.

Harry poured himself a straight scotch, not a big one, and lifted it with a shaking hand. There were times when a person needed steadying, he thought, and this was one of them. Harry remembered that he had said after lunch with Lesley today that he would ring her back about a time to meet tomorrow to go up to Westchester. He hadn't rung Lesley, however. Why not? Well, for one thing, more than half the time he didn't know where to ring her, because of her hopping around at her work. Should he try her at her apartment now? As Harry frowned at his telephone, it rang.

It was Lesley.

Harry smiled. "I was just about to call *you*."

"Did you make any arrangement about tomorrow?"

Harry said he had, and stammered out something about the train from Grand Central at 3 P.M. or a couple of minutes before. Lesley asked him why he was so nervous.

"I dunno," Harry said, and Lesley laughed.

"If you've got it all arranged with the Bucks, don't change anything, but I can't make it by three, I know," Lesley said. "Werner—you know, Werner Ludwig, he needs me at two tomorrow, and I know he'll need an hour anyway, but the good thing is, he lives near that town you mentioned."

"Gresham?"

"That's it, and he said he'd be glad to take me up with him in his car. I think he even knows the Bucks' house. So I could be there by four, I should think."

Suddenly that problem was solved, for Harry. Or postponed, he thought, the girls' meeting. At least they wouldn't be meeting in Grand Central.

They hung up, and the doorbell rang. Connie had his key (so did Lesley), but Connie always buzzed when she knew he was home.

Harry's nerves did not improve during the evening. He was cheerful, even made Connie laugh once, but he felt that his hands were shaking. When he looked at his hands, they were not shaking.

"Jitters already, and you haven't even signed anything?" Connie asked. "You don't have to take *this* house. It's the first one you've looked at up there, isn't it? Nobody buys the first thing they see." Connie spoke in her serious, logical way.

He was no good in bed that night. Connie thought it funny, but not as funny as Lesley would have. Connie had brought two manuscripts. They slept late on Saturday morning (Harry had at last fallen asleep after hours of trying to, and trying to be motionless so as not to disturb Connie), and she read one of the manuscripts after their brunch, until it was time to leave for Grand Central. They took a taxi to the station. Connie read the second manuscript, absorbed and silent, during the short ride, and was not even half through the script when they got to Gresham, doing as usual her careful job, Harry was sure.

Dick Hanson met them, not Nelson Buck as Harry had expected.

"Welcome, Harry!" Dick said, all smiles. "So it's—" He looked at Connie.

"Connie Jaeger," Harry said. "You've met her, I think. I know."

Dick and Connie exchanged "Hellos" and they got into Dick's car, Harry in the back seat, and off they went into the countryside. Twenty to four. Would Lesley be there ahead of time?

Would it be any worse than her coming five minutes *after* they got to the Bucks'? No. Should he mention now that he was expecting someone else? Harry tried rehearsing the first sentence, and realized that he couldn't have got the first words out. Maybe Lesley wouldn't be able to make it, after all. Maybe Werner had had a puncture, was going to be delayed? And what then?

"There's the house," said Dick as he made a turn in the road.

"Oh. Very lovely," said Connie, quietly and politely.

Connie never went overboard about anything, Harry reminded himself, with a little comfort.

Harry saw a car in front of the Bucks' house on the curving graveled driveway. Then Harry saw Lesley come out the front door, onto the porch, with Julie Buck.

"Well, well, they've got visitors," said Dick, pulling his handbrake.

"My friend Lesley," Harry mumbled. Did he black out for the next seconds? He opened the car door for Connie.

Much chatter, introductions.

"Connie—this is Lesley—Marker. Connie Jaeger," Harry said.

"How do you do?" the girls said simultaneously, looking each other in the eyes, as if each was trying to memorize the other's face. Their smiles were polite and minimal.

Dick shuffled, brushed his hands together for no reason, and said, "Well, shall we all go in and look around? May we, Julie?"

"Su-ure! That's what we're here for!" said Julie cheerfully, not digging a whit of the situation, Harry realized.

Harry felt that he walked into purgatory, into hell, into another life, or maybe death. The girls were stiff as pokers, didn't even look at him as they all walked from room to room. Julie gave them a guided tour, mentioning defects and assets, and as on many a guided tour, Harry felt, some of the tourists were not listening. He caught the girls sizing each other up with lightning glances, which were followed by an ignoring of each other. Dick Hanson wore a puzzled frown, even when he looked at Harry.

"What's going on?" Dick whispered to Harry, when he could.

Harry shrugged. It was more like a twitch, though he tried for a desperate couple of seconds to say something intelligent or normal to Dick. He couldn't. The situation was bizarre, the rooms, the house suddenly meaningless, their parading back down the stairs as useless as some rehearsal in a play in which no one had any interest.

"*Thank* you, Mrs. Buck," Lesley was saying with careful politeness in the downstairs hall.

Lesley's friend, who had brought her, had evidently departed, because his car was gone, Harry saw. Connie looked at him with her quiet, knowing smile. Her smile was not friendly, but rather amused.

"Harry, if you—"

"I'm afraid it's off," Harry said, interrupting Dick. "Off, yes."

Dick still looked puzzled. So did both the Bucks, maybe Julie Buck less so.

The end, Harry thought. *Ruin, finish.* He tried to stand up straighter but mentally he was on the floor, crawling along like a worm.

"Maybe you'd like to talk a little—by yourselves," said Nelson Buck to Harry and the girls, gesturing toward the library on his right, which now had more cartons on the floor and fewer books on the shelves. His gesture, his glance had included Harry and the two girls.

Did Nelson Buck think he maintained a harem, Harry wondered.

"No," said Lesley, coolly. "Not your fault, Mr. Buck. It's a lovely house. Really. Thank you too, Mrs. Buck. I think I must be on my way, because of an appointment in New York tonight. Maybe I can phone for a taxi?"

"Oh, I can take you to the station!" said Nelson.

"Or I can," said Dick. "No problem."

It was agreed that Dick would take Lesley, now. Harry walked

out with them to Dick's car. Dick went ahead of them, and opened
his car door.

Lesley said to Harry, "What was the idea, Harry? That we'd
both commute?" She laughed aloud, and in it Harry heard a little
bitterness but also a real amusement. "I knew you had a friend, but
this—It's a bit much, isn't it? Bye-bye, Harry."

"*How* did you know?" Harry asked.

Lesley had got into the front seat. "Easy," she said in her easy
voice.

"Not coming, Harry?" Dick asked.

"No. I'll stay here with Connie. Bye-bye, Lesley."

Harry turned back to the house as they drove off. Stay here
with Connie? What was *she* going to say? Harry walked back into
the hall.

Connie and Julie and Nelson Buck were conversing pleasantly
in the big hall, Connie with her hand on the newel post, one
trousered leg and sneakered foot extended. Her face was smiling,
her eyes steady as she looked at Harry. The Bucks faded away, Julie
to the rear of the house somewhere, Nelson into the living room
on Harry's right.

"I'll be going too," said Connie, not changing her stance. "I
hope you'll be happy with Lesley."

"*Lesley?*" said Harry in a tone of astonishment. It had simply
come out of him. He had nothing to say afterward.

Connie gave a silent laugh, shrugged her shoulders. "Nice to
meet her finally. I knew she existed."

Were Harry's cheeks warm because of shame? He was not
sure. "How?"

"Lots of little things. The dishes were always stacked differ-
ently when I turned up on Sundays. Different from Wednesdays
maybe. Little things." Slowly she got a cigarette from her canvas
jacket pocket, having put her briefcase with her manuscripts in it
on the floor between her feet.

Harry sprang to light the cigarette for her, but Connie swung herself slightly, out of his reach, and had the cigarette lit. He had lost her, Harry knew. "I'm sorry, Connie."

"Are you? I don't know. You couldn't have got your *dates* mixed," she said, not like a question, not quite like a statement either, something in between. Connie's serious, straight blue eyes, her shake of her head seemed to penetrate Harry's body from his head down to his feet. Connie was finished, had said good-bye to him, inside. "My taxi's there," Connie said, looking past Harry through the open front door. She went down the hall to find Julie.

Then Connie went out to the taxi, talked to the Bucks for an instant through the open taxi window, before the taxi moved off.

The Bucks came into the house, both looking puzzled, Julie barely managing a faint smile, absurd below her frown.

"Well," Nelson said, a little heavily.

The moment was relieved by Dick's car crunching up the driveway. Both the Bucks turned to it as if it were a lifesaver. How soon could he take off, Harry was thinking. Thank God for Dick! Dick could whisk him off. Unthinkable that Harry would have taken the same train as one of the girls, or both of them.

"Harry, old boy," Dick said, then added, as Nelson had and in the same tone, "Well!"

"Maybe you two would like a word by yourselves," said Nelson to Dick and Harry.

"I should be leaving," Harry said. "I thank you both—for your time."

A few more polite phrases, then Harry was in Dick's car, rolling away.

"Harry, what in the name of God," Dick began in the gruff tone of a senior brother, a man of the world who had made some mistakes in life but learned a little from them.

"I think I did it deliberately," Harry said. The words came out before his brain had formed them, or so he felt. "I couldn't make up my mind. I had to—get rid of them both. I love them *both*."

"Rubbish! Well, it isn't rubbish, I don't mean that. Something—could've been arranged . . . But my God, Harry, to bring them both like that! I had the feeling they hadn't met before."

"They hadn't."

"Come to our place and have a drink. Won't hurt you."

"No, thanks," Harry said. He knew they were heading for Dick's house. "I'd better get to the station, if you don't mind."

Harry insisted, over Dick's protests. Dick wanted to put him up for the night, have a talk with him. Dick knew the next train, and it would not be the train the girls would have taken. There were quite a few trains, Dick said, and probably the girls had taken different ones, and anyway there was plenty of room on the trains, so they needn't have ridden in the same car. On the way to the station, Dick began again his speech about there being a way to patch things up, to decide which girl he wanted, and then either drop the other girl or hang onto her in some way.

"They're both *lovely*," Dick said. "I can understand your problem! Believe me, Harry! But don't give up. You look like a guy who's just been through a war. Don't be silly. You can patch things up."

"Not with those girls. No," Harry said. "That's why I liked them so. They're different."

Dick shook his head in despair. They had arrived at the station. Harry bought his ticket. Then Harry and Dick shook hands with a hard grip that left Harry's hand tingling for a couple of minutes. Harry walked alone onto the platform and waited, then the train came and he rode back to Grand Central. Deliberately. He knew he had done it deliberately. He had somehow wanted to do this, break it all up, but what did he have now? People said the world was full of girls, pretty girls. True maybe. But not many as interesting as Lesley and Connie.

During the next week the girls came, separately, and picked up their few belongings from Harry's Jane Street apartment, each leaving her key under his doormat.

The Kite

The voices of Walter's mother and father came in jerky murmurs down the hall to his room. What were they arguing about now? Walter wasn't listening. He thought of kicking his room door shut, and didn't. He could shut their words out of his ears quite well. Walter was on his knees on the floor, carefully notching a balsa wood strip which was nearly nine feet long. It would have been exactly nine feet long, but he had notched it too deeply, he thought, a few minutes ago, and had cut that little piece off and started again. This was the long center piece for the kite he was making. The crosspiece would be nearly six feet long, so only by turning the kite horizontally would he be able to get it out his room door.

"*I* didn't *say* that!" That was his mother's shrill voice in a tone of impatience.

A couple of times a week, his father went mumbling into the living room to sleep on the sofa there instead of in the bedroom with his mother. Now and then they mentioned Elsie, Walter's sister, but Walter had stopped listening even to that. Elsie had died two months ago in the hospital, because of pneumonia. Walter now noticed a smell of frying ham or bacon. He was hungry, but the menu for dinner didn't interest him. Maybe they would get through the meal without his father standing up and leaving the table, maybe even taking the car and going off. That didn't matter.

The work under his hands mattered, the big kite, and Walter was so far pleased. It was the biggest kite he had ever tried to make, and would it even fly? The tail would have to be pretty long. He might have to experiment with its length. In a corner of his room stood a six-foot tall roll of pinkish rice paper. Walter looked forward with pleasure and a little fear to cutting a single big piece for his kite. He had ordered the paper from a stationery-and-book shop in town, and had waited a month for it, because it had come from San Francisco. He had paid the eight dollars for it from money saved out of his allowance, meaning from not going to

Cooper's for ice cream sodas and hamburgers with Ricky and other neighborhood chums.

Walter stood up. Above his bed he had thumbtacked a purple kite to the wall. This kite had a hole in its paper, because a bird had flown through it as if on purpose, like a bomber. The bird had not been hurt, but the kite had fallen quickly, while Walter had wound in his string as fast as he could to save the kite before it got caught in a tree. He had saved the kite, what was left of it. He and Elsie had made the kite together, and Walter was fond of it.

"Wally-y? . . . Dinner!" his mother called from the kitchen.

"Coming, Mom!"

Walter was now brushing balsa wood chips, tiny ones, into a dustpan. His mother had taken away the carpet last year. The plain wooden floor was easier to sweep, easier to work on when he was gluing something. Walter dumped the chips into his wastebasket. He glanced up at a box kite—blue and yellow—which hung from his ceiling. Elsie had loved this kite. He thought she would admire the one he was making now. Suddenly Walter knew what he would put on his kite, simply his sister's name—Elsie—in graceful script letters.

"*Wally?*"

Walter walked down the hall to the kitchen. His mother and father sat already at the rectangular table which had X-shaped legs. His sister's chair, the fourth chair, had not been removed, and perhaps was there just to complete the picture of four, Walter thought, a chair on each side of the table, though the table was big enough for eight people to sit at. Walter barely glanced at his father, because his father was staring at him, and Walter expected a critical remark. His father had darker brown hair than Walter's, and the straight brows that Walter had inherited. Lately his father had an amused smile on his lips that Walter had learned was not to be counted on. His father Steve sold cars, new and used, and he liked to wear tweed suits. He had a couple of favorite tweed suits that he called lucky. Even now, in June, his father was wearing brown tweed trousers, though his tie was loosened and his shirt open at the neck. His mother's blonde hair looked fluffier than usual, meaning she had been to the beauty parlor that afternoon.

"Why so quiet, Wally?" asked his mother.

Walter was eating his rice and ham casserole. There was a plate of crisp green salad on his left. *"You're not saying anything."*

His father gave a soft laugh.

"What've you been doing this afternoon?" his mother asked.

Walter shrugged. She meant since he had got home from school at half past three. "Fooling around."

"As long as he hasn't been—you know." Steve reached for his mug of beer.

Walter felt a warmth in his face. His father meant had he been to the cemetery again. Well, Walter didn't go often, and in fact he hated the place. Maybe he'd gone there just twice on his own, and how had his parents even found out?

"I know Wally was home—all afternoon," his mother said gently.

"Caretaker there—he mentioned it, you know, Gladys?"

"All right, Steve, do you have to—"

Steve bit into garlic bread and looked at his son. "Caretaker there, Wally. So why do you jump the fence? . . . If you want to go in, just ring his doorbell across the road there. That's what he's for."

Walter pressed his lips together. He didn't want to visit his sister's grave in the company of an old caretaker, for God's sake! "So what if I did—once?" Walter retorted. "Frankly—I think it's *boring* there." Ugly and stupid, all those tombstones, Walter might have added.

"Then don't go," said his father, smiling more broadly now.

Walter looked in rage at his mother, not knowing what to reply now, not expecting that she could help him either.

"*Cuck*-oo!—*Cuck*-oo!—*Cuck*-oo!—"

"And I'm goddam sick of that *cuckoo* clock!" yelled his father, jumping up from the table at the same time. He lifted the clock from the wall and looked about to throw it on the floor, while the bird kept popping in and out, announcing seven.

"Ha-ha!—Ha-ha-*haa-aa*!" Walter laughed and tried to stifle it. He nearly choked on lettuce, and grabbed his milk glass and laughed into that.

"Don't break it, Steve!" cried his mother. "Wally, *stop* it!"

Walter did stop laughing, suddenly, but not because his mother had told him to. He finished his meal slowly. Now his father wasn't going to sit down again, and they were talking about the Beach-comber Inn, whether his father was going there tonight, and his mother was saying she didn't want to go, and asking Steve if he expected to meet anyone there. One person or several, Walter couldn't tell, and it didn't matter to Walter. But his mother was getting more angry, and now she was standing up also, leaving her baked apple untouched.

Steve said, "Is that the only place in this—"

"You know that's where you were for days and nights—*that* time!" said his mother, sounding out of breath.

Steve glanced at Walter, who lowered his eyes and pushed his half-eaten dessert away. Walter wanted to jump up and go, but sat for the next seconds as if paralyzed.

"That is . . . not . . . true," said his father. "But am I going out tonight? Yes!" He was pulling on a summer jacket that had been hanging over a chair.

Walter knew they were talking about the time his sister had caught fever. Elsie had had her tonsils out a week or so before, and everything had seemed all right, even though she was home from school and still eating mostly ice cream, and then she had become pink in the face. And his mother had been away just then, because *her* mother—Grandma Page—had been sick in Denver, something with her heart, and everybody had thought *she* might die, but she hadn't. Then when his mother had come home, Elsie was already in the hospital, and the doctor had said it was double pneumonia or at least a very bad case of pneumonia, which Walter thought nobody had to die from, but Elsie had died.

"Can't you finish your baked apple, Wally?" asked his mother.

"He's daydreaming again." Steve had a cigarette in his mouth. "Lives in a dream world. Bikes and kites." His father was about to go out of the back door to the garage.

"Can I leave now?" Walter stood up. "I mean—for my room?"

"Yes, Wally," said his mother. "That police program you like is on tonight. Want to watch it with me?"

"Not sure." Walter shook his head awkwardly, and left the kitchen.

A minute later, Walter heard the car rolling down the driveway. Walter crossed the hall from his room into the living room. Here there were bookshelves, the TV set, a sofa and armchairs. On top of one of the bookshelves stood two pictures of Elsie.

In the larger photograph, Elsie was holding the purple kite lightly between her palms, the kite that later the same day had been hit by a bird. Elsie was smiling, almost laughing, and the wind blew her hair back, blonder hair than Walter's. The second picture Walter liked less, because it had been taken last Christmas in a photographer's studio—he and Elsie in neat clothes sitting on a sofa. His father had taken the kite picture in the backyard just three months ago. And now Elsie was dead, "gone away," someone had said to him, as if he were a little kid they had to tell lies to, as if she would "come back" one day, if she only decided to. Dead was dead, and dead was to be limp and not breathing—like a couple of mice Walter had seen his father take out of traps under the sink. Things dead would never move or breathe again. They were hopeless and finished. Walter also didn't believe in ghosts, didn't imagine his sister walking around the house at night, trying to speak to him. Certainly not. Walter didn't even believe in a life after death, though the preacher had talked about something like that during the service for Elsie. Did a mouse have a life after death? Why should it have? How could it? Where was that life, for instance? Could anybody say? No. *That* was a dream world, Walter thought, and a lot sillier than his kites that his father called a dream world. You could touch kites, and they had to be correctly made, just like airplanes.

When he heard his mother's step, Walter slipped across the hall into his own room.

Within two or three minutes, Walter was ready to leave the house with a red and white kite some two feet in length, and a roll of string. It was still daylight, hardly eight o'clock.

"Wally?" His mother was in the living room and had turned on the TV. "Got your homework done?"

"Sure, Mom, this afternoon." That was true. Wally went reluctantly to the living room door, having dropped his kite out of sight in the hall. "I'm going out with my bike. Just for a few minutes."

His mother sat in an armchair, and she had pushed her shoes off. "That program you like's at nine, you know?"

"Oh, I can be back by then." Walter snatched up his kite and headed for the back door.

He took his bike from the garage, and installed the kite between two rags in one of the satchels behind the seat. Walter rolled down the driveway and turned right in the street, coasting downhill and standing on the pedals.

Walter's school friend Ricky was watering his front lawn. "Going up to Coop's?" Ricky meant the hamburger-and-ice-cream place.

"Naw, just cruisin' for a few minutes," Walter said over his shoulder. Walter had no extra money at the moment, and was not in the mood for Coop's with Ricky, anyway.

The boy rolled on, through the town's shopping center, then turned left, and began to pedal harder up a long slope. The wind was picking up, and blew against him as he went up the hill. Houses grew fewer, then there were more trees, and finally he saw the spiked iron fence of Greenhills, the cemetery where his sister was buried. Walter cycled around to the right, had to walk his bike across a grassy ditch, then he walked several yards more until he reached a sheltered spot concealed from the road by a big tree. He leaned his bike against the fence, poked his kite and string through the bars, and climbed the fence, bracing his sneakers against the bars. He eased himself over the spikes at the top, dropped to the ground, and picked up his kite and ran.

He ran for the pleasure of running, and also because he disliked the low forest of mainly white tombstones all around now. He felt not in the least afraid of them, or even respectful of them, they were simply ugly, like jagged rocks that could block or trip a person. Walter zigzagged through them, aiming for a rise in the land a bit to his left.

Walter came to Elsie's grave and slowed, breathing through his mouth. Her grave was not quite at the crest of the hill. Her stone was white, curved at the top because of the figure of an angel lying on its side with one wing slightly lifted. MARY ELIZABETH MCCREARY, the stone said, with her dates that Walter hardly glanced at. The dates did not span ten years. Something below about a LAMB GATHERED. What baloney! The grass over her grave had not grown together yet, and he could still see the squares cut by the gravediggers' spades. For an instant, he felt like saying, "Hi, *Elsie!* I'm going to try the red and white. Want to watch?" but instead, he set his teeth and pressed his lips together. Trying to talk to the dead was baloney, too. Walter stepped right onto her short grave and over it, and walked to the crest of the hill. Even here the ground was not free of gravestones, but at least they lay flat on the ground, as if the owners of the cemetery or whoever controlled it didn't want tombstones showing against the sky.

Walter dropped his roll of string, took the rubber band off the rag tail of the kite and shook it out. This was also a kite that Elsie had helped him make. She had liked to cut the paper, slowly and cautiously, after he had marked it out. This tail consisted of parts of an old white sheet Walter had taken from the rag bag, and he recalled that his mother had been annoyed, because she had wanted the sheet for window polishing. Walter took a run against the wind, and the kite leapt promisingly. He stood and eased the kite up with long tugs on the string. It was going! And Walter had not been optimistic, because the wind was nothing great today. He let out more string, and felt a thrill as the kite began to pull at his fingers like something alive up in the sky. An upward current sent it zooming, took the string from his hand, and Walter had to grab for it.

Smiling, Walter walked backward and tripped on a grave marker, rolled over and jumped to his feet again, the string still in his hand. "How about *that*, Elsie?" He meant the kite, way up now. The wind blew his hair over his forehead and eyes. A little ashamed because he had spoken out loud, he began to whistle. The tune was one he and Elsie had used to hum or whistle together, when they were sandpapering balsa strips, measuring and cutting. The music was by Tchaikovsky, and his parents had the record.

Walter stopped whistling abruptly, and pulled his kite in. The kite came reluctantly, then dived a few yards as if it gave up, and Walter wound it in faster, and ran to save it. It had not landed in trees. The kite was undamaged.

By the time Walter mounted his bicycle, it was nearly dark, and he put on his headlight. The cops program his mother had talked about would still be on, but Walter didn't feel like watching it. Now he was passing the Beachcomber Inn, and he supposed his father was there, having a beer, but Walter didn't glance at the cars parked in front of the place. His mother was accusing his father of seeing someone there, or meeting someone there. A girl, of course, or a woman. Walter did not like thinking about that. Was it his business? No. He also knew that his mother thought his father had been spending all his spare time at the Beachcomber, or somewhere with "that woman," when his sister had been coming down with fever, and so his father hadn't taken care of Elsie. All this had

caused an awful atmosphere in the house, which was why Walter
spent a lot of time in his own room, and didn't want to look at TV
so much any more.

Walter put his bike in the garage against the wall—the car was
still gone—cut his headlight, and took his kite and string. He went
in quietly by the back door and down the hall to his room. His
mother was in the living room with the TV on and didn't hear
him, or, if she did, she didn't say anything. Walter closed his room
door softly before he switched on his ceiling light. He folded the
kite's tail, put a rubber band on it, and set the kite in a corner
where two or three other kites stood. Then he moved his straight
chair closer to his worktable so there would be more room on the
floor, swept the floor again, and removed his sneakers. He felt
inspired to measure his rice paper for the big kite. He walked barefoot to a corner of the room and fetched the roll, laid it on the
floor and carefully rolled a length out. Rice paper was quite
strong, Walter had read in lots of books about kites. This big kite
of course had to be extra strong, because a lot of surface would be
hit by the wind, and a strong wind would go right through tissue
paper of this area, just as surely as the bird had gone through his
smaller kite.

From his table Walter took his list of measurements, a metal
tape measure, a ruler, and a piece of blue chalk. He measured and
marked out with the chalk the right half of the kite. When he had
cut the first long line from bottom tip to the right hand point, he
felt a surge of pride, maybe of fear. Maybe such a big kite wouldn't
even get off the ground, or not get far up, anyway. In that case, he
would try to shrug off his disappointment, and he would be hoping that no one was watching at that moment. Meanwhile, Walter
whistled cautiously to himself, cut the top line, then folded the triangle carefully down the center line which he had drawn with the
blue chalk. He then traced the triangle on the left-hand side.

His mother had lowered or cut the TV and was on the telephone now. "Tomorrow night, *sure!*" came her high voice, then a laugh. "You'd better have it. Basted *and* sewn. I know it's right now. . . . What?"

She was probably talking to Nancy, her friend who did a lot of sewing. His mother did a lot of cutting—of cloth—for coats and dresses. It was a "pastime," she said, but she earned money from it. *Cutting is always the most important operation*, his mother said. Walter thought of that as he cut as surely as he could in the middle of his chalk lines. Besides making good kites, Walter would have liked to write a good poem, not the kind of silly poems his English composition teacher ordered the class to write now and then. "Tell about a walk in the woods . . . a rainstorm in summer . . ." No. Walter wanted to write something good about a kite flying in the air, for instance, about his thoughts, *himself*, being up there with the kite, his eyes too, able to look down at all the world, and able to look up at space. Walter had tried three or four times to write such a poem, but on reading his efforts the day after, had found them not as good as he had first thought, so he had thrown them all away. He always felt that he addressed his poems to his sister, but that was because he wanted her, would have wanted her to enjoy what he had written, and maybe to give him a word of praise for it.

A knock on his door startled him. Walter withdrew his scissors from the paper, rocked back on his heels and said, "Yep?"

His mother opened the door, smiling, glanced at the paper on the floor, then looked at him. "It's after ten, Wally."

"Tomorrow's Saturday."

"What're you making now?"

"Um-m—This is paper for a kite."

"*That* big! One kite?" She glanced from top to bottom of what he had cut, which did stretch almost from the far wall to the door where she stood. "You mean, you'll fold it."

"Yes," said Walter flatly. He felt his mother wasn't really interested, and was just making conversation with him. Her squarish face looked worried and tired tonight, though her lips continued to smile.

"Where'd you go this evening? Up to Cooper's?"

Walter started to say yes, then said, "No, just for a ride around. Nowhere."

"You start thinking about going to bed."

"Yep. I will, Mom."

Then she left him, and Walter finished his cutting and laid the long piece of paper, lightly folded in half, on top of his worktable, and put away in a corner what was left of the rice paper roll. He looked forward to tomorrow when he would tie the balsa strips and glue the paper, and even more to Sunday when he would try the kite, if there was a good wind.

Hours later, the popping sound of his father's car on the gravel awakened Walter, but he did not stir, only blinked his eyes sleepily. Tomorrow. The big kite. It wouldn't matter if his parents quarreled, if his mother and her yackety friends spent all evening over patterns in the living room—and in Elsie's room at the back opposite the kitchen, which his mother was lately turning into her workroom, even calling it that. Walter could shut all that out.

His father looked at the big kite and chuckled. "That'll never fly. You expect that to *fly*?"

This was just after lunch on Saturday. They were in the backyard.

Walter's face grew warm, and he felt flustered. "No, it's just for fun . . . For decor," he added, a word his mother used quite a lot.

His father nodded, pink-eyed, and drifted off with a can of beer in his hand. Then he said over his shoulder, "I think you're getting a little obsessed on the subject of kites, you know, Wally?— How's your schoolwork these days? Haven't you got final exams coming up?"

Walter, with one knee on the grass, straightened his back. "Yes . . . Why don't you ask Mom?"

His father walked on, toward the back door. Walter resented the school question as much as he did the kite remark. He was first in his class in math, without even trying very hard, and maybe second in English, behind Louise Wiley, who was nearly a genius, but anyway he had A's in both subjects. Walter returned to his gluing. When was the last time his father had looked at his report card, for that matter? Walter pushed his kite nearer the fence. He was working in a corner made by the bamboo fence, the most sheltered spot against the breeze. The grass was short and even, not as good as his room floor to work on, but the kite was too big to lie flat in his room now. Walter weighted the periphery of his kite with stones about the size of oranges which he had taken from a border and intended to put back. The breeze and the sunlight would hasten the glue setting, or so Walter liked to think. He wanted to forget his father's remarks, and enjoy the rest of the afternoon.

But there was something else disagreeable: they were going to Grandma McCreary's for tea. Walter's mother told him. Had Walter forgotten? she asked him. Yes, he had forgotten. This Grandma was called Edna, and Walter liked her less than his Grandma Page, who was called Daisy, the one who had nearly died from a heart attack. Walter had to change into better clothes and put on shoes. Edna lived about fifteen miles away in a house right on the coast with a view of the ocean. They got there around four.

"You've grown another inch, Wally!" said Edna, fussing around the tea tray.

Walter hadn't, not since he had seen Edna a month ago, anyway. He was worried about his kite. He had had to take it very carefully into his room and lean it against his worktable. Walter was worried that the glue hadn't set enough, and that something might go wrong, the paper be unusable, and he hadn't enough paper left over for a second effort. These thoughts, and the general uncomfortableness of his grandmother's living room—magazines lying everywhere, and no place to put anything—caused Walter to drop his plate off his pressed-together knees, and a blob of vanilla ice cream fell on the carpet with the slice of marble cake on top of it now instead of underneath.

His mother groaned. "Wally—you're so clumsy—sometimes."

"I *am* sorry," Walter said.

His father gave a soft chuckle. He had taken a glass and poured a couple of inches of scotch into it from the bar cart a few minutes before.

Walter was diligent with the sponge, and tackled the spot a second time. It was more fun to be doing something than to sit.

"You're a helpful boy though, Wally. *Thank* you," said Edna. "That's really good enough!" Edna took the saucepan and sponge from him. She had pink-polished fingernails and smelled of a sweet perfume Walter didn't like. Walter knew her very blonde hair was dyed.

". . . misses his sister," Walter heard his mother murmuring, hissing, as she and Edna walked into the kitchen.

Walter shoved his hands into his pockets and turned his back on his father, went over and stared at a bookcase. He declined another helping of ice cream and cake. The sooner they could leave, the better. But then they had to file out and admire Edna's rose bed, all freshly turned with black, wet-looking earth and yellow, red and pink roses all starting to bloom. Then there were more mumblings, and his mother said something about kites, while his father went into the living room for another drink.

It was after six when they got home. Walter went at once, but not hurriedly so as not to cause any more remarks, to check on the kite. He saw two small gaps between paper and wood, touched them with some of his brown-colored glue, and held them with his fingers for several minutes, standing on his straight chair to reach the spots.

From the living room Walter heard a low, grim hum, the tone that meant his parents were quarreling again. "I didn't *say* that!" This time it was his father saying the words.

When Walter thought the glue was reasonably firm, he got down from the chair, changed back into jeans and sneakers, and started making the kite's tail. He hoped an eight-foot length might do. It was the weight not the length that mattered. He had bought two great rolls of nylon cord, light and strong, each of three hundred yards' length. This purchase had been wildly optimistic, he realized, but even now he was inspired to tie the end of the first roll—which he found loose in its center hollow—to the start of the second roll. He could take them both on his bike, one in each satchel. The kite he would have to carry with one hand as he cycled. Walter cut four strands and tied these to the four wooden pieces (already notched for this purpose) at the back of his kite, joined the four ends, and tied this to the starting end of the first roll of nylon. He then uncoiled what he estimated as two hundred yards of cord, and fixed a stout eight-inch long stick in the cord, tying it with an extra piece of nylon. This was for him to hang on to, if the kite was very far up, and a stick was also easier on his hands than holding plain cord. He added two more such sticks at intervals, then decided that was enough.

The evening promised rain. Clouds and a gusty wind. But tomorrow who knew? He gazed at his kite—it was upright now, its point nearly touching the ceiling though it slanted against his table—and he bit his underlip. The long strips of balsa looked clean and beautiful. Should he turn the kite around now and write ELSIE on it with watercolor paint? No, it might be bad luck to do it so soon, like boasting. Walter's heart was beating faster than usual, and he looked away from the kite.

But the next morning, Sunday, inspired by the brilliant sunlight and the strong and steady wind, Walter wrote ELSIE in blue watercolor on the leading side of his kite. It had rained during the night. The wind came from the south mainly, Walter saw. He set out on his bike around ten o'clock. His father was not yet up. Walter and his mother had breakfasted together, his mother looking a bit sleepy, because Louise and another friend had come over after dinner, and they had stayed up late.

"Wow, *that's* a monster!" Ricky was again on his front lawn, tossing a Frisbee around.

Just at that moment, Walter had to get off his bike and take a better grip on the kite. He had made a loose but reliable noose or sling out of ordinary string by which to hold the kite while he cycled, but the bottom point of the kite was still apt to touch the ground, and the least breeze made his bike wobble. Walter said nothing at first to Ricky, and was a little embarrassed as he tried to tighten the string without hurting the kite.

Ricky was coming over to look. A car passed between them, then Ricky came nearer. "You're not gonna try to *fly* that. It'll bust!"

"And so what?" Walter replied. "But why should it bust?"

"Not strong enough, I bet. Even if it gets up, wind's gonna tear it. You think you know all about kites!" Ricky smiled with a superior air. His voice was changing, and lately he was trying to treat Walter as if he were a much smaller kid, or so Walter felt.

"My problem, anyway," said Walter, and got back on his bike. "See you, Ricky!"

"Hey, Wally, where're you going?" Ricky wanted to join him.

"Haven't decided yet. Maybe nowhere!" Walter was on his way, coasting precariously down toward the shopping center.

He knew he would soon have to start walking, and walk all the rest of the way with his big kite, because it caught so much wind, he could not control his bike. There were only two heights within reasonable distance, Greenhills, where Walter didn't want to go, and the hill beyond Cooper's, which Walter headed for. He walked his bike along the very edge of the road, holding his kite on the right side of his bike, so he could see passing cars and keep clear of them. One car driver laughed at him and made some remark that Walter didn't catch. At last he arrived at the base of the hill he wanted. The footpath faded into grass, and Walter lowered

his head and trudged the rest of the way, still holding his kite close
to his bike, and leaning his weight against the push of the wind.

At the top of the hill, Walter laid his bike on the grass, and sat
down with the kite flat on the grass beside him. He held his right
wrist in his left hand, and gazed between his knees at the splendid
view below: lots of little white houses, green lawns, winding gray
streets, and way over to the left the blueness that was the Pacific,
disappearing in a haze at the horizon. An airliner was coming in
from the north, still rather high because it was going to land south
of here in Los Angeles, but it was heading into the wind already.
The wind was from the south, as it had been earlier that morning.
Walter got to his feet.

"Hoo-o!—Hoo-o!" the wind said in his ears. It sounded
warm and friendly, nicer than a human voice.

He shook out his string, and took a position from which he
could run a few yards to launch the kite, but he did not need to.
The kite rose at once toward the north. The tail flipped around
wildly at first, the nose of the kite pointed right at him as the kite
flew flat in the wind, then the tail pulled it upright, and the cord
ran through his hand.

He held the cord with both hands, and let it slip for nearly a
minute. The kite was a flyer! He had hardly to coax it at all!

"*Yee-hoo-oo!*" Walter yelled into the wind. No one was near
him to hear, to stare, to heckle—or even to admire his kite. Walter
leaned his whole weight back against the kite's pull. Now the
pinkish diamond-shaped kite looked happy, waggling a little in the
blue emptiness, and climbing ever higher. Walter let out more
cord, until he felt the first wooden stick jump into his hands, and
he held on to it.

This was fun! He could tug slowly and hard, then feel the kite
pull against him even harder, lifting him forward, off the ground
for several feet until his weight and his efforts with the stick got
him back to earth. He was just about a match for the kite. That was
an exciting thought.

A dog barked in the distance, down where the town was. The kite looked smaller now, like an ordinary kite, because it was so high. Walter pulled at the cord with all his strength, leaning back until his body nearly touched the ground. Then the kite pulled him up slowly and gently and lifted him off his feet. Walter moved his feet, thinking to find ground under them, then the kite gave another playful and powerful tug, like a beckoning, and Walter was flying.

He glanced behind him, and saw the roll of cord dancing around on the ground, unwinding itself, and the second roll near it, as yet motionless. Then the nylon twisted, the stick turned, and Walter saw the trees on the hill diminishing under him, and a valley below that he had been unaware of before, with a thin railroad track snaking through it. Walter held his breath for a few seconds, not knowing whether to be afraid or not. His arms, bent at the elbows, supported him quite comfortably on the stick tied in the nylon. Below him he saw another stick he had tied in the cord, and he tried for this with his feet, missing a couple of times, then he had it.

Now he was twisting again, and he could see to the southwest the town where he lived, the round white dot of Cooper's hamburger-and-ice-cream place on a green rise. *The town where he lived!* That was funny to think about while he floated high up in the air like a bird, like a kite himself.

"Hey, looka tha . . . !" The rest of the faraway voice was unintelligible to Walter.

Walter looked down and saw two figures, both men or both in trousers anyway, pointing up at him.

"Wha' you . . . *doing?*" one of them yelled.

Walter was silent, as if he couldn't reply. He didn't reply, because he didn't want to. He looked up, and pulled comfortably now at the pink kite, sending it a bit higher, he thought, straight up. Walter attempted to steer it more to the right, the east, but that didn't work with this length of cord. The kite seemed to have its own ideas where to go. Walter saw one of the men on the ground running now, looking like an insect, maybe an ant, moving up the gray thread of street. Walter felt in a more beautiful atmosphere. The nylon cord hummed musically now and then in the wind. Elsie would have loved a flight like this. Walter wasn't dumb enough to think Elsie's "spirit" might be with him now, but her name *was* on the kite, he felt somehow near to her, and for a few seconds wondered if she could be aware that he was flying now, borne by a kite? Even the white clouds looked close, tumbling over themselves like somersaulting sheep.

And the ocean! Now as the cord twisted, Walter had a slow, sweeping view of its blueness. A long white ship was sailing south-ward—maybe to Acapulco! "Shall we go to Acapulco, Elsie?" Wal-ter said out loud, and then laughed. He tugged southward, westward, but the kite wanted to go northeast. Walter saw rows of fruit trees, maybe orange trees, and a low rectangular building whose silvery roof reflected the sunlight. Cars moved like ladybirds in two directions on a road down there. Walter saw a cluster of people beside what looked like a roadside diner. Were they staring up at him? A couple of them seemed to be pointing at him.

". . . *kid*, not a man!" one of them said.

"Hey!—Can you get that thing *down*?"

Walter noticed that one man in the group had binoculars, and after staring up, passed the binoculars to another person. He floated over them and beyond, motionless with his hands on the stick and his sneakered feet on the stick below.

"Sure it's a *kid!* Not a dummy! Look!"

Over more fruit-tree fields, the kite soared in an updraft, northward. A bird like a small eagle zoomed close on Walter's right, as if curious about him, then with a tilt of its wings went up and away again.

He heard the hum of a motor, thought it might be from the plane he saw coming from the northeast, then realized the plane was much too far away to be audible. The sound was behind him, and Walter looked. There was a helicopter behind him, nearly a mile away, Walter estimated. Walter was higher. He looked up at his kite with pride. He could not be sure at this distance, but he thought that every inch of his paper must be holding to the wood, that the length of tail was just right. His work! Now was the time to compose a poem for his sister!

> *The wind sings in your magic paper!*
> *I made a bird that the birds love . . .*

"*Hey*, there!" The voice cut through the helicopter's rattle.

Walter was startled to see the helicopter above and just behind him. "Keep clear!" Walter yelled, frowning for emphasis, because he couldn't spare a hand to wave them back. He didn't want the copter blades snarling his cord, cutting it maybe. There were two men in the copter.

"How're you getting down? Can you get 'er *down*?"

"Sure!"

"You're sure?—How?" This man had goggles. They had opened the glass roof of their compartment and were hovering. The copter had something like SKY PATROL on its side. Maybe they were police.

"I'm okay! Just keep *clear*!" Walter suddenly felt afraid of them, as if they were enemies.

Now the boy saw more people on the ground, looking up. He was over another little community, where twenty or more people gawked up. Walter did not want to come down, didn't want to go back to his family, didn't particularly want to go back to his own room! The men in the copter were shouting something about pulling him in.

"Leave me alone, I'm *okay*!" Walter screamed in desperation, because he saw now that they were lengthening something like a long fishing rod, pulling out sections of it. Walter supposed it had a hook like a boathook at one end, and that they were going to make a try for the nylon cord. The cord trailed away, out of sight under Walter's feet.

". . . *above!*" came one man's voice on the wind, and a second later the copter rose up, climbed to the height of his kite and maybe higher.

Walter was furious now. Were they going to attack his *kite*? Walter pulled defensively at his kite cord—which was so long, the pink kite scarcely bobbed. "Don't *touch* that, don't *touch* it!" Walter yelled with all his force, and he cursed the noisy chopping motor that had probably drowned out his words. "*Idiots!*" he screamed at them, blinded by his own tears now. He blinked and kept looking up. Yes, they were grappling with that long stick for the cord not far below the kite, or so it looked to him.

If the kite rose suddenly now, it would hit the blades and get chopped to bits. Couldn't the idiots know that? The long stick reached to the right of the copter, and slanted downward. Walter assumed it had a hook at the end—impossible to see, because the sun was directly in Walter's eyes now. Besides the copter's chopping noise, the people on the ground were yelling, laughing, shouting advice. Still, Walter screamed again:

"Keep away, *please*! Keep *awaa-aay!*"

The helicopter was still higher than the kite. The man had caught the cord, it seemed, and was trying to pull it toward him. Walter could see his tugs. The kite waggled crazily, as if it were as angry as Walter. Then there was a roar from the people below, and at the same time Walter saw his kite fold in half. The crosspiece had broken—from the idiot's tugging!

"*Stop* it!" For a couple of seconds his kite, folded and flat, was almost invisible, then the kite opened and spread, but in the wrong way, like a bird with broken wings. The kite flapped, leapt and leapt again and failed, as the beige stick drew the cord toward the copter.

Then Walter realized that he had pitched a bit forward and that he was dropping fast. He gripped his stick harder, terrified. Now the trees were zooming up, and ground also, faster and faster.

A shout, a groan like a big sigh came from the people below who were now quite close to Walter and in front of him on his right. Walter crashed into branches that punctured his body and tore off his shirt. He screamed in panic, "*Elsie!*" Upside down, he struck a heavy branch that cracked his skull, then he slid the last few yards to the ground, limp.

The Black House

An abandoned, three-story house stood black on the horizon of Canfield, a middle-sized town in upstate New York, whose industry was chiefly papermaking and leather processing, since the town had a river flowing through it. Houses and lawns in Canfield were neat and well-tended, people took a pride in keeping up their rose gardens and trimming their hedges, though none of the houses was a mansion. Canfield was composed of respectable middle-class Americans, many of whose families had been there two hundred years. Nearly everyone knew nearly everyone else, the atmosphere was friendly, people were neighborly, exchanging plants and trees from gardens, Christmas and birthday invitations, recipes and favors. They had cleaned up the river, which had used to carry yellowish refuse from the factories, at some expense and after some fighting against the government regulations that had demanded the cleaning, but now they were proud: the river looked rather clear again and certainly didn't smell sour or sulfurous when the wind blew, even though as yet there were no fish in it.

But the black house? Women chose to forget it, as if it were an eyesore they could do nothing about, but the men made jokes and told stories about it. First of all, the land was in dispute, said to be owned by a family now based in Ithaca, New York. But just who owned the land and the house? No one in Canfield really knew, though a couple of names were bandied about, Westbury and MacAllister, who were cousins, but nobody recalled ever seeing them or meeting them. The house had stood so, empty and neglected, before most of the people in Canfield had been born.

"Why doesn't somebody put a match to it?" a man would say, laughing over a scotch or a beer with his friends in the White Horse Tavern, a favorite gathering place.

"What harm's it doing anyone?" another would reply.

Another round of drinks—perhaps it would be "after church" at half-past noon on a Sunday—and Frank Keynes would relate a story of when he was fourteen with a crush on a girl in school, and he'd made a date with her to meet at nine o'clock at night at the foot of the hill to the black house, and she had stood him up. "But what do you know? Along came *another* girl who was quite willing to go up to the black house. *Quite* willing!"

The men would laugh. Was it true or not?

Ed Sanders, manager of the Guardian Paper Mills, might say, "The last time we heard that story, the *first* girl went up with you. Where are you, Frank? Whiskey's rotted your brain?"

And everyone would smile, while fantasies of boyhood, boastful tall tales, drifted through their minds like smoke, mingling together, trailing off. The men preferred to stand at the slightly curving mahogany bar. Their wives or girlfriends sat at the little tables, out of hearing, content to sip their own drinks and chatter until usually Kate Sanders, Ed's wife, would make the first move, come up to the bar and suggest that she and Ed get home for lunch, which would be ready, thanks to their automatic cooker, though she didn't have to say all this, because Ed knew it.

The youngest of the listeners was Timothy Porter, twenty-three, unmarried, a new employee of the leather factory, where he doubled as accountant and salesman. He had graduated from Cornell, tried his luck for a year in New York, and decided to return to his home town of Canfield, at least for a while. He was about six feet in height, with reddish blond hair, friendly but reserved. He rented a room in his uncle's house in town, his parents having moved away in the last years. Once he had brought an Ithaca girl to Canfield for the weekend, and they had both had a drink in the White Horse, but the girl had not visited him since. Timothy was alone one Sunday when he said, smiling, to the men at the bar:

"I remember when I was about ten, going to school here, we used to pretend that an ogre lived in the black house. Or a madman that even the police couldn't get out, and if we went very close to the house, he'd rush out and choke us to death. You know how kids are. Nothing but fantasies. But I remember aged ten it seemed very *real.*" Tim smiled broadly and downed the rest of his beer.

"There *is* something funny about the house," Ed Sanders said dreamily, perched on a bar stool. "It *looks* haunted—you know? The way that roof and the chimney tilts at the top, as if it's about to fall down on somebody." Ed saw his wife approaching, and was sorry. He was having a good time, talking about the black house. It was like being in another world, like being a boy again, twelve years old perhaps, and not a thirty-nine-year-old man with a growing paunch, knowing all about life, and more than enough.

Sam Eadie, plump, blond and balding, bent close to Ed, having also seen Ed's wife, and whispered rapidly, "I still say, because it's true, I made love *for the first time* to a girl there—when I was fifteen." He straightened and put on a smile. "Good morning, Kate! Second good morning today! I think you've come to collect?"

You're not the only one who did, Ed Sanders thought, a bit resentfully and proudly, but he couldn't say it aloud, because his wife was present. Ed only frowned for a couple of seconds at his old friend Sam Eadie.

Timothy Porter went home to his uncle Roger Porter's house for his Sunday lunch. Uncle Roger had not been to church, but then neither had Timothy, who had been walking in the woods before joining the locals at the White Horse. At Uncle Roger's house, the Sunday meal, prepared yesterday by his uncle's part-time housekeeper Anna, was ready to serve: a pork and rice casserole which Roger had been warming in the oven. Roger, in shirtsleeves, gave the final touches, Timothy finished setting the table—wine glasses and his own napkin which Roger had forgotten—and then Roger put on a tweed jacket and they sat down.

"Nice morning?" asked Tim, serving himself after his uncle. He knew his uncle had been either pottering in the back garden or going over his law office briefs.

"Not bad. And yours?"

"Sure, fine. In the woods. Then I had a beer at the White Horse."

"Lots of people? . . . Well, Ed Sanders, I'm sure." Roger smiled. "Frank Keynes too."

Why don't you join them sometimes, Tim wanted to ask, but his uncle at fifty-five was older than most of the White Horse group, and a little sad after the death of Tim's Aunt Meg about three years ago. Roger had not yet got used to her absence, and Tim knew Roger was glad of his company in the house, though Roger was not the type to put it into words. "I was wondering," Tim began, "why—"

"Why what?"

"Why the conversation in the White Horse always turns to that house they call the black house. Here. You know, the old abandoned house on the hill."

Roger looked at his nephew and smiled, his fork poised near his lips. "Because it's been there a long time, perhaps. It's our castle." He chuckled, and ate.

"But they sound like a bunch of kids talking about it. I remember too, when I was little, all the kids used to pretend to be afraid of it. But these grown men talk as if it's . . . haunted or somehow dangerous even now. Granted they've all had a couple of drinks by the time they start talking about it. But this is the third or fourth time I've noticed." Tim suddenly laughed. "And these old guys brag about taking *girls* there! When they were teenagers, I mean. It's really a panic to listen to them!"

Roger chewed reflectively, and looked into a corner of the room. His thinning brown and gray hair was neatly parted, his forehead wrinkled with thought, but his lips still smiled. "Well—they dream. They make stories up, I'm sure. After all, there was that murder there five or six years ago. Adolescent boy—body found on the ground floor of the house. Throat cut. He'd been there three or four days. Awful story." Roger shook his head with distaste.

"And they never found out who did it?"

"They never found out. Not a boy from around here. He was from—oh, Connecticut, I think. Doesn't matter." Roger went on in a more cheerful tone, "I used to play in that house when I was eight and nine. I remember distinctly, I and a lot of kids, running up and down the stairways there, telling each other the stairs would fall down with us, that there was an idiot behind the doors—things like that. The place was abandoned even in my day. Imagine."

Tim tried to imagine forty-five years back. "Why didn't somebody take care of the house?"

"Because legally speaking no one's got the right to touch the property till the case is settled, and since the house isn't a fire hazard up there on the hill with no trees around it . . . Even the trees died, I think, from sheer neglect."

They talked of other things. Roger was a lawyer, the most highly esteemed in town. He had his own office, with a couple of secretaries and a younger partner who would finally take over. Roger and Meg had had no children. Tim asked his uncle about the progress of a difficult case he was working on, which he knew worried Roger, and Roger answered him. But Tim's mind kept returning to the black house, as if it held some kind of mystery unsolved.

"Do you think there were tramps sleeping there? When that boy you mentioned was murdered?"

For an instant, Roger didn't seem to know what Tim was talking about. "Oh! The black house! No. Not at that time. Well . . . there may be a tramp or two sleeping there sometimes. I don't know. No, Tim, if you want to know the truth—" Here his uncle lowered his voice as if someone might be able to hear him. "What I'm saying was not in the papers here or anywhere. The girl in the picture was pregnant by the boy who was killed. And she and the boy had made a date to meet again—in that house. As I recall, they often met there. The story is that her father was furious. And the

boy—just a hoodlum—to tell the truth. The father left town afterward with his daughter."

Tim was stunned. Such violence hardly two miles from where
he sat now! "Do you mean the father wasn't even suspected?"

Roger gave a laugh and touched his lips with his napkin. "I
think he was. I think the judge let him off. Everyone was on the
father's side—somehow. There's something evil about that house."

There was something evil about murder too. A pregnant
daughter didn't warrant killing the boyfriend, in Tim's view, since
it seemed not at all a case of rape. "I feel like going there again—
taking a look. To that house, I mean. What is it but a lot of empty
rooms?"

"Oh-h—why go?" Roger was serving the ice cream, but he
paused to look at his nephew. "What'll you be accomplishing,
going there?" He added as he sat down, "A floor might give way
under you."

Tim laughed. "I'll test 'em with a foot first. I'm not afraid of
the place."

Roger shook his head. "You'll be gaining nothing, Tim."

Why was Roger looking at him so sternly? Tim started on his
ice cream.

The next day, Tim left Canfield Leather at exactly 5 P.M., quitting time, though he usually stayed a little later. He was eager to
drive to the black house and have a look, before it became dark.
The month was October. The house wasn't even black, he recalled,
but a dark brown or red. It was only black at night, as any house
would be without lights in it.

Tim drove his tomato-colored Chrysler up an unpaved road,
whose bends he had quite forgotten. He stopped the car at a
brambly spot where the lane ended, where there might have been
gates to the estate in the very old days, before Tim's childhood.
Now there was no sign of gates or fence. The old dark house
seemed taller, seen close now, and somehow frowning down on
him. Tim dropped his eyes from it, and watched the ground as he

climbed the slope. It was still rather light, he could distinguish pebbles, blades of grass in the patchy and dried-out lawn on either side
of the footpath that led to the front door. Had people even stolen
the paving stones that surely must have been here once?

Some ten yards from the house, Tim stopped, and looked up.
True enough, the house wasn't really black, but a dark brown.
Stone front steps, with cement pillars at the foot. A paneled front
door whose knocker had been removed or gouged out, leaving a
hole in its place. There were two windows on either side of the
door, of course with no glass in them. Was the door unlocked, able
to be pushed open? Tim smiled a little, and walked to the right,
intending to circle the house before he entered it.

He glanced at the sterile-looking ground for beer cans, sand-
wich papers, or any other sign of revelry, and found none. Tim
lifted his eyes again to the windows of the second story, the third.
Most of the windows were broken, open to the elements. Black
inside. Was some face going to look out at him in a moment, some
madman having heard his car motor, or his footsteps? Some white
ghost?

Timothy laughed out loud. His laugh sounded deeper than his
usual laugh, reassuring to him. Sure, it was an empty house, a classic, dark and all that. But why be afraid of it, unless you were a ten-
year-old child? Tim walked more briskly around the other side of
the house toward the front door. Off to the right of the front corner of the house, he did see a tossed away beer can, and he smiled
at the sight.

He went up the front steps. Even the doorknob had been
removed, he saw, but probably one could simply push the door
open. Or if it was locked, the window to the right . . . No, that was
too high from the ground to climb into easily, though it gaped
wide, glassless. Tim looked at the door, and decided to put the fingers of his right hand into the gap where the doorknob had been,
his left hand against the door, and push. He lifted his hands to do
this, then hesitated, dropped his hands, and smiled at himself. As his

uncle had said, why bother? What would he be proving? Nothing at all, and indeed he might break a leg with a first step onto a rotten floor.

Tim eased his shoulders, ran down the steps and turned and shouted up at the house: "Halloo-oo! . . . Anyone there? . . . Ha-ha!"

He trotted down the path toward his car, looked back, and gave the house a wave, as if he were waving good-bye to someone he saw at a window there, but there was nobody.

It was suddenly dark.

Tim had intended to say to his uncle Roger that he had visited the black house, walked around it, gone into it—and so what? But he felt ashamed, that evening, of not having entered the house after all, and therefore he said nothing about his visit there at dusk. Tim found himself thinking about, remembering a fair-haired little girl he had been in love with when he was nine, and she about the same age, in school. *In love*, at that age? What an absurdity! Yet the sensations, Tim realized, were much the same at nine as at twenty and so on, when one was in love. The sensation posed an unanswerable question: why is one certain person of such fantastic importance to me? Tim remembered his fantasies of asking the little girl to meet him at the empty house, as Tim remembered his contemporaries calling it. Had she ever? Of course she hadn't. What would her parents have thought, if their little eight- or nine-year-old daughter had said, after supper, that she had a date with a boy at the black house, or the empty house, maybe a mile from where she lived? Tim found himself smiling again. He could see that it would be so easy to pretend she *had* come, that they had kissed and embraced madly, and done nothing else, at that age. Yes, so easy to invent, and to come to believe that what he had invented and told to other people was true. That, of course, was exactly what the old boys at the White Horse were doing every Sunday after church, and maybe a little bit on Friday and Saturday nights too.

By the following Sunday, Tim's ideas had taken a different and more realistic form. He felt calmer and more detached, as if he were seeing the situation—even the black house itself—from a certain distance. So he was quite cool and collected as he walked into the White Horse Tavern at twenty past noon on Sunday. He wore his walking boots, twill trousers, an anorak jacket of bright blue.

The boys were here, Ed Sanders, Frank Keynes, a couple of others whose names Tim knew also, even one high school acquaintance, Steve, whose last name Tim couldn't at once recollect, though it began with a C. With a friendly nod at Ed, who had one leg over a stool, facing him, Tim walked up to the bar near the group, not as if he intended to join them, but not putting a distance between him and them either. Tim ordered a beer, as usual.

Before a minute had passed, Frank Keynes, who was standing at the bar with a Christmasy-looking old-fashioned in his hand, turned to Tim and said, "Hiking again?—How *are* you, Tim?"

"Quite well, thank you, sir!" said Tim. In the mirror beyond the row of bottles, he saw his own face, rosy-cheeked from his hike, and he felt pleased with himself, happy to be twenty-three years old, and also—in the left back corner of the room he could see reflected a pretty girl with short brown hair who sat at a table. Tim had noticed her when he came in just now, but in the mirror he could stare at her with pleasure, without her being aware of his staring. She was with two fellows, unfortunately. Tim lifted his beer and drank, and brought his thoughts back to what he intended to say to the men near him. The right moment came when he was on his second beer, and there was a lull in the conversation in which Tim had joined.

"By the way, I went to the black house Friday evening," Tim said.

Short silence.

Then Frank Keynes said, "Y'did? . . . Inside it?"

Tim quickly noticed that four men, even the younger Steve,

were all attention, and he wished very much that he could say that he had been inside the house. "No, not inside. I mean, I went up and looked around, walked around the grounds there. I didn't see any signs of tramps—or people. Just one old beer can, I remember."

"What time of night was it?" asked a tallish man named Grant Dunn, who seldom spoke.

"Wasn't night. Just before six, I think."

Ed Sanders, flushed of face, lips slightly parted as if about to say something, exchanged a glance with Frank who was standing to Tim's right. Ed said nothing, but Frank cleared his throat and spoke.

"You didn't go *in*," Frank said.

"No, I just walked *around* the house." Tim looked Frank in the eyes and smiled, though he frowned at the same time. What was all the fuss about? Did one of these fellows *own* the house? What if one of them did? "I did go up to the door, but—I didn't open it, no. No doorknob even. Is the place locked?" Tim noticed that Sam Eadie had joined the circle, drink in hand.

"The place is not locked," Frank said steadily. He had gray-blue eyes which were now as cold as metal. He looked as if he were accusing Tim of trespassing, of having tried to break in.

Tim glanced to his left toward the tables where the women sat, and his eyes met briefly the eyes of one of the wives, whose wife, Tim wasn't sure.

Ed suddenly laughed. "Don't go there again, boy . . . What're you trying to prove, eh?" Ed looked at Frank and Grant as if for approval or support. "What would you be proving?" he repeated.

"I'm not trying to prove anything," Tim replied amiably. Ed's a little pissed again, Tim thought, and felt tolerant, and quite sure of himself by comparison. A beer and a half had not gone to Tim's head. Tim took his time, let the curiously hostile glances at him die away, and finally he said, "My Uncle Roger told me about an adolescent boy being killed there." Tim had lowered his voice, as his uncle had done. He felt the coolness of perspiration on his forehead.

"True enough," said Frank Keynes. "You interested in that?"

"No. Not really," Tim replied. "I'm not a detective."

"Then—best to stay away, Tim," said Sam Eadie with a small smile, looking at Tim sharply for an instant. He turned to Frank as if for confirmation of what he had just said, winked at Frank, then said to everyone, "I'll be pushing off. My wife's getting impatient over there."

Frank and Ed smiled more broadly, almost chuckled, as they watched Sam's round figure in dark blue Sunday-best suit walk away toward a table of four women.

"Henpecked," one of the men said softly, and a couple of others laughed.

"You never went into the black house—when you were a kid, Tim?" Ed Sanders asked, now on a fresh scotch and ice.

"Yes, sure!" Tim said. "We all did. When we were around ten or eleven. Halloween, I remember, we'd take lighted pumpkins up and march around it. Sometimes we—"

Guffaws interrupted Tim's sentence. Men rocked back on their heels, those who were standing up.

Tim wondered what was so funny? The clap of laughter had made his ears ring.

"But not afterwards?" asked Frank Keynes. "Not when you were sixteen or so?"

Tim hadn't, that he could remember. "Around that time I was in—boarding school for one year. Out of town." That was true. He'd had to go to a crammer to pull his grades up enough to enter Cornell. Tim felt, and saw, the men looking at him as if he had disappointed them, missed something, failed another exam. Tim, vaguely uneasy, asked, "Is there some mystery about that boy who was killed there? . . . Maybe there's a local secret I don't know." Tim glanced at the barman, but he was quite busy over to Tim's left. "I don't mean to be prying into anything, if it *is* a secret."

Ed Sanders shook his head with an air of boredom, and finished his drink. "No."

"Naw," said Frank. "No secrets. Just the truth."

Now a man laughed, as if at Frank's remark. Tim looked behind him, to his left, because the man who had laughed was standing there. This man was a stranger to Tim, tall with neat black hair, wearing a cashmere sweater with a blue-and-yellow silk scarf, one of the group obviously. Tim glanced again quickly at the very pretty girl in the front corner, who was smiling, but not at him. Tim took no comfort from his glimpse of her. He suddenly thought of Linda, his last girl friend, who had stopped seeing him because she had met a fellow she liked better. Tim hadn't been much in love with Linda, just a little bit, but her telling him she wouldn't be coming to Canfield had hurt his ego. Tim wanted very much to meet a new girl, someone more exciting than the three or four girls he knew from college days, two of whom lived in New York.

"That story's as plain as day, sure . . ."

The jukebox had started up, not loudly, but the song happened to be a loud one, with horns and drums. Tim couldn't hear every word the men were saying. A wife came up, Ed's, and he disappeared.

"Good story!" Frank yelled into Tim's ear. "That story you mentioned. Dramatic, y'know? The girl was going to have a baby. Maybe she loved the boy. Must have—to've gone up to the black house again to meet him."

And her father had cut the boy's throat. Tim was not going to bring *that* up, not going to query the truth of it, because his uncle Roger had said it was supposed that the father had killed the boy. Two more wives came up to claim their husbands.

A few minutes later, Tim was walking to his uncle's house with a feeling of having been slighted, even laughed at by the men in the White Horse Tavern. He hadn't gone into the house, true enough, but he certainly hadn't been afraid of the black house.

There'd be nothing there, that he could see, to be afraid of. What was all the drama about, which seemed to extend from Ed Sanders to the rather stuffy-looking guy in the cashmere and scarf today? Was the black house some kind of private club that the men didn't visit any longer? Why not go in and tell them he'd gone in, and join the club thereby?

Tim realized that he was angry, resentful, that he'd best cool down and not say a word about the White Horse conversation today to his uncle. Uncle Roger, Tim knew, had a touch of the same mystic reverence for the black house as Ed and Frank and the others.

So Tim kept his thoughts to himself all Sunday. But he did not change his mind about going into the black house, walking up the two flights of stairs, and he intended to do it one night that week. By Friday afternoon, Tim felt inspired, irresistibly inspired, to visit the black house that evening, though he had been thinking of Saturday night.

His uncle Roger on Friday evening was engrossed in a television play which had not interested Tim from the start. Roger took hardly any notice, when around ten o'clock Tim said he was going out for an hour. Tim drove his car to the north of Canfield, toward the black house, and he parked it in the same place as before, on the unpaved road, and got out.

Tim had brought a flashlight. Now it was really dark, utterly black all around him, until after a few seconds he could make out clumps of trees nearby, not belonging to the black house property, which were darker than the starless sky. Tim flicked on his flashlight, and began to climb the pebbly path.

He shone the light to right and left: nothing but empty and untended ground. And then he walked up the steps. Now with more assurance, he pushed against the door, and it opened with his second thrust. Timothy turned his flashlight beam around the front room, which seemed to be a large living room without any small front hall. Empty. The gray, neglected floorboards were each some five inches wide. Tim set his left foot beyond the threshold, and the floor supported him. In fact, he saw, at least at this point, no sign of missing boards or of decay in the wood. There was a hall to the right, or a wall which partly concealed a staircase. Tim walked softly toward this, stopped before he reached the wide doorway to the stairs, and shouted:

"Hello?" He waited. "Anyone here?" He smiled, as if to put on a friendly face to an unseen person.

No answer. Not even a rustle of someone stirring upstairs or anywhere else. He advanced.

The stairs creaked, the banister and steps were covered with very fine whitish dust. But they held his weight. On the second floor there was a worn-out rug in the hall, one corner folded under. And as far as Tim could yet see, this was the only sign of furnishings. Not even a broken chair stood in any of the four rooms on the second floor. The rooms were rather square. A swallow, two of them, took flight from a room's upper corner at his presence, and made their way with audible flutter out a window which had no glass. Tim laughed nervously, and turned around, shining his flashlight now toward the stairs to the next floor.

This banister was shaky. Tim didn't trust it, not that he needed it, and stepped carefully upward more on the wall side of the steps than the middle, as this stairway seemed more sagging. Up here, there were four more rooms, and one tiny one with no door, which Tim saw had once been a toilet, though the toilet bowl had been removed. He stood on one room's threshold and shone his light into its four corners. He saw faded rose-colored wallpaper with an indefinable pattern in it, three windows with half their glass gone, and absolutely nothing on the floor except the ubiquitous pale dust. Somehow he had expected an old blanket or carpet, even a burlap bag or two. Nothing! Just space. A fine place to invite a girl!

Tim gave a laugh. He felt both amused and disappointed.

"*Hey!*" he yelled, and imagined that he heard his voice echo.

He glanced behind him at the dark hall, the darker well of the stairway down, and for an instant he felt fear at the thought of two flights of stairs to descend to get out. He swallowed and stood taller. He took a breath of air that was surely fresh because the windows were open, but he could still smell the dust.

Graffiti! Surely there'd be graffiti, considering all that had presumably gone on here. Tim focused his light on the floorboards of the pink room, tested their strength as he had tested the strength of all the other floors he had stepped on, and then he walked toward the front wall of the room. He stopped close to the wall, and moved his light slowly over a wide surface of the sun-blanched wallpaper, looking for pencil marks, initials. He found nothing. He looked over the other three walls quickly, then went into the hall, and with the same caution entered a back room. This room's wallpaper had been stripped, for the most part, curls of it lay on the floor, and the patches that remained were of a dirty yellow color. Tim picked up a dry coil of paper, and out of curiosity straightened it. There was nothing on it.

Not a cap or a glove someone might have forgotten on the floor. "Not a sock!" Tim said out loud.

Courage flowed back into him. Well, he had seen the place. The floorboards held. There were no ghosts, and not a tramp or a hitchhiker was making use of the house as a pad, even though the winter was coming on.

Tim looked at the other two rooms upstairs, found them equally unrewarding, and then made his way downstairs. He felt like running downstairs, but he went down rather slowly. An old step could still give way, he supposed, and he didn't want a broken leg or ankle. On the ground floor, he turned and looked up at the dark tunnel of the stairwell.

"Ha-ha!" Tim laughed softly.

One look into the closed room back? This turned out to be

the remains of a kitchen. A scarred white sink was still there, but no water taps projected from the wall. Four marks in the green and white linoleum showed where the legs of a stove had rested.

This was enough!

"Hal-loo-*oo*!" Tim shouted, and let his voice break, as he pulled open the front door. "Happy next Halloween!" he added.

Carefully, as if he were observing himself trying to do the right thing, Timothy closed the front door, using his fingers in the hole where the doorknob had been, trying to leave the door as he had found it.

It was good to be on solid ground again, to hear grit and pebbles under the soles of his tennis shoes.

On the familiar streets that he took driving homeward, he began to relax. Here he was, safe! Safe from what? There hadn't been one spookily creaking door in the black house, not a current of wind through a crack that could have suggested the moan of a ghost. He felt proud for having explored every room, and he realized that his pride was silly, juvenile. He had best forget his satisfaction and simply state to the men on Sunday that he had gone in and . . . looked the place over.

And what was the matter with telling them now? Tim saw by his watch that it wasn't yet midnight. Mightn't a couple of the fellows be at the White Horse? If no one was there, he'd drink a beer by himself. He turned right at the next corner.

The White Horse was indeed busy this Friday night. Tim had an impression of yellow lights everywhere, balls of yellow lights across the eaves, yellow light pouring through the door when it opened and a couple came out. Tim parked his car in the graveled forecourt, and entered the bar. The jukebox music which he had heard only faintly outside now sounded nearly as loud as that of a disco. Of course Friday night wasn't Sunday noon after church! And there were the fellows, the men, in their Sunday noon place at the back half of the bar, but in rather different clothes. Frank Keynes wore blue jeans and a turtleneck sweater. Ed Sanders was even in overalls with shoulder straps, as if he had been painting or working on his car, as maybe he had.

"Evening, Ed!" Tim shouted over the music, nodding and smiling. "Frank!"

"Timmy!" Frank replied. "Out on the town?"

Ed laughed, as if the town didn't offer much.

Tim shook his head, and when he caught the eye of the barman, he ordered a draft beer.

Then Tim saw Sam Eadie turn from the jukebox into which he had evidently dropped some coins, because he was stuffing a hand back into his baggy trousers. He had a drink in his hand. The tables were only half-filled, and these mostly with young fellows and their girls.

"Not walking in the woods this time of night, Tim?" asked Ed.

"Na-aw." Tim had his beer now, and sipped. "No, matter of fact I went up to the black house. Just now. Again." Tim smiled, and wiped a bit of froth from his lips with the back of his hand.

"You did?" asked Frank.

Tim saw that he had caught their attention at once, including that of Sam Eadie who had been close enough to hear.

"You went in?" asked Frank sharply, as if Tim's answer yes or no would be important.

Tim knew it was important, to them. "Yes. I had a flashlight. Went in all the rooms. Up to the third floor. No sign of tramps— or anything else." He had to talk loudly and clearly, because of the jukebox song which was something about *Golden . . . golden . . . hair and eyes . . . and paradise . . .*

The three stared at him, Frank frowning in a puzzled way. Frank looked a bit tight, pink-eyed. Maybe Frank didn't believe him.

"Just nothing. All quiet," Tim said with a shrug.

"What do you mean—nothing?" Frank asked.

"Oh, take it easy, Frank," said Sam Eadie, pulling cigarettes from a pocket. He brought the package to his lips.

"I just thought," Tim continued over the music, "you thought the place might be partly occupied. Not at all! Not even any interesting graffiti for all the—the—" Tim couldn't find the phrase for what he meant, which was taking or meeting girls there, making love to them on the barren floors, probably, unless the fellow or the girl had thought to bring a blanket. Tim shifted on his feet and laughed. "*Nothing* there! Empty!" He looked into the faces of the three men, expecting a smile in return, a nod of approval, because he'd gone all over the place at night.

Their expressions were a bit different, each man's, but in each was disappointment, a hint of disapproval, perhaps. Tim felt uncomfortable. Sam Eadie's face seemed to combine contempt with his disapproval. Ed's long face looked sad. Frank Keynes had a glint in his eye.

"Nothing?" Frank said. "You better step outside, boy!"

Ed suddenly laughed, though his frown remained.

Tim laughed too, knowing what Frank meant: a fight over the reputation, the charisma of the black house. What was he supposed to say, that he'd seen a lot of *memories* there? Ghosts or ghostly faces of pretty girls aged fifteen? In which room had that teenaged boy had his throat cut, Tim wondered suddenly.

The barman arrived at the tap of Sam's empty glass on the bar.

The jukebox song ended with a long drawn out *paradi-ise* . . .

"I said, step outside," Frank repeated, plucking at Tim's sleeve.

This little half-pissed middle-aged guy! Tim found himself following, walking beside the slightly wobbling Frank toward the door. Tim was still smiling, a little, because he felt like smiling. What had he done to antagonize them, or Frank in particular? Nothing at all.

Outside, as soon as Tim, who had walked ahead of Frank through the door, turned to speak with him, Frank hit him with his right fist in the jaw. Tim had not been prepared, and he staggered and fell to the gravel, but at once leapt up. Before he could get a word out, or his fists up, Frank hit him in the pit of his stomach. Then came a shove in his chest, and a loud crack at the back of his head.

"Frank, cut it out!" a voice shouted.

Tim, flat on his back, heard feet crunching on gravel, more voices.

"His head's bleeding!"

"O-kay, I didn't meant to—didn't mean to knock him *out!*"

Tim struggled to stay conscious, to get up, but he could not even move his arms.

"Just lay still, boy, we're getting a wet towel." It sounded like Sam Eadie, a stooped figure on Tim's right.

". . . doctor maybe? Or an ambulance?"

"Yeah . . . his head . . ."

Tim wanted to say, *It's a handsome house, a fantastic house. I can still see the ivory-painted moldings all covered with dust now, and the good floorboards that held my weight. I didn't mean to insult the black house, to make fun of the house.* But Tim could not get any of these words out, and worse, he heard himself moaning, and felt ashamed and afraid because he couldn't control the idiotic sounds coming from his throat.

". . . blood out of his mouth now! Look!"

A siren's scream rose and fell.

". . . that—house," Tim said, and warm blood ran over his chin.

Many more feet on gravel.

"Sh-h! Up!"

Tim's body was lifted suddenly in a sickening way, and he felt that he fainted, or maybe died. If he was dead, his thoughts, his dreams were worse than before. He saw the dark interior of a room in the black house, and Frank Keynes coming at him from a corner with a big stick like a club that he was gripping with both hands, about to take a swat at him, grinning. In a dark hall stood Ed with a faint smile, and behind him, just visible enough to be recognizable, stood Sam Eadie, hoisting his belt a little over his paunch, smiling also in an unfriendly way, as if he were about to witness something he would enjoy. *You have failed, Tim*, the men were saying. And *Nothing? Nothing?* in a scoffing way, as if Tim had sealed his doom by uttering that word in regard to the black house. Tim could see it all clearly now as he journeyed through space into hell, perhaps, into an afterlife of some kind that might go on forever.

Now he was moving through a ringing space. His ears rang, and he was jostled on the journey. Voices came through the ringing. He felt a touch on his shoulder.

"It's Ed," a voice said. "Look, Frank didn't mean to hit you so hard. He's too cracked up even to ride with us—now. He's—"

"If your name is Ed," said another deeper voice, "would you please keep quiet, because . . . doing you a favor letting you ride with us . . ."

Tim could not speak, but words came abundantly to his mind. He understood. That was all he wanted to say. The house was of great importance and he had treated it as if it were—nothing. He remembered Frank saying just a while ago, "Nothing—Nothing?" But to die for this mistake? Was it that serious? The words did not come. Tim moved his lips which were sticking together with blood. His eyelids seemed as heavy as his arms. They had given him a needle in his arm, a long time ago.

Now the two men in the ambulance with him argued, their voices came like gusts of angry wind, sometimes singly, sometimes together. And Tim saw the club in the grinning Sam Eadie's hands now. Sam meant to kill him.

Timothy Porter fell into a coma from which he did not awaken. His uncle Roger came to visit. Tim's lips remained parted, wiped free of blood which had ceased to flow, and a slender tube in one nostril furnished extra oxygen to him. His eyes were slightly open, but he no longer saw or heard anything. On the third day, he died.

Frank Keynes had to appear in the town court. He had already been to Roger Porter's house, made his apologies and expressed his grief and regret at having been responsible for the death of the young man. The town judge considered it a case of manslaughter. Frank Keynes was not imprisoned, but a fine was imposed, which Frank paid, and he was admonished not to drink any alcohol in any public place for six months, or his driving license would be taken away for two years. Chastened, Frank Keynes obeyed Judge Hewitt's orders, but he did still visit the White Horse, where he drank Coca-Cola or 7Up, both of which he disliked.

He felt that his old pals liked him less now, kept a funny distance from him, though Frank wasn't sure, because at the same time they tried to cheer him up, reminding him that he hadn't meant to cause any damage so serious, that it was a piece of bad luck that the boy had hit his head on something—the parking area curb that was made of stones as big as a man's head—when he fell.

Then came a Sunday in April when Frank could have a drink, according to the date of the calendar. Frank and his chums were gathered at the bar of the White Horse Tavern after church, as usual, while their wives sat around at the little tables. On his second scotch, which felt like four to Frank, because his wife Helen had been quite stern with him at home about not drinking, almost as if their home were "a public place," Frank said to Ed and Sam:

"Any one of us might have done it too. Don't you think so?"

Grant was standing nearby, and Frank included him in this question. Frank could see that Ed took a second to realize what Frank was talking about, then Ed glanced at Sam Eadie.

There was no answer from anybody, and Frank said, "Why don't you admit it? We were all—a little annoyed that night, same as me."

Ed leaned close to Frank, Ed in his Sunday suit, white shirt and silk tie. "You had better shut *up*, Frank," Ed said through clenched teeth.

He won't admit it. They won't admit it, Frank thought. *Cowards!* But he didn't dare say another word. As bad as they were with their wives, Frank thought, just as cowardly! And he admitted that he had to include himself here. Did they ever talk to their *wives* about what they'd all done in the black house when they were kids? No. Because the wives weren't the girls—mostly weren't, Frank was sure—that the fellows had been with in the black house. Frank understood, a little bit: they were like a club, maybe, and the club had rules. Certain things, facts, existed, but were not talked about. You could boast even, but not talk, somehow.

"Okay!" said Frank, feeling reproached but unbent. Not cowed by any means, no. He stood taller and finished his drink, glanced at Ed and Sam and Grant before he set his empty glass down on the bar. They had a certain respect for what he had done, Frank was sure. But like a lot of other things, facts, that respect was never going to be put into words by any of them.

About the Author

Born in Forth Worth, Texas, in 1921, Patricia Highsmith spent much of her adult life in Switzerland and France. She was educated at Barnard College, where she studied English, Latin, and Greek. Her first novel, *Strangers on a Train*, published initially in 1950, proved to be a major commercial success and was filmed by Alfred Hitchcock. Despite this early recognition, Highsmith was unappreciated in the United States for the entire length of her career.

Writing under the pseudonym of Claire Morgan, she then published *The Price of Salt* in 1953, which had been turned down by her previous American publisher because of its frank exploration of homosexual themes. Her most popular literary creation was Tom Ripley, the dapper sociopath who first debuted in her 1955 novel, *The Talented Mr. Ripley*. She followed with four other Ripley novels. Posthumously made into a major motion picture, *The Talented Mr. Ripley* has helped bring about a renewed appreciation of Highsmith's work in the United States, as has the posthumous publication of *The Selected Stories*, which received widespread acclaim when it was published by W. W. Norton & Company in 2001.

The author of more than twenty books, Highsmith has won the O. Henry Memorial Award, the Edgar Allan Poe Award, Le Grand Prix de Littérature Policière, and the Award of the Crime Writers' Association of Great Britain. She died in Switzerland on February 4, 1995, and her literary archives are maintained in Berne.